For

HOW TO MURDER
YOUR CONTRACTOR

Neal Sanders

Thanks for coming!

Neal S___

The Hardington Press

How to Murder Your Contractor is a work of fiction. While certain locales, references to historical events, and organizations are rooted in fact, the characters and events described are entirely the product of the author's imagination.

Also by Neal Sanders

Murder Imperfect
The Garden Club Gang
The Accidental Spy
A Murder in the Garden Club
Murder for a Worthy Cause
Deal Killer
Deadly Deeds
A Murder at the Flower Show
Murder in Negative Space

For everyone who has ever built their dream house,
discovering along the way that living through nightmares is,
unfortunately, part and parcel of achieving that dream

HOW TO MURDER YOUR CONTRACTOR

Chapter One

This is a story about avarice and greed. It is also about blatant dishonesty, casual adultery, astonishing incompetence and teeth-gnashing sloth. It will encompass a sufficient number of the seven deadly sins to satisfy both King Solomon and Evagrius Ponticus. I might add that this story will touch on snow farms and dwell on hot compost.

Mostly, though, this is a story about Joey McCoy, the worst excuse for a contractor ever to wear a tool belt. Joey thought that building my house was his ticket to unearned riches. He was wrong. Unforgivably wrong.

Where is Joey now? Let's just say that I was Joey's final customer. I can make that statement with authority.

I would start at the beginning except that I'm not certain what constitutes 'the beginning'. Maybe it was six years ago when our youngest, Noah, set off for college on the other side of the continent. That's when I first realized our house was too big and had been so for many years. Perhaps it was three years ago when my husband, Matt, accepted that I was going to 'downsize' with or without him and we began planning our new, smaller 'dream' home.

In either case, the decision was made irrevocable by two events. First, upon Noah's graduation, he sought and accepted a job in Seattle, just over 3000 miles distant. At his graduation, he gently told us that there was no further reason to keep a bedroom just for him. Second, our intrepid marine biologist daughter, Kate, got married with a minimum of fanfare and almost immediately purchased a home near her Woods Hole lab. There would be no boomerang generation under our roof.

Or, 'the beginning' could be the day when Joey McCoy came swaggering into my life.

Joey McCoy. Let me start with a question: If your parents name you 'Joseph', at what age are you no longer a 'Joey'? In my view – and it is shared by almost everyone whom I have asked – 'Joey' becomes 'Joe' by thirteen, where it can stay for the rest of your life or come full circle to 'Joseph' if you are named CEO of an especially stodgy Fortune 500 company.

But Joey McCoy was fifty years old when he first handed me his business card. The adolescent nickname still appended to a purportedly mature man ought to have set off alarm bells…

I'm sorry, I'm being rude. Allow me to introduce myself. My name is Anne Evans Carlton.

Anne *Evans* Carlton. It's interesting how an entire generation of women who would never put up with being "Mrs. Matthew Carlton" managed to marry and became comfortable folding up and packing away their 'maiden' names into some dusty, never-used storage closet. Then, starting about ten years ago, it became not just fashionable but *de rigueur* to append the surname with which they were born. Some attribute it to Hillary Rodham Clinton. That's an interesting notion, but my own theory is that in the era of Facebook, women suddenly resurrected it by necessity or choice. Through social media, they searched for and reconnected with their childhood playmates, high school classmates and college roommates, none of whom would have ever heard of 'Carlton'.

I, on the other hand, have weightlessly carried those three names for 26 years. I'm proud of my husband's career, but I am also my own person and have my own accomplishments. More about that later.

My husband, Matt, is an attorney. 'Lawyer' is for lesser mortals. Matt knows more about contract law than Charles W. Kingsfield, Jr. and his specialty is the biotechnology industry, where his name is spoken in hushed, reverential tones. His skills are in continuous demand with the result that I see him without work interruption for fewer than four or five days in any given month. Oh, he comes home every evening on the 6:36 but will disappear into his den/office until sometime after ten. He also travels internationally, especially to Switzerland and Germany. He has enough miles on SwissAir and Lufthansa to have a plane named after him. Possibly an airport.

When, three years ago, Matt realized I wasn't going to let the subject of a smaller house drop, he sighed deeply and asked what I had in mind. Matt also specializes in sighing deeply. His sigh means, "This isn't worth fighting about. We'll do it your way. But I reserve the option to resent it later." He puts a lot into a sigh.

I told him I wanted to stay in Hardington. It's the Boston suburb we've lived in since Matt got his first performance bonus four years after we were married. We went from a little house to a not-so-little house to what I call our 'starter castle' with fourteen rooms. We use four of them, but I have to clean all fourteen.

I like Hardington because it's a classic New England village with farm fields on its periphery (Trustees of Reservations properties, actually, but they *look* like farm fields), yet it is just eighteen miles from the Financial District and has express commuter rail service. It has one of the best school systems in the state (though that's no longer a selling point for us). I especially like it because Hardington lacks the hoity-toity cachet of Wellesley or Weston. I have no desire to tell someone where I live and immediately see the thought bubble with the words 'rich snob' form over their head.

In sighing, Matt also left much of the work of actually finding a house to me. And, by 'much' I mean all. Find a Realtor, find a house, establish a budget, sell our house, move our belongings. If I needed Matt for something, he would be in his den/office, probably speaking Biotechnology Contract German. He would look up and, with a pained expression, point to the phone: the universal spouse sign language for 'please figure it out for yourself'.

Wait, I just re-read what I wrote. Let me make it clear; I *love* Matt. He is my soul mate. He cherishes me. He just gets... wrapped up in his work. A lot.

For a year I looked at dozens of reasonably priced 'not so big' houses that came on the market, trying to assess what it would take to make it perfect. And, for a year I came up empty-handed. There came a time when I finally realized that our perfect home was not a renovation project: it was something we would build.

I sat down with my Realtor and asked about vacant land. She laughed. "There isn't any vacant land," she explained.

* * * * *

"She" is Alexis Hoyt. Alexis is, without question, the most dedicated and hardest working broker on the face of the earth. Hers is also the most ubiquitous face in Hardington. She's a tall, willowy blonde with hair so long and straight she could be Crystal Gayle's long-lost Viking twin. She peers up from the placard on your shopping cart in the local Roche Brothers supermarket. She smiles from below the fold of each issue of the weekly Hardington *Chronicle*. She winks at you from every web site you visit. She is a member of thirty town civic organizations where she pays absolutely no attention to the group's agenda or program. Instead, Alexis relentlessly prospects for word of properties that may soon be on the market, whether because of a career-related move, up-sizing/down-sizing, or a change of marital status.

I couldn't accept that there were no vacant land parcels for sale in a town with a population of about ten thousand people scattered across 25 square miles.

"Wetlands, town forest, town watershed, Trustees of Reservations parcels, state-owned property..." Alexis ticked off the entities that had taken my future homestead off the market. "It may not look like it, but Hardington is effectively built out. And has been for a decade."

"But I see new houses going up..." I said.

"Teardowns," Alexis said. "If you're desperate enough, you buy a house and then pay to have it torn down and carted away."

I could see tens of thousands of dollar bills sprouting wings and flying away.

We looked at the handful of vacant parcels in town. They adjoined the railroad tracks, power transmission lines, the Sanitation Department's Transfer Station, or were bisected by wetlands. In one case, all four. There were excellent reasons why no one had built on these parcels.

After another six months of fruitless searching, Alexis and I had The Conversation. The Time to Get Real Talk. The one where the Realtor drops the bomb.

"Anne," she said. "We're going to have to buy a teardown." We were having lunch at Zenith, Hardington's 'bistro' for the Ladies Who Lunch crowd. To her credit, Alexis picked up the check.

"We're going to shoot for something under $400,000," she said.

Four hundred thousand dollars.

When Matt and I started talking seriously about downsizing, I threw out a figure of $500,000 for our dream 'just the right size' house. I might add the amount included the house, the land, and a substantial budget for remodeling the house to meet our specific needs. It didn't include landscaping, but that's a different story. With the expenditure of $500,000, we would have a just-like-new house, perfectly scaled to our lifestyle.

Now, I was being told that four-fifths of that budget would be required to buy us a building lot… once we paid an additional sum to have the existing house leveled. My heart sank.

It was about that time that I noticed Alexis kept saying 'we', as though she were kicking in part of the equity. That's when it dawned on me that this was a two-step process. Step one was buying a new house. Alexis had already invested hundreds of hours in accompanying me through dozens of houses.

Real estate commissions in Hardington are five percent, divided equally between the buying and selling broker. If Alexis received two-and-a-half percent of the $400,000 sale price, she would net something like $10,000. While that's not a trifling sum, it works out to something like thirty dollars an hour. Take out the car, gas, pantyhose, clothes, dry cleaning and lunches, and she might as well get a job as a cashier at Roche Brothers.

She had much bigger game in mind. She was angling to sell our house.

Starter castles are in demand in Hardington. Football players want them. Upwardly mobile corporate executives want them. Extended families most definitely want them. The value of our home had always been in the back of my mind. I had a working figure of a million five - $1,500,000. If we paid $500,000 complete for our new 'just-the-right -size' house, we'd be able to bank more than half a million dollars, even after paying off our mortgage…

And the five percent commission on the sale of that property worked out to be $75,000. The listing broker was guaranteed half that amount even if another broker brought the buyer. Listing a big house in a hot market is the easiest money around. If Alexis helped me find the land for our just-the-right-size house, the moral calculus would demand that we award her the grand prize of the listing for our home.

And so we began looking at tear-downs in earnest. The land that is now Hardington was seized from the Wampanoag tribe in the 1650s. The hamlet was burned to the ground during the King

Philip's War but, after 1678, Europeans returned. There are a handful of dwellings from before 1700 in town. No one is ever going to tear those down. The 18th and 19th century homes are also fairly well off limits, but mostly because they have been snapped up by savvy builders who appended modern additions to the tiny saltboxes and Colonials that occupied two- and three-acre lots. A house with a placard stating something like 'Thomson-Rogers home circa 1726' is a badge of honor, even though the original family would gaze in consternation at the added-on master suite with twin Jacuzzis and 500-square-foot his-and-hers dressing rooms.

Hardington also has a sizeable stock of roomy Victorians, a relic of the town's heyday as the 'Straw Hat Capital of the World'. Those gingerbread houses, with their turrets and mansard roofs, now sport three-car garages masquerading as horse barns, as well as granite kitchens with Wolf appliances. Those houses, too, are safe from the wrecker's ball.

The gold seam for tear-downs begins with the 1930s frame houses that rose as Hardington transitioned from rural village to Boston exurb. It accelerates with the post-World War II subdivisions built when land was cheap to the point of being free, and an acre and a half allowed room for a septic tank and a huge lawn. Hardington has three such subdivisions and the sale of a 1600-square-foot Cape in one of them is a sure sign that a Patriots third-round tight-end draft pick is going to be moving in, just as soon as a suitable 4500-square-foot Colonial gets erected in its place.

There's just one hitch to all of this: the Historical Commission.

Fifteen years ago, a software mogul with more money than common sense turned a pleasant antique Colonial into a 15,000-square-foot showpiece. OK, it was his property and, to his credit, the restoration of the original structure nicely preserved the façade, though little else.

The problem was that the software mogul's daughter wanted to take tennis lessons. And so the adjoining property – another antique colonial – was purchased, torn down, and turned into a tennis court complete with a viewing stand, judge's box, and cabana. The resulting outcry produced a special Town Meeting that enacted a 50-year 'lookback' rule. If a house is more than half a century old, any alteration or demolition requires the approval of the Historical Commission.

Hardington's Historical Commission includes a mix of die-hard preservationists who vote 'no' on every application and a majority of realists who look at a property's structural integrity and figure out if it can be saved.

The system isn't perfect. The Historical Commission can delay a demolition by up to two years, but a deep-pocketed developer can wait out the process, run out the clock, and then build whatever he wants.

* * * * *

All that was going through my mind when Alexis showed me the paperwork for 131 River Street.

I have driven River Street at least twice a week ever since I moved to Hardington. It's a pleasant, meandering country road that starts just outside the center of town and winds its way to Oakley, the town just south of Hardington. River Street was superseded half a century ago by a straighter, wider road and it is the route of choice for trucks or commuters hell-bent on getting to Route 128 a few minutes faster. River Street, with its twists and dips, attracts motorists who aren't in a hurry and appreciate an occasional glimpse of water in the form of Summer Creek. I assumed River Street had houses on it, though I had paid scant attention to them.

Well, here at least on paper, was a house on River Street. A 1700-square-foot Cape set on almost two acres of land. The house was built in 1940 so it was squarely in the purview of the Historical

Commission.

"It's a dump," Alexis said. "It has been a rental for ten years because three adult children could never stop squabbling over who got what share after their parents died. It formally goes on the market in two days. I know the broker who got the listing and she owes me a ton of favors. Do you want to see it?"

"Hell, yes," I said.

Five minutes later we were on River Street and, for the first time, I looked closely at the houses along that roadway. They were little houses – Capes, ranches, Colonials – and all well maintained. They all sat on at least an acre of land and they all had been built back from the road, mostly behind pines or shrubs.

I instantly felt I could fit into this neighborhood.

Our destination house, on the other hand, was a case study in neglect. The driveway was crumbling, the exterior had not been painted in decades and the roof visibly sagged. But the lot was beautiful. It was at least a hundred feet to the house on either side and, behind the house were woods as far as the eye could see. Moreover, the lot was level.

I want this property, I thought.

"What's the asking price?" Alexis had pointedly not given me that information in advance.

"Three-ninety-nine-nine," Alexis said. The price was Realtor psychology at work on both seller and would-be buyer. Never tell a prospective buyer a house is "three hundred and ninety-nine thousand, nine hundred dollars. Leave off that ugly pair of words, "hundred thousand". And, don't say "dollars", either. "Three-ninety-nine-nine" sounds effortless; a gossamer figure. Pocket change, really.

And, for the seller, don't price the house at $400,000: the '4' in front of the price might scare off a would-be buyer. In my mind, the only buyer it will scare off is one who can't figure out that "$399,900" is four thousand, one-hundred-dollar bills stacked up in a pile, from which someone has generously taken off the top bill. Big whoop. If someone can't figure out that little bit of arithmetic, they shouldn't be buying a house; they should be getting tutored in remedial math.

We stepped out of Alexis's Lexus (every Realtor I have ever met drives a Lexus; it's spooky). It was mid-May and the air was redolent with the fragrance of lily of the valley and lilac. There was a gentle breeze against my face. I thought, *This is a sign.*

The house was even more of a disaster than Alexis let on. The center of the roof sagged two feet lower than the ends. The wooden front door was rotting. Windows flaked paint down to grey wood and the window panes were grimy in the extreme. That was the *nice* side of the house.

In back, plywood sheets that had been nailed over rotting siding were themselves decaying. Now, the plywood veneers peeled away to show siding that could no longer hold paint. A concrete-block foundation bowed ominously. This was a dump waiting to be torn down.

But the lot was glorious. It was nearly flat, sloping gently up from the street, leveling off at the house site, then sloping gently down behind the house. There were huge pines all around and, underneath the pines, a rogue's gallery of invasive shrubs, poison ivy and noxious black swallowwort.

"Summer Creek is back there," Alexis said, waving her hand toward the back of the property. "You'll own back more than four hundred feet."

I nodded. This wasn't infatuation. This was true love. I had found my parcel of land.

"What do you think we can get it for?" I asked, trying not to betray my excitement.

Alexis pulled out her phone, which transformed itself into a calculator. She tapped the screen multiple times.

"Are we talking all cash?" She arched an eyebrow.

Of course we were talking all cash. I had set aside the money months earlier for just such an occasion. Matt hadn't batted an eyelash. He knew I was serious. Cash is king. Spread hundred-dollar bills across the table like a Mafia don. No financing contingencies. Cold hard cash and just hand me the deed.

"We offer 85% of the listing price and say we'll close in three weeks."

I was working the math in my head when she said, "Three hundred and forty thousand." I noted she had dropped the fiction that the price wasn't really $400,000. "The house never formally goes on the market. It's a private sale."

Alexis knew her stuff.

"Let's write up the offer," I said.

"It's as good as yours," Alexis said, a broad smile on her face.

Chapter Two

It is amazing how much can change in 72 hours.

I drove home on a cloud of relief after we wrote up the offer. We finally had our home site. I pulled a bottle of Champagne from the cellar to await Matt's arrival home.

When Matt saw the Champagne, he smiled. He likes for me to be happy, and nothing says happy like Champagne. We drove to River Street and I showed him the house from the roadway. We went home and used Google Maps to estimate the proximity to Summer Creek. He shared my excitement.

"I know it's more than you planned," he said. "But I agree it's the perfect location. I always figured we'd bring it in for around six-fifty."

That meant we would need to build a house for roughly $310,000. I had in mind something around two thousand square feet. That meant about $150 per square foot for a house. It would be tight, but I could do that.

"Sure, my love," I said.

And I believed it.

* * * * *

Alexis delivered the offer to the other Realtor the same evening. When we hadn't heard anything in 24 hours, Alexis came to my home. I felt something was wrong. Alexis offered soothing words. "They're just quibbling about dividing the proceeds."

"Should we have offered more?"

"Relax," Alexis said. But there was a wrinkling around her eyes that told me she was thinking the same thing.

I drove by the house the next day. There were half a dozen

trucks parked on the lawn. Painters, carpenters, electricians.

They were trying to fix the place up!

I called Alexis, who had never lost her cool in my presence. "I'll call you right back," she said.

Fifteen minutes later she delivered the bad news. "There's an open house on Sunday," she said. "And an all-new price."

I braced myself.

"Four hundred twenty-eight thousand."

* * * * *

The Realtor.com listing made it sound idyllic. *"FIRST SHOWING SUNDAY 11-2. Cozy home for first-time buyer or empty-nester. Three upstairs bedrooms, downstairs master. Spacious kitchen and screened porch to enjoy nature. Huge level lot."*

We hadn't even gone inside. Why bother?

Alexis had her own showing that morning but she encouraged me to go see the house without her.

The street was crowded with cars. No, not cars; minivans. An entire flotilla of minivans meaning dozens of moms with young kids. All of them eager to get a piece of the highly prized Hardington School System for a little over 400K. If you had three kids and the alternative was fifteen grand per kid per year for private day school in order to avoid the dropout academies in whatever "affordable" town you lived in, it was like a raise in pay.

Inside, a cheerful young sales agent handed me a brochure, instantly sizing me up as one of those 'empty nesters'.

I looked around the first floor. It smelled of fresh paint and butchers wax. That team of workmen had transformed the interior into something that, at first glance, looked like move-in condition. The walls were spotless beige, the floors gleamed. The windows had been washed and the front door replaced. Of course, the "downstairs master" was a ten-by-ten room with a two-foot-by-two-foot closet and a claustrophobic half bath. The kitchen featured harvest gold appliances. Upstairs, there were in fact three bedrooms. No bathrooms, just three tiny bedrooms, the smallest of which was less than eight feet on a side. The porch floor sagged and groaned underfoot, in stark contrast to the bright white ceiling and newly installed screens.

In the basement there was sunlight from outside visible around the frames of the tiny windows. The furnace was original equipment, a hulking monster that had likely been converted from coal and now burned oil with an efficiency in the single digits. The concrete block wall was cracked and bowed. Surely, no one was taken in by the fresh paint upstairs.

Surely.

* * * * *

The email arrived Sunday evening. Alexis read it aloud over the phone. Our offer was acknowledged. We were invited to make a second offer, provided it was above $437,000.

"She's playing games," Alexis fumed, with something of a snarl in her voice. "She used our offer as the stalking horse to talk her sellers into putting some money into the house. She told them, 'spend fifteen thousand now and get back fifty thousand next week.' She's going to pay for using me like that." Another snarl.

My heart sank. The tactic had worked. In fact, it had worked twice as well as Alexis's postulated conversation between seller and seller's agent. My $340,000 offer was now low by nearly a hundred thousand dollars.

"Do you really want this property?" Alexis asked.

"I don't want it $437,000 worth," I said.

"Then make the same offer," she said. "But this time we say we'll close in ten days, no contingencies, all cash."

"What difference does that make?"

"The family that made the high offer probably did so with lots of contingencies," Alexis said. "The house has to appraise for that amount to get a mortgage, and no appraiser is going to sign on to that much value in a dump like that. It has to go through an inspection. The price won't hold."

Alexis was absolutely right. Ten days later, the house was back on the market. The new price was $410,000. We raised our offer to $350,000 with the same quick, all-cash close.

A week later, the house was sold.

To a developer.

* * * * *

I moped around the house for four weeks. Matt said I was depressed. He was right, though I wouldn't admit it.

I looked at other properties. I went through the motions. But every day I made a point of driving down River Street. I looked not just at the house I wanted, but at the houses around it. This was a *neighborhood*. These houses were well tended. I saw a mix of young mothers playing with toddlers on lawns and elderly couples planting perennials. Moreover, this was a street filled with people *walking*. On our cul-de-sac with its eleven starter castles, no one walked. One five-year-old whose family lived three doors down even had a kiddie-sized battery-powered Mercedes. It was materialism run amok.

And on River Street everyone *gardened*. I was the only gardener on our cul-de-sac. Our neighbors' properties were maintained by landscapers who applied a continuous diet of chemicals to the lawn and planted the same boring and completely predictable half dozen trees and shrubs on every lot. The people on River Street would be kindred spirits.

Meanwhile, we heard that the demolition permit for 131 River Street had sailed through the Historical Commission on a 9-2 vote. The hearing had taken, according to people there, less than half an hour.

In mid-June, I walked into Matt's study. He looked up from a much-marked-up draft agreement. He even seemed to know what I was about to say.

"Why didn't we just pay the asking price?" I said.

Note that there was no context to my statement. I could have been talking about Roquefort cheese or Red Sox tickets.

Matt put down the contract. "Because you weren't certain," he said. "You were thinking with your head, not your heart." He paused and cocked his head. "Are you certain now?"

"More than you know," I said, recalling my daily trips to see the property.

Matt nodded. Then, slowly, he reached into his back pocket and extracted his wallet. From his wallet he took a slip of paper torn from a yellow legal pad. He held it out for me to take.

"What's that?" I asked.

"The name and telephone number of the man who bought the house," Matt said. "It wasn't hard to find."

"You've already talked with him?" I asked, incredulous.

Matt shook his head. "No. You're going to call him. Negotiate with him. Buy the house from him."

I took the slip of paper with trembling hands.

"Are you sure?" I asked.

"You are a great negotiator," Matt said. "I have unlimited faith in you."

A question formed in my mind. I held up the little piece of paper. "Exactly how long have you been carrying this information around in your wallet?"

Matt shrugged. "Two days. I sensed you had made up your mind. I was waiting for you to ask."

Another question was right behind the first one. A scary question. "How much can we afford?"

Before I continue with this conversation, I need to interject the only thing I will say about Matt's and my background. Neither Matt nor I grew up with money. Oh, my parents indulged me my passion for horses, but that was the lone extravagance in our family and it was a matter of doting on an only child. Otherwise, we lived quite modestly.

Matt was a scholarship student from his freshman year through law school. He got to where he is because he is smart, not because of any family connections. When we married, our financial resources were, to put it mildly, meager. Everything since then has been a product of hard work, frugality, and a certain amount of luck. Even though Matt's career has earned us a more than comfortable living, our backgrounds continue to color our financial choices. 'Ostentatious' is not part of our vocabulary.

"You know our finances as well as I do," Matt said, and this time he was smiling. "You see the statements before I do. You know what we can afford."

"No vacations," I said. "No expensive dinners out." It was a warning of tighter belts ahead.

"Do what it takes," he said.

Chapter Three

On July 8, we became the owners of 131 River Street. Or, more precisely, we became the owners of a vacant lot that once had a sad, little house on it.

The best advice on negotiations came not from Matt but from my friend Chloe. She told me the tale of her neighbor who had put The Addition From Hell onto her house. Her neighbor wanted to expand her kitchen and add a small family dining area. Maybe two hundred square feet in all. It would mean taking down an old, tumble-down garage they had used for storage.

On the first day of construction, a backhoe clawed into the garage; the first step to preparing the area for the expanded kitchen. Fifteen minutes later, an ashen-faced equipment operator was at the woman's back door. The claw of the backhoe had pulled up the garage's concrete slab. Beneath the slab was a half-century-old oil tank, its contents oozing into the ground. No one had any idea the tank was there. It existed on no plot or house plans.

Six months and $40,000 of remediation and fines later, construction resumed. An estimated six gallons of home heating oil had escaped the tank, but the EPA treated it as though the BP Deepwater Horizon had exploded and sunk in the woman's back yard.

And so part of my negotiation was that the developer would tear down the house. If there was an oil tank underneath the house or garage, I wanted the surprise to be on their nickel, not mine.

As an aside, we never told a soul what we paid for the property; it was a private sale. But, somehow, the word got around. And then got inflated. Everyone in Hardington 'knew' we had paid more than half a million dollars for a buildable lot. It wasn't true, but rebutting the rumors would require disclosing the actual price, which I had no desire to do. I wasn't ashamed of the price; I'm just a private person when it comes to finances.

Home sellers loved us. We had just established a new floor for the sale of old homes in town. Home buyers cursed us for driving up prices.

* * * * *

We already had a house plan. Matt and I had been working on it for at least two years.

I had started with an inventory and dimensions of the rooms we actually used in our current house. We then assembled those rooms into a house plan that eliminated space-wasting hallways and dead-ends. I was aiming for 1800 square feet. Matt said 2300 square feet was still less than half the size of our current home.

We agreed that we wanted a home we could 'age into'. That may seem strange for two people in good health. It's especially strange because I'm 49 and Matt is 51. Yes, we met in college. Matt was first-year law school, I was a junior. We married three years later following a one-year engagement. Kate came eighteen months after the wedding followed by Noah a year later. For reasons I'll explain, I was hurrying things along.

But we have always been people who looked ahead and I, in all honesty, was sick to death six years ago of our 4800-square-foot monstrosity. We didn't need five bedrooms or a master suite with the dimensions and ceiling height of a basketball court. We didn't need a dining room that was large enough to accommodate a table for twelve. We didn't need a dining room at all. The same was true for the living room with its never-used fireplace large enough to roast a cow. Get rid of those suckers and take the five-and-a-half bathrooms with it.

Our hand-drawn house plan reduced our house to what two people really needed. What we were left with was a *small* master bedroom, a nicely proportioned master bath, a small kitchen I could actually cook in without roller skates, a 'great room' off the kitchen that served as a living/dining/family space, a nifty combined laundry and pantry area that I ought to patent, and an entry foyer, because Sarah Susanka's '*The Not So Big House*' stresses that every good house needs one.

We kept the identical size and layout of three rooms from our soon-to-be old house: Matt's den/study remained, because he spends his life in it. He knows exactly where to reach for every source book and I don't want to deny him his comfort. We also transplanted our screened-in back porch, because we spend five months a year out there. Finally, we duplicated our master bedroom closet for the simple reason that I love it.

And, because we are practical, the house would also have a pair of small bedrooms and an equally Lilliputian bath upstairs. Noah would have a place to stay when he came home to visit, or Kate if she and her husband stayed overnight. No dedicated beds; just sleeper sofas. In the meantime I would have a small studio to myself.

Even before the property sale was completed, two things were underway. First, we cut apart the house plan so that it made sense for the site: garage on the north end of the building, sun porch on the west; that sort of thing. In two days, we had a revised plan we both loved. Matt turned a copy of the drawing over to an architectural design firm that owed Matt a huge, life-saving favor.

The other thing we did was start shopping our 'just-the-right-size' house to contractors.

That's when the joy of wanting to build a small house on a perfect piece of land collided with the economics of building such a house in the Boston suburbs in the second decade of the twenty-first century.

I went to four builders. All came highly recommended. They had built my friends' houses. They had each done a wonderful job that came in on time and on budget.

For each builder I would roll out my plan on an 11x17 sheet of graph paper and explain that formal architect's drawings were two weeks away. The builder would glance at the drawing, listen politely for ten minutes, then look for a way to interrupt me. They all delivered the same message.

"Mrs. Carlton," they would say, "this really isn't our kind of project."

"It's a house," I would counter. "You build houses."

"It's a *small* house," they would point out.

I would give them a blank look though, by the second meeting, I knew the speech that would follow.

"Building a house – any house – ties up a lot of resources," was the starting point for the explanation. "Equipment, inventory, men, materials…"

"And your point is….?"

They would look at the plan and back at me. Trying to be tactful. Trying to let me down gently. "Our projects *start* at 4000 square feet," said the first builder. Another allowed as how they could consider something down to 3800 square feet if it was truly luxurious inside.

No one wanted anything to do with our dinky little Cape, especially if we already owned the land on which it would be built. There was no money in it. The money was in McMansions. Starter castles. Luxury suburban homes. *Huge* luxury suburban homes.

Why? Matt explained it to me after the first meeting. "A house is mostly air," he said. "It doesn't cost anything to build air, but a builder can charge huge sums for it."

It made perfect sense. To make a compelling case for a house to be worth a million and a half dollars (or one, four-ninety-nine, nine in Realtor parlance), it has to be enormous. It has to have marble vanities and a butler's pantry. In pricing a new home, appearances are everything.

The bottom line, Matt said, is that it costs as much to build a high-quality small house as it does to put up a McMansion. But you don't dare quote someone that McMansion price when what they want to build is 2100 square feet, which was the size of the house on that 11x17 sheet of paper. So you don't quote a price at all. You tell the prospective customer they should "look elsewhere."

The builder who bought 131 River Street had no such problem. He had a demolition permit in one hand and plans for a 4500-square-foot Colonial-on-steroids castle in the other. The builder could afford to pay the negotiated price for the land because the land would end up being a small part of the final cost. Not exactly lost in the round-off, but not a major hurdle, either.

The resulting 4500-square-foot house would look ridiculous alongside River Street's modest ranches and Capes. It would be a huge, hulking presence; a lava-spewing volcano among placid hills. But 'Big' was the future of Hardington. Given the inexorable march of progress, in ten years River Street would be home to a three-mile-long stretch of affluence of exactly the kind originally proposed for the site. It would fit right in.

Four builders told me with excruciating politeness to take a hike.

I was panic-stricken. The summer construction season was going to get away from us. My plan was to have a foundation in place by the end of August, build the house during the cool, dry autumn, and move in just before Thanksgiving. It was hard to keep that schedule when builders said they didn't want my business.

So, I turned to Plan B.

I have mixed feelings about Angie's List. It makes sense as a way to find a plumber for a day's work or a place to get your snow thrower repaired. I get suspicious when I see one business with dozens of enthusiastic reviews that sound too much alike. Businesses try to 'game' the system by encouraging users to write reviews and supplying suggested wording. I'd rather read one insightful review that sounded like someone had put some thought into it.

But I was also getting desperate. Matt, bless his heart, went through the listings with me just as he had sat through two of the big builder interviews.

We drew up a list of five names. These were construction firms that specialized in 'major additions' and 'whole house remodeling'. Each had at least four positive reviews and no negative ones. Each had a website and the website showed lots of activity on large projects.

I went to work on the phones immediately. Every call went to voice mail, but that was OK; I was dealing with guys who worked for a living. They didn't have office staffs.

McCoy Contracting was my third call. The company had six reviews including three from people in Hardington. His business address was in nearby Overton, so I wasn't starting with a contractor who had a sixty-mile commute to get to the job. The website was well done and included things like the owner's license number.

Joey McCoy called back a day later. I had gone through two dispiriting conversations with contractors who would *love* to build my not-so-big house… and could put me on their schedule for next spring.

I didn't want to wait for next spring. I had it in my head that Matt and I could have Thanksgiving dinner in our new home.

Joey McCoy said he could drop by to look at our plan.

He showed up at 7:30 p.m., apologizing that he had been at a site since 7 a.m. He was a nice looking guy, probably a year or two either side of fifty. Wavy red hair without a touch of grey in the sideburns. He wasn't especially tall, but he had a muscular build that made him look like he *ought* to be tall. He wore a tool belt that cinched his waist over a blue sweatshirt and surprisingly snug jeans.

On closer inspection, he was a really nice looking guy.

Matt and I greeted him at the front door. He respectfully left his boots on the mat outside. There were holes in his socks, which I somehow found humanizing.

Joey McCoy didn't look at us immediately. Instead, his gaze went to the foyer, the stairs and the floor. He nodded upward. "Beautiful crown molding. That's oak, not pine; you can tell by the grain. Good touch." He indicated the floor. "Brazilian cherry runner. I love those. That wood is astronomical now. Ten bucks a linear foot."

He hadn't even introduced himself but was instead waxing poetic about the right-hand volute on the stairs, saying it was one piece and hand-turned rather than machine made from bits of leftover lumber. I had no idea what a 'volute' was, but smiled at his keen powers of observation.

"Maybe we ought to introduce ourselves," Matt said. "Let's go into the Great Room."

Our prospective contractor continued cataloging every piece of woodwork in our house as we walked, calling it all 'exceptional quality'.

"Coffee, Mr. McCoy?" I asked.

He shook his head. "I stop drinking the stuff after lunch. And everyone calls me 'Joey'." He handed us each a card. It read:

McCoy Contracting
Joey McCoy, President

As if on cue, I pulled out my 11x17 sheet and explained, as I had to the big construction companies, that formal architect plans would be forthcoming in – now – about a week.

Joey handled the sheet as if it were one of the Dead Sea Scrolls. Touching only the edges of the page, he gingerly turned it sideways and immediately started asking questions.

"The garage – do you want it to be column-free? Because, if you do, we're going to have to pitch the roof…"

This man wanted to build our house.

He was polite. He was respectful. He spoke to both of us or to each of us in turn. Matt did not receive special attention; there was no 'guy' thing in the air. He made half a dozen suggestions for ways to simplify and speed the construction process, then offered to put those ideas on paper and email them to our architect.

I broached the critical – at least to me – question: "Mr. McCoy – Joey – if we agreed on a price and a work schedule, could you have us in our new home in time for Thanksgiving?"

Joey scratched his chin. He stared intently at the diagram, his mind working on permutations and combinations of events that could unfold.

Before committing to a response he asked about cabinets, countertops, and appliances. I pulled out the 'perfect house' binder I had been compiling for three years. He tapped a few of my choices and said, "Very long lead time on this." He then offered, for each item, a just-as-good alternative that was available with no backlog.

After fifteen minutes of back-and-forth questions, he gave his chin a final scratch.

"I want my 'A-List' crew on this; not some pick-up guys with hammers and saws," he said. "I want to be able to watch this project every day and be able to say with confidence that I oversaw every detail, no matter how minor. Can I do that and also deliver a house for Thanksgiving? Yeah, I'm certain I can do that."

We talked a while longer about logistics and possible construction shortcuts that could be taken. At nine o'clock, he looked at his watch. "My son is part of a night baseball league. I have to pick him up in fifteen minutes."

Matt had said little during the past few hours. Joey was doing almost all of the talking. At the door, though, Matt said, "I'd like to talk to half a dozen references."

"Sure thing, Mr. Carlton," Joey said, flashing a broad, toothy smile. "I'll get those to you tomorrow."

When we heard his truck pull out of the driveway, I hugged Matt. "I think we found a contractor," I whispered.

Matt returned the hug, but expressed reservations.

"He's selling, Anne," Matt said. "We're seeing him in his salesman's mode where all things are possible, no budget is too modest, all deadlines can be met or bettered, and all things are shiny and wonderful. That is what a salesman does. Let's see what his references have to say about the reality of building a house."

* * * * *

Joey McCoy's references arrived the next afternoon via email. Matt was tied up on the kinds of things that paid our bills, so I was left with the task of contacting those six people. I got voice mail on the first two but a real, live human answered the phone on my third call. It was a man's voice who said, 'hello'.

"Mr. Berry?" I asked, and proceeded to explain why I was calling,

Harold Berry sounded like a man in his seventies. He spoke in a low rumble. I could see him in what was probably his spacious library, a newspaper – likely the *Wall Street Journal* – spread out on the table, with a Keurig system hissing out a cup of his favorite fair-trade Kenyan coffee blend. The timbre of his voice said this was a man of leisure.

"Joey and I go way back," Berry said. "Twenty years, easy. The man saved my bacon more than once. Best damned carpenter I ever saw. I give him a picture of what I want and he builds it."

"Has he done major work for you?" I asked. Carpentry was a good skill to have, but this was bigger.

Berry laughed. "Joey has probably tripled the size of this house over the years. A new kitchen here, a garage there. Yeah, that's major work."

I started working down my list of questions. On time performance? Quality of work? Quality of subcontractors? Berry put a tick mark on each item. Joey McCoy was a stickler for detail and a man of his word.

"Finished price versus up-front quote?" I asked.

That last question seemed to confuse him.

"We have a handshake agreement," Berry said. "There's no contract. I just tell him what needs to be done."

"So, you never put anything in writing ahead of time?" I asked. I was also writing '*no contract*' on my yellow legal pad.

"Never had to. His price is always fair; especially for the quality." Berry seemed adamant on that point.

"How do you pay him?" I asked.

"I write checks as we go along," Berry replied. "Joey says, 'Hey, Mr. B, I gotta pick up a load of lumber and tile for the master bath. Can you write me an advance?' Then we settle up at the end."

We chatted for another ten minutes. Joey was a whiz kid with a lathe. Joey was always cracking a joke. Joey showed his grandson how to operate a lathe and hand-sand a stubborn wooden junction. Joey avidly kept up with injury reports not just for the Patriots, but for every NFL team. Joey could cite Boston Celtics statistics going back to the Bill Russell/K.C. Jones/John Havlicek era and knew the starting lineup and batting averages of Red Sox teams going back fifteen years.

I ended the call with a nagging sense of disappointment. I got the sense that Harold Berry was a lonely guy, probably widowed, and probably with a lot of money. He put on additions to his house to keep himself busy; and possibly for the company.

But a guy like Berry would also know if he were being fleeced. Matt had put it succinctly several times: "Wealthy people have a sixth sense for that. If they don't have that sixth sense they hire lawyers to write contracts for them. Otherwise they don't stay wealthy for long."

Two of Joey McCoy's other references returned my call that day. Both, like Harold Berry, were long-time customers. They both said more or less the same thing: Joey was a peach of a guy who did great work. The only change from the script came from Phil Vonn, who warned me about the painter Joey had used for a new master bedroom wing.

"The guy showed up late, didn't clean up after himself, and played the radio loud enough to cause bleeding from the ears," Vonn said. "Almost everything he did had to be re-done."

"Who paid for the re-work?" I asked. "You or Joey?"

"Joey swallowed the cost of the new painter and apologized," Vonn said.

I thought to myself, *'but if there was no contract, how did you know you weren't paying for both painters?'* But I didn't ask the question of Vonn; you don't challenge people's intelligence when you're checking a reference. But I wrote it down on my pad.

By the end of the next day I had spoken to all six references. They were all men, all nice guys. They were all satisfied, long-term customers. Joey hadn't built a house for them, but he had extensively remodeled two. Everybody loved Joey. Joey was a walking sports encyclopedia. Joey was the greatest thing since sliced bread.

I had two voices perched on my shoulder. One of them was jumping for joy. I had a contractor with satisfied customers. One of those customers said he would leap at the chance to have Joey build a house from scratch. The other voice sat there like a grump, telling me that I had a lot more work to do.

Matt had flown to Zurich – it is not uncommon for him to come home from work an hour early and casually mention that he has booked a flight on that evening's SwissAir 10:45 nonstop – but I caught him in his hotel room. He listened carefully to my concerns. "Anne, it's a huge decision," he said. "It's also an exceptionally *expensive* decision. Is being in a new house for Thanksgiving that critical? Or, could we wait until spring to get one of the other contractors?"

My husband. Mr. Logic. Spock without the funny ears. I told him I feared that waiting would "increase our uncertainty", which was a phrase Matt frequently hurled at clients who had trouble making up their minds.

Without missing a beat, Matt said, "Then call the clients he hasn't put on his list."

"How do I find them?" I asked.

"Anne, you are one of the most resourceful people I have ever met," my husband said. "If you can't find those other clients, he doesn't have any."

Which I think was his way of one-upping me for using his patented 'uncertainty' line.

* * * * *

I knew Joey had other customers because there were ratings on Angie's List. But those were all positive. I could predict what they'd say. So, it was on to Facebook.

I don't know if it is true of other towns, but Hardington has an on-line yard sale 'community' on Facebook. Are you looking to sell your lawnmower? Post a photo and name a price. In fifteen minutes you'll know if there's interest. Want to buy a piano? You'll have half a dozen leads in an hour.

I typed, *"Has anyone had experience with an Overton contractor named Joey McCoy on a major home renovation or, better yet, building a house from the ground up?"*

Then I went to the grocery store and did a week's shopping. Watching Facebook for new posts is an invitation to get swallowed up into an activity from which you may never again come up for air. I have friends who spend an unhealthy amount of time commenting on endless series of posts or watching kitten videos or maybe regularly texting somebody they vaguely knew in the sixth grade. Whatever it is that they find so fascinating, I don't get it.

I checked back two hours later and found I had three responses.

The first was from someone named Amanda, who said Joey had competently remodeled their dining room two years earlier. That was interesting, but it was too small a job to tell me what I wanted to know. The second was from Lucy who said Joey had built a two-car garage, master bedroom, and basement extension the previous year. That was more like what I had in mind, but "Lucy" didn't offer an opinion. So, I sent her a message asking if I could speak with her on the phone.

The third response was from "Candy". Her sole comment was "Creep." Was Joey McCoy a creep or was I a creep for asking about him?

Whoa. I wanted to talk to Candy.

I messaged her, asking if she would like to expand on her comments, explaining that I was building a house and considering him as my contractor. She did not reply.

In the meantime, Lucy – her last name was DiGinnario – messaged me back and provided a phone number. I called her immediately. She told me she was a stay-at-home mom, and that she and her husband had decided to expand their house rather than moving when she became pregnant with their third child.

"No contractor is perfect," Lucy said. "Joey got the job done but, boy, did his attention wander toward the end."

I asked her to tell me more. My pen was poised to record every nuance.

There was the sound of two boys squabbling in the background, appealing to Mom to settle a dispute. Lucy ignored them. "In the beginning, Joey was at our house every day. He got the foundation poured and the addition framed. He got a roof on and had the siding installed. But then it came time to do the interior and Joey apparently got busy on another project. Instead of being…. Excuse me." Lucy put down the phone and interceded in the boys' intra-family squabble. In the background, I could hear her say, *Mommy needs to talk. Go to your rooms.* It made me exceedingly glad we had a boy and a girl and made me not miss the Terror Years between four and six.

"I'm back," Lucy said. "Anyway, here I was, seven months gone, and Joey went from being on site every day to showing up every other day. His subcontractors were doing most of the work, but Joey needed to tell them what to do. So I'm waddling around trying to speak fractured Portuguese to all-male crews who honestly believed with all their heart that taking orders from a pregnant woman was going to make them go straight to hell."

"What did you do to get things back on track?" I asked.

"My husband and I caught Joey on a day when he was here, and we were about to have one of 'those' talks," Lucy said. "You know, the one where you threaten to take them to court and destroy their reputation unless they shape up. Well, we never got to say any of it. Joey beat us to the punch. He was all apologetic and explained that his daughter had an emotional breakdown and had left college for a semester. He was as sorry as he could be that a personal issue had interfered in his business and he said it wouldn't happen again. That kind of took the wind out of our sails. We told Joey to take the time he needed to deal with his daughter, but to please wrap up the job as soon as possible."

"Did things get better?" I asked.

"Marginally," Lucy said. "He'd still miss days without explanation, but he finished up just a few weeks after the target date. The job turned out exceptionally well."

"How about price?" I asked.

"There were a few surprises," Lucy said. "Paul – my husband – said that's par for the course. I think he was about fifteen percent over his quote. Some of it was stuff we asked for. We have a master bath to die for – we really went overboard on that – but most of it was stuff where Joey came back and said prices had gone up or the town had demanded something that wasn't in the specs. I forget the specifics."

"But you'd hire him again?" I asked.

There was a pause. "I guess so. I mean, he got the job done – apart from the thing with his daughter. And his cat."

"His cat?" I asked, consternation apparent in my voice.

"His cat ran away," Lucy said. "We lost Joey for, like, four days because the family cat didn't come home and his son was out of his mind with worry. So, Joey spent four days putting up posters and driving around looking for the cat."

I didn't know whether what I was hearing was appalling or endearing. I came down on the former. "He just stopped being a contractor and started being a one-man lost and found service for his son's cat?"

"He found the cat," Lucy said. "I mean, the cat came home. And Joey was extremely apologetic."

The tone of her voice said that she accepted the contractor's explanation. As much as I am a sucker for a furry face, I'm not certain I'd consider putting up 'lost kitty' posters more critical than finishing a customer's job. If he had a daughter in college, the bereft son ought to be at least in middle school or high school and therefore perfectly capable of going out with hammer, nails, and posters to let everyone know about Kitty. I let it drop, though.

I finished with a few more questions – like how Joey got progress payments and how much was held back pending final approval. The last question completely stumped Lucy: she had no idea that a customer had to be satisfied with a job before final funds were released. I told her it was standard practice.

"Huh, Joey said all final payments were due as soon as the town signed off on the work," was all she had to say.

"Most people hold something back," I said. Changing the subject, I asked, "Have you had reason to call him to fix anything?"

Another pause. "No." That was it. No expansion of the thought, no wiggle room.

I thanked her for talking with me. As I was about to hang up,

I heard her say, "Oh, if you want a current opinion, you may want to talk to the Harrises over on Chestnut. I've seen Joey's truck there half a dozen times over the past two weeks."

I thanked her again, said goodbye, and promptly found my little Hardington phone directory. There were multiple families named 'Harris' in town but only one Harris on Chestnut Street. I tapped in the number.

There followed the strangest conversation I have ever had:

She: "Hello?" The tone was suspicious. If she had caller ID, her phone would say "Anne/Matt Carlton". But she would still have no idea who I was. I would have answered the phone the same way.

Me: "Ms. Harris, my name is Anne Carlton, I live here in Hardington, and your name was given to me by another client of Joey McCoy. I wanted to ask you…"

She hung up.

OK, I thought to myself. *I didn't express myself sufficiently well. I sounded somehow threatening. I had called her 'Ms. Harris' which sounded like a sales call.*

I pulled down a second Hardington directory – somehow, the demise of the monolithic phone companies had instigated a demand for publishers that are intent on blanketing America with a plethora of town-by-town mini-directories – this one listing residents by street in addition to alphabetically. It included the first names of adult residents, and I found that 14 Chestnut Street was the home of Ashley and Stuart Harris. I punched the number again.

Me: "Ashley? Hi, this is Anne Carlton. I was just calling to ask…"

She: "I know who you are and I know why you're calling. Don't you ever call this number again."

I heard the slamming of a phone onto a handset.

Wow, I thought to myself. *I have wandered into wacko land. I do not know who this woman is, and I do not want to know what her problems are, because there are certainly more than one.*

I took stock of my progress. I had six glowing references supplied by Joey. I had an honest, generally positive reference from a recent customer. I also had someone who had replied to a bland query with the mysterious shorthand, 'creep'. And I had a woman who was in serious need of anti-psychotic drugs.

And, yes, I know exactly what you're thinking. Run, do not walk away from this guy. Hang out in front of 14 Chestnut Street and see if a truck bearing the name 'McCoy Contracting' is there several times a week and, if so, is there contracting going on or something else? Track down 'Candy' and see exactly why she responded 'creep' to my earlier query. Keep trolling for customers, happy or unhappy, until you have a firm idea of what kind of builder Joey McCoy is. And, if in the view of everyone with whom you speak he isn't completely solid, scratch him off your list and move on to the next builder.

But you have to put yourself in my place. I wanted to build our dream 'just-the-right-size' house now. I had now owned the land for four days and desperately wanted to start seeing a house rise there. I wanted to serve Thanksgiving dinner in my new, smaller home; not in the baronial banquet hall that passed for a 'dining activity center' with its table for twelve. I didn't want to wait until next spring and take occupancy sometime after Labor Day.

Plus, I didn't have a fallback position. There was no 'next builder'. Four of the five names on that list had responded that they would be pleased to put me on their project list for next spring or summer. Two gave foundation pour dates of early May. Two said only, 'sometime in May or June, weather and schedule permitting'. The only builder ready and willing to meet my occupancy-this-November date was Joey McCoy. When it came down to the nitty-gritty, Joey was the only builder in all of New England who said he could meet my schedule.

That evening, Matt (speaking from the Park Hyatt Zurich

where it was two in the morning, bless his heart) and I called Joey and told him he was our preferred contractor, and that we needed a detailed estimate and timetable. Joey asked for ten days to get together all of his numbers. We agreed to meet on July 22 to discuss and finalize our arrangement.

The biggest wheel had just been set in motion, and I didn't know whether to be deliriously happy or frightened to death.

Chapter Four

I want you to imagine this: you are standing at the edge of a windswept chasm with nothing below you for a thousand feet. Fifty feet across that chasm is *terra firma* and the place you need to go. Someone hands you a blindfold. You put it on. They tell you to take a step forward, off the edge of the cliff. They tell you it is safe to do so because, though unseen by you, there is an invisible bridge that will carry you to the safety of the other side.

You take that step.

The decision to put your house on the market while simultaneously building its replacement is an action just like stepping off the cliff expecting against all reason and experience that there will be an invisible bridge across that chasm.

You make that decision as an act of faith, knowing that everything comes down to sheer luck and timing. In a perfect world, you put your house on the market, it sells in a reasonable period of time, and the sale closes the same week that you get your Certificate of Occupancy on your new abode.

But the world we live in is wildly imperfect. Someone may walk into your first open house, fall in love, offer full price, but demand to close in five weeks. If that happens, you will be scrambling for a place to live while your imagination runs wild at what kind of firetrap roach motel will rent someone a furnished, one bedroom apartment for two months. You will also be beseeching a mover to store your furniture for two months while your new home is completed, and wondering how many treasured family heirlooms will arrive in fragments because they were moved twice.

But that's a high-class problem compared to the alternative:

that your house squats on the market like an unloved toadstool for six months with no takers; your new house is ready for occupancy but sitting empty, and you're left with the excruciating decision of either continuing to live in the old house so it doesn't have the taint of belonging to a 'highly motivated seller', or else moving to the new home and leaving behind an empty shell of a house that has only dust bunnies as furnishings for prospective couples to imagine as their new dream home.

To sell a house, you need a broker. To sell an expensive house for its asking price and on a timetable, you need a marketing-savvy shark.

We have several friends who are Realtors and even more acquaintances that have sons and daughters who ply the real estate trade. All of them smelled the opportunity. Each of them surfaced in the weeks before we put our house on the market. Unbidden, they sent us baskets of fruit, high-end chocolates, Starbucks gift cards emblazoned with their photos, and handwritten letters on creamy stationery. And they were unanimously miffed when we didn't choose them or their niece. Some are still not talking to us.

There was never any question but that Alexis Hoyt and Hardington Properties would represent our home. Not only had she devoted two years to shepherding me around during my search for property (for which she received bupkis because we bought the River Street house in a 'private sale' with no brokers' commissions), she also sells more million-dollar-plus homes in Hardington and surrounding towns than any other broker. Alexis isn't the *only* broker with such credentials, but her track record stood out.

We did, however, ask for a marketing plan and, on July 13, Alexis showed up at our home with three one-inch-thick packages of information. Matt was two hours off a plane from Europe, yet looking fresh and alert. I guess first-class upgrades will do that for you, but I was overjoyed that he had made it home in time for the meeting.

Alexis was no longer the friend in blue jeans and a casual sweater. She showed up in a black pencil skirt, a red silk blouse, and an Emilio Pucci silk scarf. Her jewelry was matched and her makeup perfectly applied. She brought a sleek, ultra-thin laptop with a Powerpoint program ready to go. She was, to borrow Matt's terminology, in her full-blown selling mode.

"We start with the value of your home," Alexis began. She then proceeded to show us photos of every property for sale in a five-mile radius that bore even a superficial resemblance to ours. That was followed by a tutorial on every house that had sold in Hardington over the past eighteen months, the number of days those houses were on the market, and an impressive graph showing the crucial spring season and how it skewed results.

"Spring is everything," she said. "Houses show their best, people have been cooped up for four months, and they're thinking about getting their kids into local schools for the fall term. In Hardington, it's also when the Patriot draft picks sign their contracts and start spending their bonuses."

Alexis then did something even more surprising: she showed us photos of ten houses that were *about* to come on the market. "These are people who are working with either me or someone in the office," she said. "Not all of them will choose to be listed but I'd say you're looking at your competition."

She dissected the assets and liabilities of each house. In my admittedly biased opinion, our house was far and away the best looking.

She then showed a screen with a photo of one house. It wasn't ours, but it was somewhat similar. A big Colonial on two acres. "This is the Bradley house on Poplar Lane."

Everyone knew about the Bradley house on Poplar Lane. Zack and Zöe Bradley were a couple in their early thirties with two young children. With financing assistance from the First National Bank of Mom and Dad, they had bought a five-bedroom, four-and-a-half-bath home on one of Hardington's 'premier' streets about a mile away from where we were now seated. They had paid $1,499,900 for their home. At the time of the purchase they were thirty-two and thirty-three years old. What in the hell were they thinking?

It was entirely possible that they had signed the binding purchase and sale agreement on the house on the Saturday afternoon of the weekend when Boston-area housing prices hit their zenith. On their way home from signing the agreement, the Bradley's likely passed billboards proclaiming that the housing bubble had just burst. Anyone with an ounce of common sense would have found a way to back out of the deal because, by the time the sale closed, housing prices were already down two or three percent and economists were offering dire warnings of much worse things to come.

Six months later, Zack Bradley lost his hotshot Generation-X marketing job with some ephemeral dot-com startup. When Zack went job hunting, he found there were several thousand people just like him looking for the same, non-existent job. But those job-market competitors didn't have a $7500 a month mortgage to meet. Those people lived in cheap apartments in Quincy or Allston and, if they couldn't meet the rent, they moved into Mom and Dad's basement.

A year into Zack Bradley's still-fruitless job search, the family made matters even worse by going public with their misfortune. They started calling reporters. The *Boston Globe* did a sympathetic piece on a young, once-affluent couple's plight of descending into the ranks of the long-term unemployed while carrying far too much debt. Producers from ABC and CNN saw the *Globe* piece and sent out TV crews.

The TV cameras captured in unblinking detail what the *Globe* had glossed over: a house laden with every expensive toy a child could want including a pink electric Jeep for a three-year-old. Zöe

– a stay-at-home mom – had a walk-in-closet full of designer-label outfits, some with the tags still hanging off them. Zack had a hand-crafted canoe and three sets of premium golf clubs (he would subsequently say they were hand-me-downs from his father-in-law). Matt and I watched the resulting TV segments and had the same reaction as everyone else in America: how on earth did Zack and Zöe think they were going to pay for this stuff? And, hadn't either of their parents ever opened a dictionary and showed their offspring the definition of the word, 'thrift'?

Zack and Zöe apparently thought the exposure would bring them job offers, gifts from strangers, or manna from heaven. Instead, it made them objects of scorn and, worse, poster children for the inexcusable excesses of the offspring of Baby Boomers.

Six months after their media exposure, the Bradley's put their Poplar Lane house on the market – for exactly what they had paid for it two years earlier. The price of houses, by this time, was down ten percent from its peak, meaning their asking price was at least $150,000 above what was probably already too high a figure. But if Zack and Zöe sold the home for what it was now worth, they would be out an amount greater than their down payment. They were what the housing industry calls 'upside down'. Instead of getting a check at their closing, they would have to *write* a check to their mortgage lender. They couldn't afford to sell their house for its current market value.

The only visitors at open houses were there to see the Ping golf clubs and the pink electric Jeep.

Over the course of eighteen months and three different brokers, the asking price fell, but the house was always $50,000 or more above its competition. Eventually, the Bradleys declared bankruptcy, moved out, and separated (news of the Bradleys was the conversation opener at every dinner party given in Hardington for three years). Caught in perpetual legal proceedings, the now-empty house deteriorated and the lawn devolved into a foot-tall tangle of weeds and vines.

Finally, nine months ago, the house had sold in a foreclosure auction. The price: $605,000.

"This is the house that still hangs over the market," Alexis said. "You can tell the story and explain it as an outlier to every customer who balks at your asking price, but there's no getting around the fact that when someone looks at the 'comparables' for high-end Colonials or sees the average selling prices in Hardington in your price bracket, the Bradley house pulls everyone down."

I felt a splash of ice-cold water was about to be thrown on the proceedings.

"Before we talk price, let's use that days-on-market to figure out when we need to formally put your home up for sale," Alexis said, and reached into her briefcase to pull out what looked to me to be a scroll.

The scroll turned out to be a three-foot-long, continuous twenty-week calendar that started at the beginning of July and ended at the close of November. Alexis spread it across our Great Room coffee table.

From her briefcase, she also extracted what looked like a radio antennae, but which telescoped out to become a pointer.

She tapped Thursday, November 24. "That's Thanksgiving Day. You want to be moved into your new home and serving dinner to your family." She moved the pointer just to the left. "So, we assume that we close on the sale of your present home on November 23. That's nineteen weeks from today. Let's work backwards."

She began moving her pointer up the calendar. "From the day you get an acceptable offer to the time your buyer gets a mortgage commitment is two weeks, which gives time for inspections. And, from the time that mortgage commitment is issued until closing is typically four weeks." Alexis reached down and removed three pieces of paper that had cleverly and invisibly been affixed to the calendar. October 12 was now revealed as the date for the binding offer, October 26 was the date of the mortgage commitment, and November 23 was the closing date.

Alexis went back to her Powerpoint deck and popped up a slide. "For million-plus homes in Hardington, the average days on market this year is seventy-two days."

I was catching on. I counted up ten weeks and two days. August 1. I waited for Alexis to pull off the next piece of paper.

Instead, Alexis tapped the next slide into place and the house-by-house listing of days-on-market divided itself into two color-coded groups. "But that seventy-two days is weighted by the spring selling season." She tapped the green-colored lines which showed numbers as few as ten days." Now she tapped the orange lines, several of which showed houses selling after more than a hundred days.

"You have a great house on a desirable street, but we're going to be marketing into the summer and autumn season, where there are far fewer buyers. We need to add ten days." She reached down and pulled off July 22. That was nine days from today. Alexis must have seen my jaw drop.

"And, to shorten that days-on-market time to eighty-two days or less, we need to do a first-rate job of positioning it. Before the first prospective buyer walks through the door, we need to have it staged and photographed. We need to bring up a website, and we need to get the house on the Caravan calendar."

"How long does that take?" I asked.

"It should take two weeks," Alexis said without missing a beat. "We're going to get it done in nine days." She pulled off the last piece of paper. It was for today. The space on the calendar now read, 'Start marketing'.

Matt had been silent through much of the presentation. His folder included a copy of the Powerpoint presentation, to which he had appended many notes. Now, he spoke. "And what's your professional judgment for an asking price?"

Wordlessly, Alexis took out a notepad from her briefcase. She wrote on a sheet of paper, tore it off, folded it twice, and handed it to Matt.

He unfolded it.

It read *'$1,339,900 - $1,359,900'.*

"Blame the Bradley's and the summer market," Alexis said. "You'll have fewer buyers because it's too late to get their kids into school for the fall session. That will cost you a hundred thousand of value. The Bradley's comp drags down the asking price by another fifty thousand."

You may remember that I had a figure of $1,500,000 in mind as the value of our home. Alexis had just slashed its price by ten percent. But I had a question in mind.

"Why didn't any of this psychology come into play when we were bidding on River Street?" I asked.

Alexis grimaced. "The low end of the market is a completely different dynamic. There, it's a seller's market. And you were right in the middle of the spring selling season."

Two thoughts popped into my head. The first was that there was something terribly amiss when $400,000 homes were considered the 'low end' of a town's real estate market. The other was that we were inverting that oldest of real estate maxims.

Buy high, sell low, I thought to myself.

* * * * *

Matt and I talked at length after Alexis departed.

"I remember when I thought that by downsizing we were going to pay off our mortgage, own our new house free and clear, and put several hundred thousand dollars in the bank," I said glumly.

"You may remember that we're still going to make a substantial profit on this house," Matt responded. He was right, of course. We had paid 'in the sevens' for our house 'way back when. To be bluntly honest, we had purchased more house than we needed specifically because the price was so attractive relative to what else was on the market at the time.

"You're *happy* about getting ten percent less than the house is worth?" I countered.

"We could wait until next spring," Matt replied. "Put the house on the market in February. The Bradley's house would be a distant memory and the buyers would be paying top dollar. Or, interest rates could go up and the market could tank, and we'd find ourselves with two houses."

"You always manage to put things in such an interesting light," I said.

"It's a gift," Matt said and smiled. "It takes two of us to make a decision, but I think Ms. Hoyt is a professional who ought to be listened to."

"Can we at least pick the high end of the range?" I asked.

Matt smiled. "Yes, my love. We'll pick the high end of the range."

Chapter Five

Two days later, a woman appeared at my doorstep. She was so thin I thought she might be collecting for an anorexia charity. Her emaciation was exacerbated by her clothing – three shades of taupe that hung off her like bedsheets – and a hair style that to be polite could have been called a Dutch pageboy but looked for all the world as though someone had affixed a mop to her head. She was likely sixty-something but her hair or wig was jet black and unnaturally shiny, as were the thick-framed glasses she wore.

Did I tell you I took an instant dislike to her?

"I am Estelle," she stated, producing a business card – also in taupe – from a jet-black leather folder. I glanced at the card, which at least has the courtesy of including a last name. "Alexis has hired me to stage…" At this point, I thought I heard an audible sniff of disapproval. "…this house."

Still standing on my doorstep, she turned and gestured left and right at my courtyard garden.

Before I continue with this story, let me say that the courtyard garden at which Estelle was gesturing is my pride and joy. It is my interpretation of an English cottage garden. In the middle of July it was a sea of color with orienpet lilies, astilbe in multiple hues, bright yellow heliopsis and coreopsis, white and lavender stokes aster, purple geranium and a fragrant Daphne. All of these perennials were augmented by a dozen container gardens filled with a riot of annuals overflowing their pots.

"You need to get rid of at least half of these plants." Estelle said, waving her hand as if to make my offending garden go away. "They're too much. They hurt my eyes."

We were not getting off to a positive start.

Standing behind Estelle at the bottom of the steps was a much younger woman, similarly dressed in ecru and beige, but with an aura of subservience about her. She carried what were either suitcases or sample cases. She, at least, appeared to be looking at the garden with admiration.

"I have only two hours," Estelle said impatiently, tapping her wrist to indicate a ticking watch, except that there was no wristwatch or other timepiece in evidence. "I must get started."

I noted that Estelle spoke with what I would describe as a Continental cadence, as someone would speak whose first language was not English. But the words coming out of Estelle's mouth were accented with pure New England dipthongs.

"I certainly don't want to detain you," I said, rather coolly.

"Good," Estelle said, failing to pick up on the irony. "Behind me is Missy. My assistant."

"Hello, Missy," I said, smiling.

Missy only nodded. She had a wary look on her face and apparently was expected never to speak; only to follow orders. I tried but failed to make eye contact. Missy was not allowed to interact with clients. She was an appendage.

We were now standing in our two-story foyer. Behind us was an open staircase that bent twice in its way to an open walkway and railing above the foyer. Estelle glanced left and right to the formal dining room and living room.

"Too much artwork," Estelle said to Missy. "Take it all down and we'll pick one or two pieces to keep."

I should add that our living room and dining room feature some superb nineteenth-century oil paintings. They're small, delicate, and a delight to behold. I collected them over a dozen trips to Europe. They're not Corot or Millet and they're not worth millions, but they're superbly executed and excellent pieces of art.

Missy began obediently taking down every painting and piling frames on top of one another on the floor.

"Please don't do that," I said to Missy. "You could damage the paintings and those antique frames are delicate."

Estelle waved an imperious hand. "Find some dust cloths." I didn't know if she was saying this to me or to Missy.

Estelle walked through the living room to the double-doored entrance to Matt's study. She opened one door and walked in.

"All this must go," she said. "Too much clutter. This is terrible. I want to see one or two chairs and things for children. This will be a children's playroom."

I think Matt might have other plans for the room for the next nineteen weeks.

"This is my husband's study," I said. "This is where he does his work in the evening and on weekends. He can't be without this room. It's how he makes his living."

"Families want a playroom for their children," Estelle said, ignoring every word of what I had just said. "Where do you have stored your children's furniture? Where are the toys? Bring them out so I can choose. Please do not waste my time."

"My children are grown and out in the world," I said, trying to keep my voice calm. "There has not been any 'children's furniture' for nearly two decades. In fact, I'm reasonably certain we didn't move it from our last house."

Estelle sniffed. "Missy, take notes."

She then opened a door to a half bath. "The color," she said. "It hurts my eyes." She then added, "Missy, the swatches."

Missy obediently opened one of her cases and extracted six oversize pieces of colored paper. All of them were shades of gray and gray-brown.

"This one, I think," Estelle said, holding a gray swatch against a wall that was painted a warm, daffodil yellow.

Missy wrote down a number.

Estelle walked into the kitchen. "This will not do."

"Is there a problem?" I asked.

"Your appliances," she said. "They're….. white."

"So I've noticed," I replied.

"*No* one has white appliances. This is not acceptable. These must be changed." She began touching the refrigerator and ovens, as though she might have the power to make them disappear. Then she gasped "The cabinets. The hardware. This is impossible. Missy, make notes. It must all go."

Then she was in the Great Room. This is the room that Matt and I live in. It is a space that is full of light year-round. It has walls of windows that open onto the rear gardens and skylights that ensure that even the darkest days can be enjoyed without artificial lights. It is the first thing that visitors notice in our home and the room that draws the most compliments.

"This room requires drapes and window treatments," Estelle said. "I want to see attractive, wooden louvered blinds for a unified look, and drapes that will give the room a magical touch. We will use accent lights. Missy, take notes."

"Won't that defeat the purpose of all those windows with views of the gardens?" I asked.

Estelle gave another dismissive wave. "We need to create drama to sell this house. This must be a dramatic yet introspective space." She then turned and saw the back wall of the room that rises two stories. It was our 'memory wall'. On it, Matt and I had hung souvenirs of travels and special events. There were a series of photos of the two of us on the Great Wall of China, a poster-size shot of us in a hot air balloon at a New Mexico festival, and a matador's cape from Matt's foray into a bullring in Spain. All in all, I would say there were a hundred objects and photos rising to the top of the wall some eighteen feet above the floor.

"All of this must go," Estelle whispered. "This is useless. No one will be able to envision this as their home." To Missy, Estelle said, "The swatches." She then began trying various shades of taupe against the wall. "This one," she said to Missy. She returned to the kitchen. "This one," she said, holding up an ecru swatch to the kitchen wall.

To me, she said, "You do not understand. This is no longer *your* home. You may love these things, but they all read 'old'. The family that buys your home will have *young* children. If *they* cannot imagine themselves *here*, they will go to a home where *they* are comfortable."

She turned her attention to the oversized sofa in the Great Room and its flanking rattan chairs. "These I like," she said. "But you must buy pillows. Bright, colorful pillows. Fill this room with bright pillows and a young family will be at home. I also want to see large, clear-glass table lamps. Those read young and modern."

She swept her hand along the table behind the sofa. It housed the best of my pottery pieces, collected in Asia, Europe and South America. "Hide all of these things. They read 'old'. Let the buyer see themselves in the room. You must trust me."

Missy was writing furiously, of course.

We went upstairs and two rooms hurt Estelle's eyes. Beige was the prescribed antidote. And pillows. Lots and lots of matching, oversized and over-stuffed pillows on the beds. And a down comforter. My beautiful and exquisitely made Amish quilts were banished. Need I say that they read 'old'?

I snapped when we got to the Master Bath and Estelle called for a complete set of new ecru towels, the replacement of brass fixtures with nickel steel and the banishment of my Corian counter.

"I think I've had enough," I said, not trying to hide the annoyance I felt. "Declutter. I get it. De-personalize. I get that, too. But I'm not ripping out counters that don't show a scintilla of wear just because you decreed that Corian is out. And my windows overlook gardens, not a brick wall of the building next door. I want to show off that view, not hide it."

"I am trying to help you sell your home," Estelle sniffed. "This house is all clutter. It does not read young. I can make it attractive to a young family with children."

"The last young family with children that bought a house like this got divorced, went bankrupt, and had their lives destroyed," I said. "Their name was Bradley. You probably staged the house they bought. It was on Poplar Lane. Was that your work?"

"I do not have to listen to this," Estelle hissed. "I am paid to help you."

"This house is going on the market next week," I continued. "It will probably close in early November. What young family with young children is going to buy this house in August or September?"

"I know what sells," Estelle said, her eyes narrowing and hardening. "I know good taste. I know what people want. Without me, your house will sit on the market *for years.*" A supercilious smirk accompanied that last phrase.

"Estelle," I said, "I think your work here is done. Get the hell out of my house before I forcibly throw your scrawny ass out one of those windows you so desperately want to cover up."

Estelle showed no response. Missy, on the other hand, definitely reacted. Her eyes widened, her face went red, and her hands went to her mouth. She was suppressing a laugh. Fortunately, Missy was standing behind Estelle.

"*We* are leaving, Missy." Estelle said. "Come."

Estelle wordlessly walked by me and out the door. Once outside and on the sidewalk, she stopped and turned around.

"I was wrong," she said. "It is not half these plants that must go. It is three-quarters of these hideous plants in this atrocious space you call a garden."

* * * * *

An hour later, Alexis Hoyt was continuously ringing my doorbell while pounding on the door.

"What on earth did you say to her?" Alexis said, near to hysteria. "She said she'll never stage another home for me as long as she lives."

"I told her what I thought of her ideas," I said coolly. "She was brutally frank with me. So I was brutally frank right back."

"She's trying to help," Alexis said, her tone one of exasperation. "She's one of the best in the business."

"Alexis," I said, guiding her to a seat on the living room sofa, "I don't know where Estelle is getting her ideas, but she thinks the solution to every problem is to paint it beige. She wants to repaint every room in the house, replace all of the appliances, and tear out the counters. I think I'm smart enough to understand the basics of what staging is. We will take down the personal stuff. That's logical. We'll make the rooms look less cluttered. We'll store away as much art as we can. But I can't turn Matt's study into a nursery. And I'm not going to put in marble counters."

Alexis started to speak and I held up my hand. "The family that buys this house is going to have a fair amount of disposable income, otherwise they'll never get approved for a mortgage. That means they're smart. They can look at a yellow wall and envision it as green or blue. They can look at white appliances and envision stainless steel. And, if I were looking to buy this house, I would be *wary* of seeing brand new appliances, because I know that if *I* were the one doing the selling, I would be putting in the cheapest stuff I could find from Lowes. If I'm the buyer, I think walking into a house and finding ten-year-old white appliances is perfect. It gives me negotiating room."

I nodded, opening the floor to rebuttal. Alexis shook her head. "I see hundreds of buyers," she said, her voice firm. "You and I can walk into a room and mentally paint it a different color. These young kids in the market today, they can't. They'll turn down a house because they don't like the way the furniture is arranged. They can only see things one way." She again shook her head. "Things have changed since you and I were that age."

"Then where is the money coming from?" I asked. "Estelle

could only see one kind of buyer: a pair of thirty-two year-olds with a two-year-old daughter and a four-year-old son, and one more in the oven. Where could they possibly get a $350,000 down payment and how do they qualify for a million dollar mortgage? Nobody pulls down that kind of salary at that age and no family with children could possibly have put away those kind of savings."

Morin just shook her head. "All I know is, they have the money and they get the mortgage. And this is the kind of house they want." She gave me a plaintive look. "The photographers are coming on Tuesday. We won't repaint and we won't rip out appliances and counters. But give Estelle time to stage the major rooms. If what she does annoys you, feel free to put everything back the way it was the minute the photography is done. But the photos that go on the website and into the video are critical. That's what generates traffic at the open house. Thirty-somethings look at a hundred video walk-throughs and choose the three or four homes they'll visit in person. Please give me that." There was pleading in her voice.

"We can put back everything," I said. I wasn't asking a question. I was making a statement; repeating her words back to her.

Alexis nodded.

"Deal," I said. "We're waiting for our contractor to give us our firm numbers. Tonight, I'm going to take Matt shopping for pillows and lamps; an activity he loathes and for which he'll extract payment sometime when I least expect it. We'll drop off anything we find here at the house. Sunday is Matt's birthday and I'm taking him up to Maine for a long weekend. You can have the house for three days, and if I can get our room for an extra night, we won't even bother you on Tuesday."

"Go to Pottery Barn," Alexis said. "They'll have what you're looking for."

I said I would find the nearest one.

The look of relief on Alexis' face was palpable. But it was quickly replaced by one of concern. "If I can get Estelle to come back," she said. "She said she would never set foot in this house again."

"Does she get paid if she doesn't stage?" I asked.

"No," Alexis replied. "I only pay her for a completed job."

"She'll come back," I said with full confidence. "But if she touches my garden, I'll come after her with a chainsaw."

* * * * *

I have been taking Matt away for his birthday for twenty years and he has learned that it is best to clear his schedule. He has come home to find his suitcase packed for a long weekend in Santa Fe, four days in London (both wonderfully successful), five days in Montserrat (not a nice place to visit in July), and three days on Prince Edward Island (the jury is still out; I think he enjoyed himself more than he let on). Mostly, though, I book someplace on the New England coastline with good food and cool breezes.

And please don't remind me that, when I said we were going to pay an arm and a leg for the River Street property, I made it clear there would be no vacations or expensive dinners out. Matt's birthday is special and there are different rules. Plus I had booked the inn back in April and I don't pay cancellation fees.

Matt thought he was at least going to have one quiet evening of reading contracts, so he was surprised when I said we were going pillow shopping. We drove to Chestnut Hill, where Google told me I would find a full-service Pottery Barn retail outlet.

As soon as we walked into the store, everything fell into place. *This* was where Estelle got her 'design esthetic'. Everything in the store was in shades of brown and gray. The walls were ecru and taupe. Window 'treatments' in the form of curtains, blinds, and shutters completely obliterated the windows behind them. All accents were steel and glass. The beds were stacked high with pillows and comforters. All the lamps had basketball-size clear glass bases. There wasn't a book to be seen.

Alexis' stager apparently stopped into Pottery Barn every few months, swiped a catalog, and then, for a thousand dollar a pop, forced hundreds of innocent home sellers to remake their property to look just like the store's catalog.

We weren't being staged, we were being 'Pottery Barned'.

And on a Friday evening the store was swarming with people, all in their twenties and thirties. They were avidly purchasing horrendously overpriced duvets and shamelessly marked-up bric-a-brac.

I tried to think back where I shopped when I was in my late twenties. I had two young children to feed and clothe, and Matt was stuck as a 'Senior Associate' at a firm that pointedly refused to hand out partnerships to anyone under the age of seventy. I probably shopped at K-Mart. Or yard sales.

We left the store with half a dozen items that, for no reason I could discern, were on sale. My purchase of those items proved to myself that I was willing to meet Alexis half way. As we left I put half a dozen catalogs in my shopping bag and vowed to leave them scattered around the house so that Estelle was certain to find them. However, given that subtlety was not Estelle's strong suit, it was unlikely that she would get my message. At least Missy would pick up on my dig.

* * * * *

We spent a peaceful, romantic three days in Boothbay Harbor. I got to see the Coastal Maine Botanical Garden in its mid-summer glory. Matt got to take long walks along the beach and put comfort letters, exclusion clauses, and joint and several liabilities out of his mind for a few days while contemplating what it felt like to turn fifty-two.

I surreptitiously phoned Alexis on Monday evening and was assured that if we arrived home after 1 p.m., the photographers would be packed up and gone.

* * * * *

We arrived home Tuesday afternoon after enjoying a final seafood gorging in the form of fried clams and lobster chowder with onion rings at J.T. Farnham's in Essex. I was in a great mood right up until the time I opened the front door.

Our house had been hit by a taupe tornado. The furniture had been re-arranged and half of it was simply missing. Two-thirds of my art was gone, what was on the wall were not the paintings I would have chosen, and all of my treasured ceramic pieces had disappeared. Matt's study consisted of a rocking horse I had never seen, two chairs from the basement, and a handful of books, chosen for the color of their jackets.

An antique Provençal doll, acquired a decade ago at a shop in Exe and carried on my lap on the flight home, lay on a low bookcase shelf where it could be picked up, beheaded, and thrown at a wall by the first cranky three-year-old who encountered it. At least five hundred books had utterly vanished. The pitiful few books that had been permitted to remain did not sit normally on the shelves. Rather, they were positioned artfully, sometimes cantilevered precariously into space.

Feeling ill, I found my phone and called Alexis. She answered before the first ring was completed.

"I know what you're thinking," she said before I had an opportunity to get out a single word. "The photos are gorgeous. I'm looking at them right now. Your house glows. This is going to be a killer walk-through. You're going to be mobbed on Saturday."

"Where is our stuff?" I asked. I didn't raise my voice. I was too stunned to muster any anger. I suppose that would come later. I genuinely didn't know how a house full of personal belongings had vanished.

"The garage and the basement," Alexis said. "You can put it all back if you want. But I'd beg you to wait until after Saturday."

"Please tell me you made a list of where everything is," I said. "Please tell me the boxes are numbered. Please tell me there are *boxes*. Please tell me everything was carefully wrapped."

There was a pause on the other end of the phone. "We used newspapers and towels to wrap the delicate items," Alexis said. I didn't believe her. Not for a heartbeat.

I ended the call with a tap, not bothering to say goodbye. In something of a daze, I went down into the basement.

And started crying.

Our art, ten paintings deep, leaned against basement walls that were probably damp. My pottery was on the floor, one layer deep covering more than hundred square feet, every piece touching at least three other pieces. Matt's books and our library were simply thrown in stacks three and four feet high. Almost everything that had been on my kitchen counters was piled by our downstairs freezer.

It was vandalism. Estelle had gotten her revenge. And Alexis either had willfully not noticed or else hadn't bothered to show up to supervise.

I went back upstairs, numb. In the garage, surplus furniture covered the floor and, when whoever moved it ran out of floor space, they stacked furniture and accessories two and three pieces high.

Matt found me in the garage. Wordlessly, he took my hand and then embraced me, holding me tightly for more than a minute. There were no words exchanged. Words were unnecessary. Words would have gotten in the way. Matt understood my pain.

When at last we pulled apart from one another, I said, "I realize now that I can't trust Alexis. She isn't really on my side. She simply wants to get the house sold so she can collect her commission."

Matt nodded agreement. "That's how it is in any commission-based business relationship. She gets paid only if and when the house sells. And, once the house is sold, it's just a notch on her pole and money in her back account. She isn't your friend, all those hours she spent with you notwithstanding. What she did was an investment in getting this commission. Our house is a product. She has maximized its salability, though at the price of hurting our feelings. Obviously, she values salability over our feelings."

He kissed me on the cheek. "There is a bright side," he said. "We've known all along that most of our furniture won't fit in the new house. I suspect you've been giving some thought to what stays and what goes. This is a great opportunity to get rid of the surplus."

He was right as far as it went. Much of the furniture would go to charity and this was the time to perform that triage. But I wasn't going to discard paintings or ceramics. And to hell with 'reading old'. It was my house.

It was *my house*. And, instead of crying, I decided to take back my house.

I found my phone and scrolled through my contacts for friends with high-school-age teens. In an hour, I had assembled a crew of five brawny boys and two girls who not only were on the Hardington High School lacrosse team, but had also impressed me with their superior organizational skills.

At five o'clock, I had them in the remains of my living room, organized into three work crews where I explained the task at hand. I said we would start at eight the following morning and that I would provide lunch. The pay was fifteen dollars an hour with a bonus if the project was completed in one day. They eagerly agreed.

The next morning, Matt took the train into Boston and my crew and I went to work. Last year we had taken extensive photos of our home's interior for insurance purposes. Now, those photos were shown larger than life size on a bare wall using Matt's digital projector. One three-man (well, two girls and one boy) crew was charged with recreating Matt's study with every book and knickknack in its exact place.

A second crew carefully bubble-wrapped artwork that was not being returned to the walls. A third did the same with certain of my ceramic pieces and non-essential kitchen items. All bubble-wrapped items were carefully placed in storage boxes I acquired at the Overton U-Haul franchise and each box was numbered and labeled for content. After lunch, when the library project was nearing completion, I pulled off one of the girls to make an Excel spreadsheet of the contents of each box.

When the boxes were neatly stacked, I turned the two all-male crews over to the task of measuring, photographing and wrapping surplus furniture and then moving it into the basement.

At four o'clock the eight of us did a walk-through of the house. I gave a few final assignments. Teenagers scurried to do as I asked.

Matt's study was exactly as it had been when we left for Maine. When he came home this evening, it would be as though no one had ever touched his inner sanctum. Just as important, rooms had been 'decluttered', but now held items that were significant to Matt and me. The art now on display was – in my opinion – our most beautiful pieces. I had pulled out quilts that I thought complemented bedroom decors. If it read 'old', then to hell with it.

I assembled my crew at five o'clock and passed out stacks of twenty-bills that I retrieved from my bank's ATM at the same time I picked up lunchtime pizzas for everyone. In all, I gave out $1,120. Please understand that I do not splurge. I have never purchased a thousand-dollar outfit and I have never had a thousand dollar dinner, no matter how many guests were involved. I fly coach unless miles are involved or someone else is picking up the tab. I am not a tightwad; I just recognize the value of money.

But, in just one day, these seven kids had not only given me back an acceptable semblance of my own home, they had helped me organize the next several months of my life. Without them, I would have spent hours anguishing over what to keep and what to discard; what to 'depersonalize' and what to retain on display. Now, those critical tasks were not only done, the results were carefully boxed up, labeled, and accessible at any time via an accurate spreadsheet.

All things considered, the price was a bargain.

* * * * *

The next morning, Alexis phoned and asked if she could come over to see me. She sounded excited and said she had something important to show me. If there was any contrition in her voice for what she had allowed to be done to my home, it was not apparent.

Fifteen minutes later, my doorbell rang. I dispensed with the usual thirty second grace period and immediately opened the door. I wanted to see the expression on Alexis' face before she had time to pull down her professional mask.

Alexis walked in, smiling broadly. But her smile was *too* broad; it was a fake smile, pre-pasted look.

But even that phony smile evaporated when she looked at the foyer, living, and dining rooms. I had created my own staging. But this was a look that I could endure for the next eighteen weeks.

"What did you *do*?" she gasped.

"I decluttered, like you asked," I said, a pleasant smile on my face. "I depersonalized the place. I barely recognize it as my own house. You said I could put back everything the way it was, but I figured this was better."

Alexis walked from room to room. She stopped only at Matt's study. "You know people really want that children's play room," she said.

"I bet it's in the video," I said. "When they get here, they can use their imagination."

Alexis shook her head. I don't know if it was sorrow or disgust.

"You said you would do just enough to make the house work for the video," I continued, exchanging my smile for the kind of look you give children who have just been caught in a lie. "Instead, you pulled the house apart and just threw everything down into the basement. You expected, with everything in disarray, I would just fold and leave it the way you wanted. Well, I didn't." My voice, while not cold, was certainly not warm and friendly.

"It isn't the house people are going to expect to see," Alexis said, almost but not quite gritting her teeth. "This isn't... bad... but it isn't... what people want. You're supposed to trust me to know what I'm doing."

"And you're supposed to know that Matt and I have to live here," I said. "All Estelle knows is what she sees in a Pottery Barn catalog. That's not taste; that's just copying what a chain store sells. You want to save yourself a thousand dollars on each listing? Just give your client the catalog and say, 'copy this'. But also remember: next month, Pottery Barn may be touting this look. No one wants to live with taupe forever."

Just for a moment, I saw the 'real' look on Alexis' face. Resignation. We were going to be 'difficult' clients. We were going to be the couple that insisted on doing things differently. Against the odds, I had pulled together my own look. Maybe the thirty-somethings would flee in horror. Maybe they would see it as the look they wanted. Maybe, just maybe, they would look past whatever décor was in front of them and envision the house the way *they* wanted it.

"We'd better look at the website and video," Alexis said, pulling her computer from her briefcase. "It goes live tomorrow morning. There's a Realtors' open house at 11:30 and I want to bring through a few brokers for one-on-one viewings." She looked around the room and added, "God only knows what they're going to be telling one another after they leave."

I was hearing the sound of a woman who realized she was going to have to earn her commission.

Chapter Six

If there is a day in this saga that stands out as a positive one, it is July 22. That was the day, sometime after midnight, that our home hit the Internet. At six in the morning, I clicked through Realtor.com, Zillow, Trulia, and Homes.com. There we were: 32 beautiful photos, a gorgeous five-minute video with pans and zooms set to music, professionally-produced floor plans, the distance to schools and shopping, and enough comparison information to tell everyone that our home was fairly priced. Because our listing was new, we were at the top of all of the sites.

I also studied the competition. Two other Hardington homes would have their first showing over the weekend. One was similar in size and price, the other a step down in both measures. The direct competitor looked nice on the screen, but I knew its dirty little secret: the house was in Metacomet Estates. Metacomet Estates is a 1960s-era subdivision of poorly-built ranch houses on acre-size lots. Maybe a third of those houses have been torn down and replaced with newer, larger homes, but the one for sale was on a block where all the other structures were fifty years old and looking tired.

Through the morning, Alexis emailed me viewing statistics. More than seven hundred people had viewed the page, eighty-seven had watched the complete video and fifty-one had bookmarked the listing. Could a bidding war be brewing?

At 10:45 I left the house and went grocery shopping. The homeowner is not allowed to be around for the brokers' open house.

In the early afternoon, Alexis emailed again with a summary of brokers' comments. The positive ones were music to my soul: 'immaculate', 'fairly priced', 'love the woodwork', 'intelligent floor plan' and my favorite, 'great home in a great neighborhood'. While most liked the house there were negatives: 'white appliances', 'décor not neutralized', and 'not child friendly'. I disregarded those, but paid attention to one that read, 'garden beautiful but intimidating'

In the middle of the afternoon, Alexis called to make certain I had read her emails. She sounded subdued. "A lot of brokers like the house, but they don't have a lot of clients looking in this price range right now," she said. "It comes down to who shows up tomorrow."

* * * * *

July 22 was also the day Joey McCoy hand-delivered the cost proposal for our home. "I knew you'd have questions," he said when he came over that night. "I want to be able to respond to any issues fully and fairly." It was a hot evening following a day when temperatures had hovered in the mid-90s. Joey had slimmed down to shorts and a well-worn black souvenir tee for 'The Ramones in concert'. His waist was still cinched by that tool belt.

The proposal ran to eight pages and there was a copy for both Matt and myself. Matt, I noted, started reading at the top of page one. I did just the opposite: I went straight to the number on page six.

There were two numbers mid-way down the page: $409,227 and $424,553.

I gulped and started back at the beginning of the proposal.

McCoy Contracting is pleased to provide this estimate for the construction of a new residence for Mr. Matthew Carlton and Mrs. Anne Carlton at 131 River Street, Hardington, Massachusetts…

The first two pages were feel-good words about using the highest quality materials and licensed subcontractors of long experience that were well known to McCoy Contracting. There were paragraphs about adhering to the highest building standards, building 'green', and going 'above and beyond code requirements' in order to ensure peace of mind for the homeowner.

Page three launched into a description of the work McCoy Contracting would provide: site preparation, digging and pouring a foundation, framing the home… the list was exhaustive. Everything, in turn, tied back to the 'architectural plans supplied by the client on July 17.' Joey's proposal stopped only at the 'final and finish grade from foundation to street and a 25 foot perimeter around the sides and rear of the home. This was good; I had said I wanted to be responsible for our own landscaping.

Several parts of the proposal included 'allowances'. There was a $14,000 allowance for kitchen appliances, $25,000 for cabinetry, and $9,000 for granite and/or marble. If we went over that allowance, I assumed, we paid the excess. If we were under, the cost of the house came down.

My eye fell on the paragraph labeled, 'Timetable'.

McCoy Contracting enters into this project fully aware that the clients seek to occupy their new home before Thanksgiving Day. We will make every effort to expedite construction to deliver a finished home 120 days from the date an agreement is reached.

I felt my toe start to tap involuntarily. Thanksgiving was, by my count, 125 days away.

"I have a few questions," Matt said, breaking the silence. Joey and I looked his way.

Matt has a way of disarming people. He starts with a simple question, something everyone can agree on. It's the kind of question to which the answer seems so obvious that the people on the other side of the table wonder, at least initially, if Matt is really all that smart.

The last time we went shopping for a car, Matt's opening question upon getting a quote from the showroom salesman was whether the spare tire was full size or one of those temporary tires good for a hundred miles. The brochure for the car made it clear the car had a full-size spare and, just half an hour earlier, the salesman had lifted up a panel to show it to us. And so the salesman reassured Matt that the car came with the same size and model tire that was standard equipment on the car's four wheels.

That first question was just part of what Matt called, 'wearing down the other side'. Forty-five minutes later, Matt had chopped nearly twenty percent off of the quoted price and the salesman was sweating from every pore on his body. I almost felt sorry for the salesman. Almost.

"You're not going to put vinyl siding on this house, are you?" Matt asked.

Joey grinned and leaned back in his chair. "It's right there on page five, Mr. Carlton," Joey said. "'Premium cedar siding to be used for all house exteriors'. You're getting nothing but the best."

"Primed on both sides?" Matt asked. McCoy Contracting's quote had been silent on the subject.

"You bet, Mr. Carlton," Joey said, still grinning. "That's the way to do it right."

Matt lobbed a few more softballs, then started getting serious.

"Can we buy our own appliances and have the store install them?" Matt asked. "It would get that whole 'allowance' thing out of the way and make the total price a lot easier to take. It would also free up your time for more important things."

Joey nodded. "Sure," he said, "I don't see a problem there."

Except that there was a problem – for Joey McCoy. Every time a contractor touches something, it gets marked up. In theory, the lumber yard or the appliance store gives contractors a discount roughly equal to the markup the contractor will take so the customer sees no price difference. But for the contractor, it's a hit to the bottom line. Assuming the markup was fifteen percent, Joey had just given away $2,000 of his profit. But Joey didn't seem to notice, he just kept nodding his head; saying yes to each of Matt's questions. It was fascinating to watch.

An hour went by and Matt's questions continued. Ice tea was served. Each time Joey answered, Matt made a note on a legal pad.

At 9 p.m., Matt scratched his head. "I guess if we're going to do a proper contract, then we ought to talk about a payment schedule, including some funds to get you started."

This was something Matt and I had discussed via transatlantic calls and emails. I stressed to Matt that Joey's clients apparently never had a contract with him. Matt laughed and said, "We'll take care of that oversight."

What Matt had just done was to dangle a carrot with a hook in it. An 'if-then' hypothesis, but with the carrot and hook reversed. Note he didn't say, 'If we're going to talk about a payment schedule, including some funds to get you started, then we ought to talk about a contract.' No. That would scare off Joey. Instead, the contract was assumed.

And Joey bit. Hard.

"I'd probably need ten or fifteen thousand to get started," he said.

Matt merely nodded and jotted something on his pad. "What do you think are the right trigger points for progress payments?" Matt asked.

Joey's face showed confusion. "I usually just get an advance…"

Matt shook his head and smiled. "This isn't a fifty-thousand-dollar remodeling job. This is a half-million-dollar house."

Matt had just bumped up the cost of the project – at least in Joey's mind – by nearly twenty percent.

"Then I guess…," Joey said with hesitation, "we need to talk about those trigger points."

I have had the pleasure of sitting in on a handful of Matt's big contract deals. Sometimes I was there as, frankly, a prop. Sometimes I was just there because Matt invited me to go along with him to a negotiation being held in an especially nice place. Think Hawaii or Paris. I stayed in the background, I listened, and I learned. Matt is exceptionally good at what he does.

Over the course of half an hour, the three of us hashed out a payment schedule, always determined as a percentage of the total job. When we said 'good night' at 9:45, I am quite certain Joey stopped at a wine store to buy a proper bottle of Champagne for his wife, took it home, and told her they were about to become wealthy because a couple in Hardington wanted to throw money at them.

Actually, as I learned later, Joey did something quite different after leaving our home. But that's a story for another time.

* * * * *

Our first open house was on Saturday. We weren't there, of course. Homeowners are told to stay as far away from the action as possible. Afterward, Alexis gave us the summary. We had nearly forty people including four families accompanied by brokers, which in Alexis' mind was a sign of high interest.

Half the people spent less than twenty minutes in the house. These were the 'lookey-loos'; the people who went from one open house to another just for the thrill of seeing what the inside of people's homes looked like. A few others spent more time in the garden than they did in the house. In Alexis' view, people who looked primarily at gardens were not serious buyers.

She identified five 'qualifieds', meaning they were people who had toured the house thoroughly, asked intelligent questions, and volunteered names and information about themselves. Two were 'relos' moving to Boston – one from Chicago, the other from the San Francisco Bay area – and in for the weekend to look at houses. Two of the 'qualified' were those infamous thirty-something families with two kids, both armed with mortgage pre-approvals. The final 'qualified' was a Hardington family looking for a larger home.

"I'll circle back with them and let you know what happens," she said. I tried to pull from her whether she was elated or disappointed by the number of 'qualified'. She wouldn't say. "It's the first open house. I have other brokers bringing clients through next week. Let's see what they say."

It was a thoroughly unsatisfying conversation.

* * * * *

On Monday, Matt presented Joey with a simple, three-page document. The contract incorporated as 'schedules' our architect's plans and Joey's proposal. The document then carved out a handful of exceptions to Joey's proposal – a vague list of things we said we'd buy on our own – laid out a payment schedule and penalties in the event either side failed to deliver things on time, and specified that a Massachusetts board set up to adjudicate disputes between remodelers and homeowners would settle any problems that couldn't be worked out by the two parties.

There were no 'parties of the first part' or other legalese. It was all quite simple and straightforward. Anyone could understand it. Anyone, of course, except Joey McCoy.

"I don't see why we need a contract," Joey said. He was in our great room, a glass of iced tea and some biscuits spread with Nutella on the table in front of him. He seemed to be sulking. While he scarfed down the biscuits with abandon, he had glanced through the contract just once and didn't seem to even want to touch it.

Matt took the objection in stride, but nodded his understanding. He picked up his copy of the contract and pointed to an item on the second page. "Let's take just one item. Say you complete the framing of the house on September 15 as per the schedule," Matt said. "According to the contract, framing completion is a trigger point for me to write you a check for $50,000. You've got two subcontractors standing there with their hands outstretched, expecting to be get paid for their work. But when you come to see me to get the check, I tell you that I'm going out of town for two weeks but I'll write you that check just as soon as I get back, say, on October 1. Is that all right with you?"

"Well, no," Joey said, clearly considering the image of burly, angry subcontractors hefting pieces of lumber in a menacing manner because he had not paid them promptly. "That wouldn't fly in my kind of work."

"Of course not," Matt said. "And you don't want to dip into your own cash reserves to pay a sub. You should get paid when that part of the job is done so that you can stay on good terms with your crews."

That statement, of course, made the assumption that a contractor kept $50,000 lying around in a checking account on the off chance that it might be needed to fend off those cranky subcontractors.

Matt continued. "What the contract says is that if you finish the framing on September 15 and I haven't cut you that $50,000 check by September 16, I owe you a daily penalty of a thousand dollars. That's an awfully strong incentive for me to pay you on time."

Matt's example was brilliant. But that's what he does for a living: make people see a contract for the benefits it bestows on them while not pointing out what penalties come into play for slips on the other side. It's what Matt didn't say – or point out – that was even more brilliant. Getting the framing done by September 15 kept the house on its date-of-occupancy target. And to get the check, Joey had to do more than just say the framing was finished. He had to have a signoff from the town building inspector. Only when we saw that signature did we cut a check. And, for every day that McCoy Contracting missed that September 15 deadline, we had the right to withhold $500 from the final amount due. Joey had agreed to the dates two nights earlier. Now, he was being asked to adhere to them.

The biggest piece of legerdemain on Matt's part was right there for everyone to see if they knew where to look. The brief contract Joey McCoy was about to sign included, by reference, Joey's own eight-page proposal. As part of that proposal, Joey had included all the feel-good language about using the best materials and highest standards of workmanship. He was now obligated to adhere to those standards.

Let me make this clear: our goal wasn't to screw Joey McCoy or to not pay him what he was owed. Our goal was to get our house built on time, on budget, and with the quality we expected. The contract was a way of keeping Joey's attention focused squarely on our house. If he got sidetracked, the contract would get him back in line. If he thought the contract somehow did not apply to him, he would find out – in an excruciatingly painful way – that he was wrong.

Chapter Seven

And, just like that, our house was sold.

Well, not exactly 'just like that' and maybe not even 'sold', but for a few breathless moments, it felt like we had pulled off the fantastic feat of selling a million-dollar-plus house in a weekend.

Remember those five families from the first open house? One of the 'relos' extended their weekend house-hunting trip and came back for a second look on Monday morning. The Hardington family looking for a larger home made two additional visits in three days.

The 'relos' were coming east from Silicon Valley. It was a husband and wife and they couldn't believe how inexpensive real estate was in New England; much less that the office where one of them would be working was just fifteen minutes at rush hour from our driveway. Their current thirteen-mile commute to Menlo Park could take up to an hour.

The Hardington family consisted of a husband, wife and three kids, the youngest of which was eight and the oldest a rising junior at Hardington High. They had a nice, three-bedroom Colonial on the south side of town, but three kids meant the two youngest were sharing a bedroom. Plus there was all the sports equipment. Plus there was a need for a home office…. You get the idea.

On July 30, we were presented with two offers. Alexis brought them over. She was in high spirits, almost giddy with delight at her coup. She presented the first letter: The 'relos' were offering fifteen thousand below our asking price. Given the asking price of our home, in real estate parlance, they were offering full price. Moreover, theirs' was an all-cash offer. There was no financing contingency and, thus, no nickel-and-diming bank appraisal that would force them to lower their offer.

In fact, there was just one lone, teensy-weensy complication: the closing date. They wanted to close before Labor Day so their kids could be in Hardington schools.

In thinking about when to put our home on the market, Matt and I had struggled with the possibility of an interim move. We asked ourselves ·whether we willing to live in an apartment for several months – assuming we could find someone willing to give us a short-term lease. Did we want to put our furniture in storage? Were we willing to subject our valuables to two moves?

We had talked it through. It was an excruciatingly painful decision; one we had spent an evening weighing pros and cons, just in the event something like this happened. We explained our thinking to Alexis, who could barely conceal her anger that we would turn down a full-price offer.

She was even angrier that we would deny her a near-effortless $54,000 payday, because the Silicon Valley relos were not working with a broker and would be fine with Alexis representing both sides of the transaction. Her argument was that we would actually get more than our asking price because Matt had worked a sentence into the contract stating if Hardington Properties represented both buyer and seller, the commission would be four percent instead of five.

Alexis said she would go back to the California couple and try to see if a closing date in November could be arranged. If I squinted, I could see the steam coming out of her ears.

The Hardington family's offer was $25,000 below asking price and it, too, came with one of those tiny little stumbling blocks: there was a sale-of-home contingency. But their closing date was flexible. Late November would be fine. After all, it was a cross-town move.

"Their house will sell in a heartbeat," Alexis assured us,

recovering from what she thought had been a slam-dunk sale. "Great neighborhood, perfect size, beautifully maintained. This is the offer you want."

We had, of course, learned to take anything Alexis said with a large dose of caution.

"You've seen the inside of their house?" Matt asked. "You know what they'll be asking for their property?"

Alexis started to speak and then thought better of it. After a few moments hesitation, she said, "I had a long talk with their broker, who assures me they're exceptionally reasonable people."

Matt pressed forward. "So, their house isn't even on the market."

"But it will be, now that they've found the house they want," Alexis countered. She was a little flustered and also more than a little combative.

Matt cocked his head – an indication to me from long observation that he had just found a flaw in someone's argument – and delivered the *coup de grace*. "So, if they want, say, $700,000 for their house but they get offered only $650,000, and if *that* sale is contingent on the sale of yet another house, are they still obliged to go through with the purchase of our house?"

Alexis' mouth hung open for several moments as she parsed Matt's question.

"No," Alexis said. And I admired her for her honesty. "They could withdraw their offer without penalty."

Matt nodded. He already knew the answer. "So we don't really have a viable offer from this Hardington family and putting up an 'Under Contract' sign in front of our house for the next four months would not be a wise thing."

Alexis allowed that the offer might be a bit tentative.

"Why don't you go back to them and explain our concerns," Matt said. "Tell them – and tell their broker – that if they are certain their house will sell quickly, then they should have no qualms about removing the sale contingency. If they want to re-present their offer, we'll carefully consider it."

The look on Alexis' face told me that she harbored no illusions about the outcome of that discussion.

Later, we would learn that the Silicon Valley couple found a move-in-ready house in Weston, priced at just under two million. The local family, as far as I know, never got an acceptable price for their home and stopped going to open houses.

And so, just like that, our house was un-sold.

* * * * *

Prospective buyers continued to come through our house during the week and another 'open house' sign went up for the following weekend. Alexis has been candid in telling us that we might be asked to leave the house on as little as half an hour's notice, so we created a 'thirty-minute check list' and I never made plans for elaborate dinners.

On Wednesday afternoon, I got one of those calls from Alexis, asking – or rather, telling, me – that Matt and I should plan to not be at the house between six and eight that evening. So, I called Matt and told him he was taking me out to dinner.

At a quarter to six, I backed my car out of the garage and, out the passenger window, I saw a man walking in the courtyard garden. I stopped the car.

"Can I help you?" I asked.

A tall – better than six feet - lanky man waved at me and looked sheepish. He wore glasses and looked to be somewhere between his late thirties and early forties, but what stood out about him was his shaved head. He jogged over to the car.

"Just trying to figure out what these plants are," he said. "This is quite a garden." He pointed at my fragrant, wildly blooming Daphne. "What's that one?"

It was a reasonable opening for a conversation, except that 'can I help you' is more or less universally understood as the polite way of saying, 'who the hell are you and what are you doing on my property?'

"It's a Daphne – Transatlantica, if memory serves," I replied. "May I ask why you're in my garden?" It was hard to be angry at this guy, clad in running shorts and a Nike tee, his head bobbing as though listening to some soundtrack playing in his brain.

"Oh," he replied, "I'm here to see the house. I just got off my shift and came straight here. My wife is going to be intimidated by this garden."

A buyer, I thought. Alexis, of course, had made it clear the day we signed the contract that we should never have any contact with a prospective buyer. Such contacts were inevitably the precursor to lawsuits and hard feelings over verbal promises that were deliberately or inadvertently misinterpreted.

"Your wife doesn't like to garden?" I asked.

"She wants to, but she's never had time," the man said. "This garden may be a lot more than she can handle. But it's beautiful."

"Tell her that the purchase price includes two hundred hours of personal horticultural guidance," I said. "I won't do the gardening, but I'll show her what needs to be done. It isn't a lot of upkeep."

The offer of gardening help just popped into my head. And, yes, the part about low upkeep was a bit of a stretch.

"You guys aren't leaving the state?"

"Downsizing," I said. "Building a house on the other side of town. Our retirement home. The kids are gone and it's time to find something for two people."

He peered into the car window. "You look awfully young to be retiring."

"Gardening keeps me looking young," I said and smiled. "By the way, I'm Anne Carlton."

"Oh, jeez," the man said. "Pete Pollard." He stuck his hand through the car window and we shook.

"You said you're getting off your shift," I said. "What does that mean?"

"I'm a surgeon," Pollard said, his head bobbing. "Orthopedics. Knee replacements. You play tennis?"

"Not really," I said.

"Glad to hear it," Pollard said. "Women watch a few Wimbledon matches on TV and decide they can run down a ball like Serena Williams. Guys over fifty deciding to take up marathons. That's what keep me busy."

"What interested you in our house?" I asked.

"Loved the video and it's a great neighborhood," he said. "We've been stalking Hardington and a couple of other towns for the past six months, looking for the right property."

"You say 'we'…" I said.

"My wife," Pollard said. "She's coming with the Realtor." He paused and I saw his mind trying to form words. "Look, if we like the place, could we come by and see it without the Realtor?"

I smiled. "Alexis would scream, of course. But, sure. If you like the place, give me a call." He copied down my cell number.

I pulled out of the driveway and passed Alexis' Lexus driving toward our house, a second Lexus behind it, presumably bearing the second Realtor and Mrs. Pollard.

Matt was both interested and amused by my telling of my encounter with Pete Pollard. "You're right," he said, "Alexis would blow a gasket. She has a deep-seated and somewhat disturbing need for control of every situation." Then he added, "Of course we should see them. If they buy the house, it will annoy Alexis no end."

* * * * *

The next morning, Alexis called to tell me that a 'nice young couple' currently living in what they called a 'shoebox of an apartment' in Boston's South End had appeared to like our house and might want a second viewing. She would keep me posted.

An hour later, my phone chimed again. It was Pete Pollard. "Could Brooke and I come out to talk to you?"

Brooke Pollard turned out to be a tall, stunning blonde who made her husband look homely by comparison. She was a speech pathologist by training and a full-time mother of a two-year-old.

Brooke and I walked the garden while sipping wine, talking of gardening, motherhood, schools, and moving. Matt and Pete went through the house, talking heating systems, floor joist loads, and probably football. Brooke told me their move to the suburbs was a combination of concern that their daughter, Tenley, had few neighborhood children to play with, and an opportunity to shorten Pete's commute to the suburban hospital where he worked.

She looked up at the back of the house with its imposing screened porch, deck, and thirty-foot-long wall of windows in the Great Room. "It's what we want, but it's scary," she said.

"You could start smaller," I offered. "Move up when you're more comfortable."

Though we were alone, Brooke leaned in and whispered, "This time next year, it will be a family of four. I have zero desire to move twice. I want this to be my dream house for a long time."

"You'll have to paint the walls," I said. "Our stager was furious that we didn't paint everything gray."

Brooke burst out laughing. "Pete and I agreed we'd make an offer on the first house we saw that *didn't* have every room smelling of fresh, gray paint. You have no idea how many houses do that."

"You know you couldn't have possession until the end of November," I said.

"That's when our lease is up," Brooke grinned. "Karma at work."

They stayed for dinner and we described the neighbors, the town, the schools and the back-road commuting short-cuts. By 9 p.m., I knew these were people who would love our home. Brooke might be initially overwhelmed by the garden, but she wouldn't rip it out for an acre of lawn.

* * * * *

On August 6, a Saturday morning, we were presented with an offer from Peter and Brooke Pollard. The price was fair, they were pre-approved for a mortgage, and they sought a December 1 occupancy. We accepted and cancelled that day's open house.

And just like that, our house was sold. This time, for real. The agonizing over whether the house would sell at all or whether we would be in a Residence Inn for two months was ended. It was a perfect outcome.

Now, all we needed was to get our new house built.

Chapter Eight

Our foundation was poured on August 19. In addition to the not-so-small matter of getting our house sold, I had spent the four weeks leading up to that event pulling every string with everyone I knew in the Hardington town government to obtain permits, get us moved up on the Environmental Review Board agenda, complete wetland surveys, and comply with anything else anyone at Town Hall could conjure up by way of throwing a roadblock in our construction plans.

I spent upwards of two hours every day on the phone with town officials, pleading for them to expedite our applications. I explained our need for speed by saying that we were getting a late start on construction and didn't want the project shut down by any freakish early winter weather. And, miracle of miracles, they listened and they went along with what I asked. I thanked them profusely. I sent baskets of fresh-picked vegetables to the Conservation Commissioner and two town selectmen. No one can call six fresh tomatoes, four zucchini, three peppers and half a dozen ears of corn a bribe.

Thanksgiving Day was November 24. That gave us 97 days to put up a house. I had a four-month calendar on my refrigerator with each target date on it outlined in red. The pour date for the foundation was the hardest to meet because it had what Matt called "so many moving parts." But each part had fallen into place because I summoned my Inner Bulldog and would not accept 'maybe' for an answer.

The best part was that Joey – he was now just 'Joey' to all concerned – appeared to be fully on board. I spoke with him twice daily. He updated me on subcontractors and materials. We worked through potential choke points and changed specifications to ensure that products of comparable quality would be on site when needed. I never needed to remind him of something he had promised to do; he always ran down a check list of open items.

Whatever nagging feelings of concern I may have harbored were long gone. I was already mentally deciding what size turkey to buy.

We had set up a tent to watch the foundation being poured and invited some of our close friends to share the event. Matt and I are not big entertainers but, when we do, we do it right. For a hot August afternoon we had lobster rolls, a good-but-not-ostentatious sparkling wine, beer for those who insisted on it, chips, and a large tub of super-rich chocolate chip ice cream from a place called White Farms up in Ipswich.

Allow me to introduce my friends and, in the process, fill in a few of those blanks about myself.

I haven't had a résumé for more than two decades. Competently raising two kids puts a crimp in a career track. But I do have a fairly interesting *curriculum vitae*.

For example, in the bedroom that I call my office in our starter castle home, there is a framed gold medal. At the age of seventeen I was the United States Equestrian Federation National Junior Jumping Champion and ranked as one of the top ten junior riders in the world. That medal was the culmination of twelve years of formal training and encouragement by my parents. Having won at the Prix des States, it was assumed that, with a few more years of experience and training, I was a shoo-in for the U.S. Olympic team and would be covered in medals in Seoul in 1988.

That medal was far from the first one I had ever won, but it was the most impressive. It was also the last one I would ever win. Two weeks after the Championships, I was thrown by a friend's horse during a casual ride. I landed hard on my back with a six-inch rock pressed into my spine. I spent four months not knowing whether I would ever walk again, let alone ride. I missed the first semester of my freshman year and spent the next two years trying to catch up academically.

With surgery and therapy I made a full recovery, but I have never been on horseback since. It hasn't been just superstition. Both the surgeons and rehabilitation specialists who got me walking again made it clear that I could have been paralyzed from the chest down by that fall. They also told me, bluntly, that my spinal cord would always be a weak link. Riding, and especially jumping, is hard on the spine and another fall might well undo all that surgery. I got the message: my 'normal' life was a gift that could disappear in an instant.

That injury and my subsequent lengthy rehabilitation answers one question many people have about me. In an era when college-educated women seldom marry before their late twenties and postpone childbearing until their mid-thirties or even later, why did I marry Matt a year out of college and start having kids before my mid-twenties? The answer, at least to me, is obvious. When you've come as close as I did to spending the rest of your life in a wheelchair, your perspective about postponing the things that are important to you changes dramatically. Marriage and children were high on that list. I have no regrets in that department.

And I got lucky with Matt. Twenty-year-olds aren't supposed to know diddly-squat about long-term relationships and compatibility. You date three dozen different people over ten or fifteen years, learning by trial and error what does and doesn't work. When you meet Mister (or Ms.) Right, you cohabit for a year or three before taking the plunge. By the time that ring goes on the third finger of your left hand, you're well into your thirties.

I suspected Matt was the right guy after two dates. It wasn't just looks; he was warm and funny and took me seriously. But he also looked like Kevin Kline in *The Big Chill*. Twenty-six years after we were married, he carries a little more weight around the middle and his hair has turned silver (men can do that, it's called 'distinguished'). Come to think of it, he still looks like Kevin Kline. Maybe even better.

I'm sorry, I got distracted.

I may have gone off the jumping circuit but I did not lose my friends from my equestrian days, and Dover, Massachusetts, which is not all that far from Hardington, is a veritable hotbed of serious horsemanship.

Chloe Barnes was also deeply into the junior riding circuit and we reconnected after college. She went on to medical school, was a practicing physician until two months before the birth of her first child. Despite two kids she has the figure of someone in her early twenties and, with her smooth, oval face and perfect hair, she can still pass for someone twenty years younger than her actual age.

The lone disappointment in Chloe's life, I would suspect, is Jeff. He is the Top Ten surgeon you want if you need to have your chest opened up, but he eats, sleeps and breathes medicine. Any conversation, no matter what the subject will, after five minutes, devolve into a discussion of managed care reimbursement rates or new treatment options for arrhythmia. I sometimes see Chloe roll her eyes when Jeff launches into a passionate critique of the Affordable Care Act.

Another entry in that *curriculum vitae* is that, at the age of 30, I was a five-day champion on *Jeopardy*. It was pure whimsy. Matt invited me to go along with him to a contract law working group conference in Los Angeles. I have long been a *Jeopardy* fan and, after two days, was bored to tears with southern California. Back in those days, the *Jeopardy* qualifying test was not online. Rather, unless *Jeopardy* came to your city looking for contestants, you went to Culver City, sat in a room, and answered a battery of questions on a written test. If you scored well, you were invited to play a few practice rounds. If you did well on those, you were invited to appear on the show a few months hence.

Here's what else you need to know about *Jeopardy*: women are scarce commodities on the show. And, at the risk of sounding vain – which I am not – *attractive* women are even scarcer. I was still filling out my application when a parade of staff members began casually wandering through the room to size me up. I aced the test and the practice rounds. The producers pounced. I was back in California six weeks later armed with multiple changes of clothes.

Winning on *Jeopardy* is a matter of skill and reflexes. The questions aren't especially hard. It's a matter of pressing that signaling button at exactly the right instant. Riding show horses gives you excellent trigger instincts – just as you and your horse are one being during a competition, so my brain and thumb were one with that signaling button.

And, the reason women don't win more often on *Jeopardy* is that, usually, they're lousy bettors. They hit a Daily Double, have second thoughts, and end up betting the value of the clue. They go into Final Jeopardy and play it safe. In short, they play for second place. In six days I hit a Daily Double nine times and, seven of those times, I said, "Alex, let's make it a true daily double." I answered the clue correctly on six of them and it proved to be the winning edge. On the seventh time, I tripped up on a Shakespearean quote; something I knew was wrong as soon as the words were out of my mouth. Brutus and Cassius were my undoing.

There is a six- to eight-week lag between when a show is taped and when it appears on your local station. My shows were still airing when I got the first call. It turns out there's a sorority of multi-day female *Jeopardy* winners, including more than a dozen in and around Boston. They welcomed me into their circle and several became good friends. The nicest part is that the circle continues to grow.

On that hot afternoon, three of my 'sorority sisters' were

present. Emily Silverstein won the Teachers' Tournament several years ago and, yes, she continues to teach middle school English on the North Shore. (She's the one who brought that delicious ice cream, packed ingeniously in dry ice.) She's my age, has a wonderful sense of humor, and can converse intelligently on any topic. She's also about fifty pounds heavier than she ought to be and I worry about her heart, but I've long since stopped judging people that way.

Maria Olivera is the knockout of the group. She took home $140,000 in five days and I would swear that the producers were picking categories tailored to her. She went on the show the first day in a fuzzy pink sweater and showed off a 'C' cup top on a 24-inch waist. She swung her boobs around with excitement every time she answered a question correctly. The overnight ratings probably went through the roof for those five days and she came back every day in a different-color but just as curve-enhancing sweater. She lives in Newton, is an executive at Biogen and, in my humble opinion, ought to be running the company.

My third *Jeopardy* guest was the newest addition to the sorority. Michaela McDermott is just 28, but she nailed answers in every category the Clue Crew could throw at her. She humbled a two-day winner by running the 'current culture' categories that held the Daily Doubles while the incumbent champion – a nerdy guy in a velour jacket and bow tie – fumbled Beyoncé lyrics. Michaela was on top for three days earlier this year and came home with more than a hundred thousand dollars. She's a paralegal with a bright, maybe even brilliant, future.

The final bullet point on my mythical *curriculum vitae* is that I'm a serious gardener. It started twelve years ago when I took the Master Gardener course and found a group of kindred spirits. Matt encouraged me to keep studying and I found myself at lectures at Tower Hill and Arnold Arboretum. My garden became my homework and then my passion. It would be a fair statement that

I am almost as excited about starting a new garden from virgin soil as I am about building our new just-the-right-size house.

Two of my Master Gardener buddies were there to savor the day. Susan Williams lives, breathes and eats gardening. She may not be completely certain of what grade her eleven-year-old is in, but she can rattle off Latin binomials with an ease that is ever so slightly spooky. She's also Kerry Washington's separated-at-birth twin: cocoa skin, tall and perfectly proportioned, with silky black hair. She would be even more of a knockout if she weren't usually dressed in overalls and an oversized man's tee shirt. She had skipped the overalls this day because of the heat, but her tee read, 'It takes *malus* to make a good apple pie'. As gardening humor goes, it was pretty good.

The last woman on hand was Gwyneth West. Gwyn is my twin sister. Well, not literally, but we took the Master Gardener course together and, one day over lunch, discovered we were born on the same day. In addition to gardening, Gwyn is a cycling fiend who logs close to two hundred miles a week. She has usually done a warm-up ten-mile ride before her husband and boys are up. She is high-energy in the best sense of the word and goes through life with the confidence of someone who still slips comfortably into a size four outfit at age 49.

The seven of us are a noisy group, and I guess I'm the common bond that holds us together. We've done girls' weekends in New York and leave-your-husband-at-home dinner parties. We have an annual Christmas luncheon in Boston and do wine tastings on a few hours' notice. It is good to have friends who can share your life events, large and small.

I had hoped Matt would have a similar guest list, but his friends don't have the luxury of taking a day off to watch something as monumental as someone's concrete get poured. They're flying to Singapore or buying Google or something similarly world-changing. The male contingent consisted of Lew Faircloth and

Matt. Lew is a fellow attorney who is also Matt's tennis buddy. Lew is an older guy, a criminal defense lawyer who has handled a lot of high-profile cases, many of them hopeless clients who have already been tried and found guilty in the media. Last year, his defendant was a Wellesley Hills housewife whom everyone in New England knew with absolute certainty had managed the impressive feat of getting her adulterous husband to die in the arms of his mistress by spiking his Little Blue Pill with a deadly drug chaser. We all know how that one turned out. Matt and I have dinner with Lew and his wife, Phoebe, at least once a month, and the two of them regale us with tales of how they tie unprepared prosecutors in knots.

On reflection, the idea of a party to watch concrete being poured into forms ought to have been filed with a star on the list of 'Weird Anne Events', but I wanted to share the day – and the first tangible evidence that a house was about to be built – with friends. Plus, I never turn down an opportunity to have a lobster roll in the summer.

And the progress was wonderful, albeit noisy. A conga line of concrete-bearing trucks rambled across the front of the property. As the concrete was poured, Joey and his 'Concrete Guy' – all of his subcontractors have identifying nicknames like 'Framing Guy' and 'Roofing guy' – poked poles into the goop to make certain it was all going in smoothly.

I took my friends on tours of the property, showing them where I planned to locate each garden, where the patio would be placed, and the path the asphalt-free driveway would follow from the street to the garage. When they tired of hearing my spiel, I went on my own walks, dragging a piece of rebar to better fix in my mind the location of future perennial borders and a vegetable garden.

About one o'clock in the afternoon, I overheard a fragment of a heated conversation between Joey and his 'Concrete Guy'. I was on one of my solo walks and probably fifty feet away, but there was no equipment noise and the wind must have been blowing in just the right direction, because I heard every word with perfect clarity:

Joey: But you said there wouldn't be any need for a pumper…"

Concrete Guy: "That was before your idiot excavator put the stockpile right in the middle of the access…"

Joey: "So just have your guys go around the stockpile."

Concrete Guy: "Have you ever seen a truck with thirty yards of concrete tip over? You want to pay for a pumper or you want to pay to clean up thirty yards of stuff?"

Joey: "I'm not paying for either one."

Concrete Guy (shrugging): "Then I'll come back with the rest of the trucks when your guy moves the stockpile."

Joey: "You know we can't do that."

Concrete Guy: "I can have a pumper here in half an hour. Or I can come back in three or four days (another shrug)."

Joey (pleading): "I don't have a pumper in the budget."

Concrete Guy: "Not my problem. Call me to reschedule the rest…"

Joey: "Get the damned pumper. I'll figure it out."

Even from a distance of fifty feet, I could see the smile of Concrete Guy's face as he reached for his phone.

I wasn't certain what a 'pumper' was or what they meant by 'stockpile', but there were three huge mounds of dirt and boulders left over from the excavation of the basement, one of which was between the foundation and the woods where the site engineer had placed a silt barrier topped with an orange fence. I had a suspicion that the mound of dirt and rocks was the 'stockpile' and that Joey had failed to specifically indicate to his 'Foundation Guy' where to leave access for trucks to get around to the forms on the back side of the house.

Half an hour later, a new truck arrived, this one with an impressive array of ducts and pipes. In fifteen minutes, the pipework had extended over the top of the front of the foundation and concrete was pouring into the forms that would become the rear foundation walls of the house.

Joey had made numerous trips – more than fifteen by my count – to the tent over the course of the morning. He had snagged four or five lobster rolls and two or three beers. He introduced himself to everyone and was especially attentive to the younger and more attractive women. He was, in short, his charming self; making small talk, explaining the work ("I guarantee the back corner of the basement will be within an inch of the plan presented to the Conservation Commission!"), and making the construction of our home sound like the greatest engineering achievement since the iPhone.

But after the pumper truck arrived – the purpose of which Joey did not explain to the assembled crowd – his mood changed. He grabbed a beer, looked at but declined the ice cream, and generally had as little to do with the group as possible. He especially avoided Matt and me.

At three o'clock the foundation wall forms were filled, as were several smaller columns in the center of what would become the basement. Concrete Guy poked a rod into the goop for the last time and pronounced everything acceptable. The tops of the forms were smoothed off. I saw him write out and hand to Joey an invoice, which Joey glanced at, grimaced, and pocketed.

Matt and I said goodbye to our friends. The basement floor would be poured in two days, after the forms came down. The Hardington building inspector would pay a call, sign off on the work, and we could hand Joey his second check.

Somehow, though, I sensed a change in the air. Joey said his farewells to us as he left, but it was clear that the charge for the pumper truck was on his mind. He hadn't said a word and he had no way of knowing that I had overheard his conversation with Concrete Guy.

Maybe he was going to give the bill to 'Foundation Guy' and

take it out of that part of the budget. Maybe he was going to swallow the cost – whatever it was – as an expensive lesson in proper project management.

What I knew he was *not* going to do was hand the bill to us and expect payment. Matt had made it crystal clear that "the price is the price."

Chapter Nine

"But there was absolutely no way to have predicted this," Joey said. "Your tent was in the way, the trucks couldn't get around the other side, and I wasn't going to tell you and your guests to go somewhere else." Joey's voice had a pronounced, pleading edge on it. This conversation had been going on for five minutes.

It was the next morning – Saturday – we were at the work site. Joey had said he wanted to discuss the 'next steps' on the project.

From the time he spotted us, it had taken Joey exactly two minutes to produce the invoice from Landini Brothers Concrete for $1900 for a 'supplemental pumper truck and ducting apparatus'. Matt had glanced at it, handed it back, and said, "You're showing this to me because….?"

"I need to get reimbursed for this," Joey said, his voice full of confidence. "It's an upcharge."

'Upcharge' was a word I had never encountered before. I wasn't formally part of the conversation although I was standing next to Matt. Joey apparently had decided Matt was the right avenue to a quick approval. It was a guy-to-guy thing.

"There are no 'upcharges' on this job," Matt said, with no hint of apology in his voice. "This is a fixed-price job as defined by our contract. The foundation is part of the project. You get a progress payment as soon as the town signs off the work."

"But this is special," Joey countered. "I didn't count on this expense. And, besides, I incurred it because of your party."

Matt raised an eyebrow. "We needed a supplemental pumper because we invited friends to watch the concrete get poured?"

"You put up your tent right where the trucks needed to get to the back of the foundation." Joey said this with a perfectly straight face. It's obvious he had rehearsed this conversation. He had made it our fault.

I should add that, when we went home that afternoon, I related the conversation between Joey and Concrete Guy. Matt listened, nodded sagely, and said, "Let's see how Mr. McCoy handles this."

"Our fault?" Matt asked, emphasizing the 'our'

"Yeah," Joey said, apparently sensing that he had his wedge. "You pitched your tent right where the trucks had to drive."

"You're aware you watched us put up that tent," Matt said. "You even graciously offered your assistance to help put it up at that particular spot."

"But I didn't know it was the truck route," Joey said.

"You also visited us in that tent innumerable times," Matt added. "You didn't think to say, between helping yourself to lobster rolls, that we needed to move the tent?"

"That would have been rude," Joey said. "I couldn't just tell you to tear down your tent,"

"Oh, but you could have," was Matt's reply. "You are the contractor. We are the clients. It is the affirmative obligation – meaning, it's the job – of the contractor to tell the client when the client's actions are costing the contractor money."

I could tell Matt was relaxed and enjoying himself. Joey was flailing away, a little kid trying to throw punches while an adult holds the kid's head at arm's length. Which was when Joey said he couldn't have predicted the additional expense and his tone went from a request to a plea.

"Aren't there two ways around to the back of the foundation?" Matt asked. He pointed to the far end of the now-filled concrete forms. "There wasn't a tent over there. All I see is a pile of the rocks and dirt your subcontractor dug out of the cellar hole."

I saw Joey's face go red. "That's the designated area for the stockpile, Mr. Carlton. The Conservation Commission *made* me put it there." Joey was winging it now, 'they *made* me do it!'

"I also see two other piles," Matt said, pointing a bit to the right, his tone taking on the hint of a lawyer moving in for the kill. "Are those also areas where the Conservation Commission demanded your crew put the stockpile?"

"Your tent was in the path," Joey said, shifting from foot to foot and looking at the ground. Either he was nervous or he needed to pee. "It's only fair that you pay it."

"Here's what I think happened," Matt said. He was switching gears, his voice was now lower and almost kindly. "I think you made a mistake. People make mistakes all of the time. We're not perfect. You should have had your excavation contractor put all the debris from the cellar hole in one spot. But he didn't, and you didn't make him move it from the truck access path. Fortunately, as mistakes go, it was relatively inexpensive – under two thousand dollars. You can make that up by working smarter on other areas of the job."

Matt continued. "But what you *can't* do is to hand me a bill and tell me that I have to pay for your mistake. That isn't the way it works. You're going to have to get used to doing things according to the contract."

"Then let's split the cost," Joey said, trying yet another tack. "You absorb nine hundred and I take the hit on the rest. I've learned my lesson. Really."

This was apparently Joey's fallback position: negotiate for a reduction.

I saw Matt resist the urge to laugh. "No, Mr. McCoy," he said. "The bill is yours to pay. Work smarter and make it up. Now let's go over the rest of the work schedule…"

Which is what we did, but I could feel the resentment brewing in Joey. He threw several glances in my direction. I suspect he was wondering if he ought to have come to me instead of to Matt. I have a pretty good poker face and I certainly wasn't showing him any sympathy.

Joey told us the basement slab and stairs would be poured on Monday and that the town inspector was due by at noon to sign off on the progress.

"Can I get my check then?" he asked, his voice showing equal parts apprehension and resentment.

Matt nodded, "You'll have your check the moment I see the signoff from the town."

* * * * *

Back at home, the message light was blinking on our phone. It was Emily Silverstein, my *Jeopardy* Teacher's Tournament winner friend. She was calling to thank me for a wonderful day in Hardington. Then she added with something of a laugh, "Give me a call when you get time. There's something I'd like to share with you."

Which, of course, prompted me to call her back immediately. I thanked her for bringing the ice cream.

"What I wanted to tell you – and it didn't seem proper leaving the message on your phone – was that I laughed all the way home thinking about your contractor," Emily said.

I was confused. "What about him?" I asked.

Emily chuckled. "Don't tell me you didn't notice it?"

"I honestly don't know what you're talking about," I replied.

"All the time he was talking to Maria, Chloe and Susan," Emily said, expecting a light bulb to click on.

"You lost me," I said. "Was he doing something to annoy them?"

Emily laughed again. "I want you to think back to middle school, when boys' voices were just starting to deepen and they started noticing girls' chests. There is a particular stance that thirteen- and fourteen-year-old boys take when they talk to girls. They hook their thumbs through their belt loops and casually point their first fingers. Those two fingers make a 'vee' that invariably triangulate down to their crotch. The current term for it is, 'pointing out the family jewels'. They can talk to a girl for half an hour and shift every other part of their body, but the fingers remain inextricably hooked through those belt loops – or pants tops – and that 'vee' never wavers from due south. Fortunately, it's an affectation that boys outgrow."

Emily took a breath. "Except for your contractor. Every time he visited the tent – which seemed to leave him precious little time for actual work – he made a beeline for Maria, Chloe, and Susan, and immediately assumed that stance while he talked to them. It was all I could do to stop from laughing."

"I didn't see it," I said. "Honestly, I had no idea." Meanwhile, I was wondering, first, how I missed it and, second, whether Chloe, Susan and Maria noticed it and if they were offended.

"Does he consider himself some kind of 'ladies' man'?" Emily asked. "If so, I think he needs to update his moves."

"He's never come across that way to me," I said. And immediately started thinking about the bizarre phone call with Ashley Harris on Chestnut Street, where Joey's truck has been seen parked many afternoons.

Maybe Joey *did* think of himself that way…

"Well, I just wanted to share that with you," Emily said. "It was so damned funny seeing a full-grown man doing that."

We said our goodbyes with a promise to get together in the next few weeks.

* * * * *

On Monday at noon, a remarkable and life-affirming sight greeted me when I drove by River Street. There were stacks of lumber everywhere. Factory-built roof trusses were being off-loaded from a flat-bed trailer by four burly men. And a forty-foot-tall crane had magically appeared in an open space at the front of the property.

This was the beginning of my new house.

Behind those stacks of lumber, I could see Joey and another man whom I assumed to be the Building Inspector walking the foundation. I hadn't been invited, but I hadn't been told to stay away. I parked out on the street and joined the walk-through.

When parents name someone 'Bruno', there ought to be a gene pool to support at least 250 pounds of pure beef and rippling muscles. And, when the family's name is 'DiNapoli', that gene pool needs to produce an olive complexion and tough, southern Italian good looks.

Mr. and Mrs. DiNapoli didn't get that memo. Bruno DiNapoli, Building Inspector for the Town of Hardington, stood an erect five feet two inches in what were probably elevator shoes. He tipped the scale, including wallet and car keys, at maybe 120 pounds. Most surprising, he looked about as Italian as Monterey Jack cheese. He looked to be about forty with short brown hair and an intelligent smile.

He shook my hand in a firm, official-like manner and had a business card in the other. "Mr. McCoy and I have just been going over a few 'heads up' issues about last year's changes in the building code," DiNapoli said.

"Do they affect the foundation?" I asked, probably with worry around the edges of my voice.

DiNapoli swung his head in an exaggerated side-to-side fashion. "No, we're fine on that. You're good to go. But Hardington got placed in a 100 mile-per-hour wind zone last year. Everyone who has built in town in the past five years got the specs. My job is to assume not everyone reads them."

"Were there any surprises, Joey?" I asked, turning my attention to my contractor.

"None at all," Joey said, smiling broadly. "I pay real close attention to those things. A good contractor knows the code as well as the inspector."

While Joey and DiNapoli went over building code changes, I

walked the perimeter of the foundation, then toured the piles of lumber. I couldn't have guessed where to begin. Expert craftsmen, on the other hand, would treat this as a Monday Sudoku. They'd grab exactly the right truss and stack of two-by-fours and start gun-nailing things into place. In thirteen weeks, this would be my home.

Fifteen minutes later, Joey was at my side. He was all smiles and, in his hand was a signature in the second block of the building permit. '*B DiNapoli*' was signed in red. "Your husband said I'd get paid right away," Joey said.

And, while the contract said we had twenty-four hours to pay, I had come prepared. I reached into my purse and found the folded check for $35,000, payable to McCoy Contracting. I handed it to him. Joey looked at the check carefully, then beamed.

"You watch how fast this house goes up," he said. He turned as if to leave, then snapped his fingers and wheeled around to face me. "There's one thing you can do for me if it isn't a problem."

"Tell me," I said. *An opportunity to be of help*, I thought.

"Things around here are going to get really busy for the next several weeks," he said. "Can you take care of talking to the gas company? They don't accept applications until the foundation is in and you can end up spending an hour or more getting to the right person. I'd rather spend that time here, keeping my guys on the straight and narrow."

I smiled. "I think I can do that."

"Aw, that's great," Joey said. And then he did turn around and start shouting instructions to the four men unloading roof trusses.

Chapter Ten

Have you ever had one of those *Alice in Wonderland* experiences? The kind where you fall into a rabbit hole, nothing makes any sense, and the more you try to explain, the worse it gets?

I had gone home from River Street, turned on my computer, and found the telephone number for 'new residential connections' for MassGas, the natural gas utility that serves Hardington and a dozen surrounding towns.

Even though there was a separate telephone number for 'single-family homes', I immediately found myself in a voice-activated telephone tree that started with "Please say 'business' or 'residential'," and then, "multi-family' or 'single-family'. Six more queries – many of them interrupted by the random interjection of "I didn't understand that. Would you please repeat it?" got me to a live person. Elapsed time: 18 minutes.

'Felicity', if that was her real name, sounded like she was in a call center. She also sounded tired, though it was not yet 3 p.m. She took the name and address and verified that this was new construction and that a foundation was in place.

Then, Felicity said, "I can schedule that for the end of April."

I nearly dropped the phone.

"It's August 22," I said. "The house is going to be finished in mid-November. I'm serving Thanksgiving dinner." The last statement sounded a little irrational, but I had a point to make.

"Yes, ma'am," Felicity said. "But we're scheduling crews ten weeks out. October 31 is ten weeks from today and you haven't been visited, let alone approved by Engineering, and we don't schedule a crew until Engineering approves the site. We shut down the connections crew on October 31."

"Why?" I asked, incredulously. "What's magical about Halloween and gas connections?"

"Because the ground is frozen and the likelihood of snow," Felicity said matter-of-factly.

I thought back to last Halloween. We didn't get a lot of trick-or-treaters on our cul-de-sac, but I remembered our next door neighbors' little girls coming over. Both were dressed as Disney princesses; one was Ariel, the other was Jasmine. They weren't even wearing sweaters.

"The ground doesn't freeze until sometime in December," I said. "And, if we get a snow in October, it melts in about twenty minutes."

"That's our policy, ma'am. We do our first connections on April 20, weather permitting. I've already booked a couple of dozen appointments."

"MassGas believes there's going to be a foot of snow on the ground in Eastern Massachusetts after October 31 and the ground will be frozen solid until April 20," I said.

"Also, the towns won't allow road cuts because it's too cold to lay down asphalt," Felicity added.

I was having an out-of-body experience.

"Felicity," I asked, using my friendliest voice. "Where exactly are you?"

"That's not important, ma'am."

"Humor me," I pressed. "You're telling me I can't have gas in my new home until eight months from now. The least you can do to soften that blow is to tell me where you're located."

"Dallas, ma'am."

"Dallas, Texas," I said. "MassGas processes residential gas connection requests through Dallas, Texas."

"This is corporate headquarters, ma'am," Felicity said. And now I began to hear what had, until now, been a well-disguised southern twang in her voice. "Well, truth be told, corporate headquarters is downtown and we're a couple of miles west."

"MassGas is headquartered in Texas?"

"It's actually Reliable Energy, ma'am. MassGas is just the name we use up there - up your way."

"Felicity," I said, keeping my voice calm. "I'm 'up there' as you say in a town called Hardington, Massachusetts. Contrary to what anyone in Dallas believes, the ground doesn't freeze until the middle of December at the earliest. Our town DPW still makes cuts in the road in November and asphalt still sets. Please take my application. I have gas heat and a gas range in my new home and I plan to cook Thanksgiving dinner for my family. I have a son flying in from the west coast."

There was a long pause on the other end of the phone.

"I can email you the application, ma'am, but I can't promise anything."

I asked, "What happens after I send you back the application?"

"It goes to Engineering," Felicity said. "Someone goes out and looks to make certain the site is ready to trench for a pipe and put in a meter."

"How long will it be before someone from Engineering comes out?"

"About two weeks, ma'am."

I clenched the phone so hard I could feel my hand cramp. "So, had I called two weeks ago and made the same request, someone from Engineering would be coming out today to see my foundation, and sometime in late October I'd be getting my gas installed."

There was another long pause. "Was your foundation poured two weeks ago?"

Truth or lie? "It was poured two weeks ago today," I said, putting all the regret I could muster into my voice. "My idiot of a contractor didn't think about gas because all the houses he usually builds are electric or oil."

Of course, if a competent contractor knew it took two weeks for Engineering to send out an inspector and they also knew that connections were cut off at the end of October, they would have made this call two week ago.

Which led me to two questions. First, had Joey already made this call, gotten the bad news that it was too late to install gas, and decided that it would be a whole lot better if I were the one to tell *him* the bad news rather than the other way around?

The second question was one that was truly frightening: had I placed the building of my house in the hands of an incompetent contractor?

Felicity was speaking and I missed the first part of what she said. "…get that application back to me today and I'll pin an explanatory note to it when I send it over to Engineering. I still don't promise anything, but that's just plain awful."

I thanked Felicity profusely. There was a glimmer of a chance. But I needed to turn that glimmer into reality.

* * * * *

Monday was also delivery day. One weekend each year, usually toward the end of August, the Massachusetts state legislature, in its infinite wisdom, chooses to waive the state's 6 ¼% sales tax. Originally, the Tax Holiday was created to help spur back-to-school buying, but the real impact is a tsunami of purchases of electronics and other big-ticket items.

As soon as the contract was signed, Matt took everything in my 'wish list' binder and started contacting purveyors of those items. He wheeled and dealed on pricing, then added the final request: to record the sale on Saturday or Sunday of the sales tax holiday. Not one retailer objected. Everyone wants in on the action.

The result was the purchase of nearly $60,000 of kitchen and laundry appliances, tile, bathroom and lighting fixtures, mirrors, carpeting, countertops and blinds. Some of it would be held at the suppliers' warehouses until we called for it. Most of the merchandise, including the appliances and bathroom fixtures, required immediate delivery to qualify for the sales tax holiday.

To us, it was an opportunity to save $3,600 in sales tax plus what Matt achieved by way of product discounts. For Joey, however, it meant foregoing a 15% handling fee representing more than $9,000 of instant, never-get-your-hands-dirty profit. The contract specifically allowed us to purchase things for the house that Joey, in turn, was obliged to install.

All morning long, trucks had been disgorging refrigerators, toilets and lighting fixtures that disappeared into our cavernous basement. A few hours earlier I had actually felt sorry for Joey. He undoubtedly assumed we had inserted that contract language because we were going to purchase a few toilets at Home Depot. As pallets of items were offloaded from the trucks, I had been thinking of ways to soften the blow; perhaps by offering to pay Joey for the installation of things like tile.

With the discovery that Joey had almost certainly screwed up on obtaining gas for the house, that reservoir of good will evaporated.

In due course, Joey would be told about all of the things we had purchased, and that the cost of our house would be $60,000 lower and his profit $9,000 less. If I had to spend the next twelve weeks begging a utility to install something that should have taken a simple phone call, depriving Joey of his handling fee was fair compensation for my time.

Chapter Eleven

On Wednesday morning, with the floor of the basement poured and cured, construction began in earnest on our house. Joey's 'Framing Guy' spoke minimal English and his crew spoke only Portuguese, but they were the most energetic workmen I had ever encountered. They arrived at 7 a.m. – the earliest outdoor work is allowed in Hardington on a weekday – and by noon the crew had framed the exterior walls on most of the first floor. In the afternoon a crane went to work lifting those pre-built trusses into place. By 6 p.m., there was the outline of a house.

The day was a cacophony of power saws, drills, and nail guns. I stayed and watched because I wanted to understand how a house was constructed, but also because I wanted the people building my new home to care about the quality of what they were doing.

Accordingly, I had brought three 'Boxes of Joe' and two dozen doughnuts from Dunkin' Donuts. The coffee and donuts were accepted gratefully. At noon I had half a dozen foot-long submarine sandwiches and sodas delivered, only to find that the workmen had brought their own meals, which they wolfed down in fifteen minutes and then returned to framing. Lesson learned: coffee and sweets – good. Lunch – not so good. (And because I don't throw away perfectly good food, I ate refrigerated and increasingly soggy submarine sandwiches every day for the next two weeks. Lesson *really* learned.)

Joey was already at the site when I arrived. He introduced me to his 'Framing Guy' but otherwise oddly kept his distance. He did not ask if I had called MassGas and I didn't enlighten him. I had a strong sense he was waiting for me to say something.

Well, he had a hell-freezing-over length wait in front of him.

I realized there was an urgency to this part of the project. Late summer is a time of fickle weather in eastern Massachusetts. It isn't the temperature or the humidity: it's the threat of drenching thunderstorms that can blow up in the afternoon and drop an hour of torrential rain on one spot. It's one thing to have such rain falling on a completed house. It's quite another to have it come cascading down on hundreds of unprotected sheets of plywood and thousands of linear feet of lumber.

Weather was on my mind because I had watched the previous winter as a townhouse condominium project in Hardington shut down construction for the season. When bad weather set in, the end unit was only partially completed and was left open to the elements. For four months snow, rain, and ice poured though the shell of the building. To my horror, in the spring the builder finished the townhouse as though no time had passed. The condo sold to a relocating family that had no idea that the plywood, lumber and sheetrock in their new home had swollen and dried multiple times. On the surface it looked perfect. Underneath, it was a disaster waiting to happen.

I got lucky – or else 'Framing Guy's' crew was exceptionally conscientious, quick-like-a-bunny fast, and stayed until darkness fell each evening. Before the end of the week there was a shell of a house in place, wrapped in Tyvek and with plastic sheeting over the roof and covering the holes where windows and doors would be installed. If and when the heavens opened up, the interior of my house would be perfectly dry.

On Friday, Joey could no longer contain his curiosity.

"How did you make out with the gas company?" he asked innocently.

"They told me I can't have gas until next spring. Late April."

Joey feigned incredulity. "That's horrible!" Then he added, much too quickly, "I guess we can bring in bottled gas for the winter."

"The remarkable thing," I said, ignoring his proposed solution, "is that it didn't have to be that way. If someone had called the gas company just two weeks earlier we would have been fine. It takes two weeks to get someone from Engineering to come out to look at the site. If someone had called, say, the first or second week of August, the Engineering guy would have been here this week. He would have seen a foundation in place and we'd be on the Construction calendar for October."

"Yeah, but they won't take an application unless the foundation has been poured."

"Is that what they told you when you called?" I asked.

"I have no idea what you're taking about," Joey replied coolly, not missing a beat. "Calling the gas company was your responsibility. Do you want me to make arrangements for a couple of LP tanks, or will you do that?"

"I submitted the application," I said. "They took pity on me. I told them the foundation was poured in early August but my contractor forgot to call. The Engineering guy should be here in a week or so. Maybe we'll get lucky."

"Huh," Joey said, and then walked away. I don't know if he thought he won or lost that round. What he ought to have understood was that, if he thought he could shift the blame onto me, he had failed miserably. And by not 'manning up' when confronted with fairly clear evidence that he had screwed up, Joey had made himself a little less trustworthy.

* * * * *

The next week was a blur of construction. The exterior of the small second floor was framed and roofed, and the complicated gables and roof pitches that gave our home its distinctive look went from roughed-in plywood to shingled reality. The exterior was still Tyvek, the garage was just a foundation, and the front and rear porches were just spray-painted lines on the ground; but this was unmistakably a house. Inside, floor joists were laid and three quarter-inch plywood subflooring quickly went down over them. Stairs were framed and studding appeared like a bark-less pine forest.

In case you're wondering, I was at the site every day. Not all day and no longer at 7 a.m. when the crews arrived, but I was there five or six hours every day, six days a week. I made coffee runs, I picked up nails from the ground, and I threw into the dumpster the little pieces of scrap wood and cardboard boxes that littered the site. This was my house and I was damned proud of it. I loved watching it come together.

I quickly got to know the principal subcontractors: 'Framing Guy' was Julio, 'Roofing Guy' was Primo, and 'Window Guy' was Estêvão. Paul was the electrician; Fred, the plumber.

In the Boston suburbs and where non-union labor was the rule, the unlicensed building trades were almost all from Brazil. They worked visibly hard, took minimal breaks, and thanked me profusely for the small favors I did. I stayed out of their way and seldom bothered them in any way. To the crews, I was *senhora do chefe com café* – the boss lady with the cofee. I liked the title.

When I arrived at the site on Wednesday of that week, I found Estêvão offloading a truckload of windows. I waved and he waved back. The previous day he had shown up with two members of his crew, reviewing the installation schedule for the roughly thirty windows going into the house. Today was the day that thirty plastic-covered holes would become a series of beautiful double-hung and casement windows.

Joey had not yet arrived. Since that previous Friday when we had our standoff over gas, his visibility at the site had been somewhat sporadic. He had to 'run out for supplies' or 'run a quick errand'. He would be back two hours later, bearing a sandwich and a container of coffee which he would consume in his truck while making phone calls with the engine running the entire time.

Matt – whose week-long trip to meet with clients in Zurich made it easier to spend my days on River Street – was of the opinion that a good manager doesn't need to look over every subordinate's shoulder every day. But that begged the question of whether Joey was a 'good' manager, an assumption that was starting to be suspect. On the other hand, everyone seemed to know what they were doing and no subcontractors were tripping over one another. The house was rising nicely.

Something, however, prickled at my subconscious about Estêvão and the windows. The big cardboard boxes disappeared into the house and there was soon the sound of saws and hammering.

I was performing my morning sweep for nails when one of Estêvão's crew came out with a load of boxes. He handily tossed four cartons into the dumpster, gave me a wave and a smile, made a coffee-cup-tipping motion with his hand, and disappeared into the house.

I make no claim of paranormal powers, but my Spidey-sense went on full alert. As soon as Estêvão's helper was out of sight, I was on tiptoes looking into the dumpster. All I saw were four large cartons, each marked as having contained a double sash window of a particular size.

I looked harder. After thirty seconds, it hit me: it wasn't what I saw, it's what I *didn't* see.

Two years earlier, we had ice damage in a bedroom of our starter castle. Ice backed up from the eaves, melting water got into the walls and we feared mold. A contractor ripped out a section of interior wall and confirmed that we needed to replace the wall and windows. We did and, on the contractor's advice, chose a top-of-the-line Andersen 400-series window with Low-E glass and enough insulation to keep out an arctic gale. When we designed our just-the-right-size house, we mentioned to our architect that we were quite happy with those Andersen windows and she incorporated them into the design specs. It was right there in black and white on the materials list.

What I didn't see was that distinctive orange-and-black decal that had been on the window boxes when our contractor put in those new windows two years earlier.

Instead, these boxes said, 'Shur-Tite Windows'.

There were two possible explanations. One of them was that Estêvão had purchased the wrong windows through an honest mistake or communications error with Joey. The other was that either Estêvão or Joey had made a deliberate decision to substitute a lesser window for the ones called for by the architect – and I had no doubt that 'Shur-Tite Windows' were a cheaper substitute.

Was this Joey's way of making up for the two thousand dollar cost he had been forced to swallow of that pumper truck?

I am by narture someone who has no problem with taking swift and decisive action. I immediately fished out the four cartons and took them to my car. That was Step One.

Step Two, though, called for some circumspection. It was 8:15 in the morning on the east coast of the United States. It was six hours later in Zurich. I snapped a picture of one of the Shur-Tite Windows cartons and emailed it to Matt. I appended the note, *'Call me as soon as you can. Potential trouble.'*

* * * * *

At that moment, Joey's truck pulled up.

Psychologists say that what we drive speaks volumes about both who we are and how we want to be perceived by others. Automobiles are an extension and a reflection of our personality. Let it be said that nearly all contractors drive pickup trucks. Joey drove one: a brand new Dodge Ram 3500 Longhorn. Let it be further stipulated that the preponderance of contractor-driven trucks are black. Joey's was black, but his was a glistening, evil black that could be achieved only with multiple coats of some expensive, clear-coat gloss. And, Joey's truck never had a speck of dirt or mud on it. He arrived every morning in a vehicle that looked as though it had been detailed overnight. The 3500 Longhorn features chrome (or whatever passes for chrome in the new millennium), and that chrome shone as though it had been buffed to a dazzling brilliance by someone with an electric polisher. Even the over-sized tires sported some kind of a shining agent. Joey's truck said he was someone you didn't mess with.

I quickly closed the trunk of my car. I didn't want any of my 'evidence' to disappear.

Joey got out of his truck and stretched languorously. He swiveled his neck and head multiple times as though he had been driving all night. Then he reached into the cab and pulled out a Starbucks cup, indicating that his arduous drive had, in reality, been roughly half a mile and had taken three or four minutes.

He gave me a quick wave and a half-smile. I walked over to his truck where he was strapping on his tool belt. In the morning heat, he had opted for a tight, bright green tee that showed well-toned muscles.

"Your window guy got here a little while ago," I said.

Joey glanced at the white truck that said *Goncalves Door and Windows – Framingham.*

"All my guys start early and get the job done," he said. "That's why they're my guys."

"Why don't we go see how they're doing?" I suggested.

Joey paused. "They don't need to be interrupted," he said, squinting as he looked toward the construction. "And, while it's your house, I'm getting a lot of pushback from my guys over the fact that you're here all the time. They think you're checking up on them and don't trust them. They think the coffee and donuts are just a ploy."

Which might have been believable had Julio, the Framing Guy, not gently suggested just yesterday that his crew infinitely preferred the Colombian Extra Dark Roast from Starbucks to the House

Blend from Dunkin' Donuts. And, did I know that Honeydew offers Bear Claws?

"Well," I said, "Let's risk annoying them and have a chat with Estêvão."

"Let me ask him if it's OK," Joey countered.

"Let's both ask him," I said, and started walking toward the house.

Joey hurried to keep up with me.

We found Estêvão and his crew getting ready to install the first of the three, oversized library windows.

"How's it going?" Joey asked. "We just wanted to see that you have everything you need."

Without waiting for an answer from Estêvão, whose knowledge of colloquial English probably did not extend to parsing the meaning of Joey's question, particularly when it came out as 'howzit gowun', he turned to me. "Satisfied? Let's leave them alone."

"I want to check something," I said. One of the unboxed windows was leaned up against a sheetrock wall. "It should be down here."

I ran my finger down to the bottom right-hand corner where, in a barely visible image, there should have been an Andersen logotype, window model number, and such information as 'Low-E' meaning we had paid about fifty bucks extra per window for a low-emissivity coating to make the glass better reflect back outside heat.

"I'm not certain what's going on here," I said. "I wanted to make certain we had the Low-E glass. Instead, I can't find the Andersen logo or that information."

Joey shifted from one foot to the other and tugged in his belt.

"They just put that stuff on some windows," he replied quickly.

"Well, it ought to be on the box," I said. "Let's check the boxes."

I saw Estêvão's eyes tracking the exchange as though it were a soccer match. The worried look on his face said he understood the gist of the conversation all too well.

Joey quickly placed himself between me and the unopened boxes. "These guys need to get back to work."

"No, Joey," I said. "These guys need to install the correct windows. The architect's bill of materials calls for a really high-quality window.· I know because I worked with them on the specification. You agreed to install the exact products on that list. Instead, you sent out Estêvão to buy a truckload of the cheapest crap you could find."

"I have no idea what you're talking about." Joey crossed his arms, a symbol of defiance.

"Shur-Tite Windows," I said, crossing my own arms to match his stance. "Just turn around and look at the boxes."

"Oh, that," Joey retorted, not bothering to turn around. "The windows your architect wanted are out of stock and backlogged about six months. I've been using these windows for twenty years. They're identical to Andersen. Maybe better. Probably better. I'm sure they're better. I'm just making certain you got into your house on time."

"Out of stock?" I asked, then had an inspiration. I took my phone out of my pocket and tapped the screen. "Siri," I said, "Check in-stock inventory of windows at Home Depot in Overton, Massachusetts." I added the size and model number.

Joey and I stared at each other for about five seconds. Joey was about to say something when Siri, in her happiest voice, came back with, "Home Depot in Overton has 22 Andersen windows in stock matching that description."

God, I love Siri.

Joey started at my phone and blinked, his mouth still open to utter whatever comment had been forming in that vast, empty space he called a head. After a moment he said, "I don't have an account at Home Depot. I do all my business at a professional builder's supply house. I get a much better discount that I can pass along to you."

"Joey," I said, "you just got caught in a lie. Just like you were lying last week when you said you hadn't spoken with the gas company." I walked over to the Shur-Tite window and placed my hand on it. "My question is, is this your first lie about materials or have you been substituting substandard lumber and supplies right from the time you poured the foundation?"

I swear I saw sweat break out on Joey's forehead. His eyes darted left and right.

"How about the roof shingles, Joey?" I asked. "As I recall, the specifications are for GAF Timberline with the 50-year Golden Pledge warranty. If that isn't exactly what you installed, you realize those shingles are coming off tomorrow, and you're paying for it."

"That's what I bought," Joey said, his eyes bulging. "I swear to God. I've got three leftover packages around here somewhere." Sweat was pouring down his face.

"Then how did we end up with these windows?" I patted the sash. Of course, I didn't accept his word that the shingles weren't something he found as an overstock at a liquidation house.

"I was pissed off," he said in a whisper. He quickly glanced at Estêvão before returning his gaze to me. "This is between you and me."

"Estêvão," I said. "Could you and your crew take a break for a few minutes?"

Estêvão nodded and motioned to his crew that it was time to go outside. By this afternoon, of course, each and every one of Joey's contractors would have heard the story that the *senhora do chefe com café* had ripped Joey a new one. A week from now, Joey would likely have a new corral of 'A-List' subcontractors.

"Your husband wouldn't pay for the pumper truck," Joey said when it was just the two of us. "That's two grand out of my pocket.

Then, he said I could make it up by working smarter. Well, the windows are working smarter. They're high quality. They'll last as long as the house."

"I think what he had in mind by 'working smarter' was to do work yourself that you would have otherwise paid a subcontractor to do," I replied. "Joey, I don't think you get it. There's a bill of materials attached to the architect's plan. That plan is part of the contract you signed. That contract may be just three pages long, but there's a paragraph that says you can't substitute products off that list without our written consent. Do you know that paragraph is in the contract?"

The blank look on Joey's face told me he had no idea there was such a paragraph.

"Joey, we could fire you right now. And we wouldn't owe you another penny. Every hour of labor your subcontractors have put in on this job would be out of your pocket, and then we'd come after you for the cost of replacing everything that was different from what the architect specified..."

Joey burst out, "I swear to God it's just the windows!"

"Then give me your receipts for everything that has gone into the house."

Joey started to say something but apparently thought the better of it. Instead, he said, "Sure."

"And I want the receipts today," I said. "It means you do two things: you tell Estêvão to take back these windows and bring back the right ones. And then it means you go home or back to your office and you collect every receipt for this project."

Joey stared at me. I wasn't certain if the look on his face was one of defeat or one masking a plan to deal with a setback. But he said, "If I do that, am I still on the job?"

It was my turn to pause, and a million conflicting thoughts were going through my head. On the one hand, I knew that Joey needed to be fired because I could never trust him again. Joey lied, and he lied so smoothly that he left no telltale trail behind. It meant that every time Joey did something, I would have to check to see that he hadn't pulled a fast one.

The reason I knew this was because, if I didn't fire him now; if I let Joey stay on this job, *he* knew he had something I wanted badly. And that 'something' was to get my house finished. He knew he was my only chance, and he would use that to his advantage every chance he could.

More than anything, I wished Matt was here. Matt, with decades of real-world experience dealing with inveterate liars, would know what to do. And, what I was certain he would say was, *"Anne, I know this is hard but we shut it down until next spring. We've got a foundation, we've got a solid start. We get someone competent to finish it."*

But he wasn't here. It was just Joey and me. And dammit, I wanted my house. Every time I walked around the foundation or through the construction, I could *feel* that this was the house I had wanted for the past five years. I may have hired the wrong contractor, but I could force him to build *my* house the way *I* wanted it.

"If the windows are the only substitution, and if Estêvão is back here today to install the Andersen's, then you're still on the job," I said. "And if you screw up even once, Matt is going to go after you with every bullet in his lawyer's gun. And from past experience I know he'll enjoy doing it."

Joey gave me a hangdog look as he murmured, "OK." But even as he did the contractor equivalent of putting his tail between his legs, I could see, just for an instant, a look in his eye. It was a look that said he had gotten away with it; that he had found the chink in my armor.

And that he would find a way to get even.

Chapter Twelve

Joey had his conversation with Estêvão and the windows disappeared. I, of course, still had the four Shur-Tite window cartons in my truck. If Estêvão or his helper came looking for them, I would plead ignorance. Joey, too, disappeared, but not without peeling out of the site spewing dirt, rocks, and an oily haze in his wake.

Then two things happened in quick sequence: Matt called from Switzerland and a MassGas truck arrived.

I explained to Matt what had happened and what I had done. He asked a lot of questions and, though he said nothing directly, I could sense the disappointment in his voice. Instead, he adopted his counselor's mantle. "You put nothing in writing," he said. "You did not agree to alter the contract. The same options that were open to us before that conversation are still available tomorrow or any day in the future."

"But he knows he's the only game in town," I replied, almost in a wail. "I have screwed up so badly…"

"Anne, he signed a contract," Matt said in as soothing a voice as I've ever heard from him. It was the kind of balm that made nervous clients climb down from ledges and write enormous checks to his law firm. And now he was using it on his wife. "That contract is air-tight; there are no loopholes. He has to perform or he doesn't get paid, and he doesn't get paid until *after* he performs, plus he needs to have a signoff from the town. Were he to walk away from that contract tomorrow, he would be stuck with at least $50,000 of bills. He can't afford *not* to do it our way."

Except that I knew Joey was going to do something. To be

afraid of ignoring what was in a contract, you first had to be smart enough to comprehend that breaching that contract could ruin you. In the few weeks that I had known him, I had discovered that there were hundreds of words and phrases that could describe Joey, but that none of them included the word 'smart'.

Which is when I saw the MassGas truck pulled into the makeshift driveway

"Matt, the gas company is here," I said. "Let's talk tonight."

I do not hang up on my husband without a really good reason. This constituted the best kind of reason. I tapped the 'end call' icon.

* * * * *

It was a woman who got out of the light blue truck. Since I embarked on the building of this house, she was the first woman I had encountered. I walked over to her with my best smile.

She was tall and twenty-something. A little older than my daughter, with long brown hair underneath a powder-blue safety hat. She was in slacks and a windbreaker that seemed designed to hide curves.

She returned the smile and held out her hand. "I'm guessing you're the homeowner," she said. "I'm Kelly."

"What you are is a sight for sore eyes," I said, meaning every word of it.

Her gaze took in the house in its present state. There seemed to be approval in that look.

"I've promised my family I'll serve them Thanksgiving dinner here, and I've paid good money for a gas range," I said. "Please tell me I haven't lied to my family."

Kelly didn't answer. Instead, she flipped through the application I had emailed down to Dallas. The application included a diagram showing where the gas would run from the street to the house. She turned the page to another, unfamiliar diagram and studied it.

"This was a teardown, right?" Kelly asked.

I nodded.

"The guys who did the demolition tore out the old gas line." She made it a statement. Then she walked in a circle about fifteen feet across, feeling the ground under her no-nonsense safety shoes. Her eyes went back to the street and she seemed to be looking for something telltale in the macadam.

"You don't need a road cut," she said emphatically.

"I don't?"

She shook her head. "When they tore down the house, they made the cutoff at the property line. The town has a ten-foot easement. You're in luck. The cutoff is on this side of the street. There's no need to tear up the road. This is a three-man, four-hour job, not a full-day, four-man crew."

She went back to the first page of the application. "Mrs. Carlton, here's what I'm going to do." She looked up at me in the way she might have looked at her mother. I hoped that she and her mom were on great terms.

"I'm going to mark a line and spray a meter site," she said. "Then, I'm going to mark this 'approved' and send it on to Construction."

She must have seen the look of relief on my face because she shook her head and the look on her face changed to one of caution.

"Don't get too comfortable. That just means you're over one hurdle," Kelly said. "The big one is getting on the schedule."

"The one that's already completely full for the rest of the season," I said.

She nodded and then asked, "Who do you know?"

I blinked.

"Who do you know who has pull? Who do you know that can make a call that will get a crew to work a little faster so they can schedule one more appointment; dig one more trench. Install one more meter."

"What kind of person has pull?" I asked.

Kelly shook her head. "You never know. Your town selectmen, your congressional liaison office, someone who is a big wheel at the gas company, someone in the state government who regulates the industry. Try them all. There is nothing standing in the way of your getting gas this fall except a bureaucracy. Figure out a way around the bureaucracy. If you do, you'll have gas in October. If you don't you'll have gas next April. I've done my part."

She gave me a firm handshake and then got back into her truck. Seconds later, she was away and out of sight.

I hoped Kelly's mother was exceptionally proud of her. I had a sense she had crashed down a wall to get into that blue truck. It was the kind of position that requires brains rather than brawn but it was also a job had been done exclusively by men for a century.

Maybe she expected to drive up and see a vacant lot without any evidence of a foundation, in which case she would have kept on driving. Or, perhaps she expected a bare foundation without a glimmer of a chance of being ready for occupants before the end of the year.

Or, maybe she expected to see what she saw, but also was ready for the person greeting her to be Joey McCoy, leering with his thumbs in his tool belt, making that infamous 'V'. And, instead of dispensing advice on beating the system, she would have cautioned that the schedule was full, so all she was doing was ensuring that 131 River Street got connected in mid-April instead of early May.

I felt it was a sign.

* * * * *

I was going to need help keeping tabs on Joey. I enlisted Susan Williams, my Master Gardener buddy. Susan's son was at camp for two weeks and she did most of her gardening at 6 a.m. Three hours later she would be showered, refreshed, and looking better than any 42-year-old human being has a right to look. She, of course, loved the idea of playing 'house detective'.

When I obliquely asked if she remembered Joey's 'thumbs on the tool belt', Susan laughed for about thirty seconds. "I felt like I was back in middle school," she said. "I didn't know whether to be grossed out or amused. What I definitely was not, was flattered. Your contractor is a first-class jerk."

I then made the mistake of asking her how she would react if her own son attempted such a 'stance' when he turned thirteen or fourteen.

Susan pondered the question for a moment before responding. "The first time I caught him, he'd go 'analog' for a couple of weeks. No computers, no games, no phone; just an opportunity to reflect on his poor behavior. I think that would cure him."

"What if there were a second time?" I asked.

She thought about that question as well. "Castration would certainly be one of the options," was her response.

We spent three hours poring through receipts provided by Joey and comparing them to the architect's materials specification list. Then, armed with the suspicion that Joey might have purchased one set of materials only to return them for cheaper substitutes, we then performed a further check by examining construction materials in the house and pulling discarded boxes out of the dumpster.

The relief was that, apart from the windows, Joey had strictly followed the letter of the agreement. Of course, apart from a handful of items, everything so far used in building the house was fairly standard contractor-grade material. Still, we checked.

Susan also listened to the tale of the windows and offered her own opinion. "It's like you're dealing with a little kid," she said. "Joey always expects to get his way and, when he doesn't, he acts out. He tests the limits of your patience, looking for the chink in the armor. He'll keep testing it. You took away his allowance for bad behavior, and he's going to use every means at his disposal to 'get even'."

"So it isn't going to end with the windows," I said, glumly.

Susan laughed. "This guy is just warming up," she said. "Your problem is that you haven't had a kid around the house for a while. Their goal is to wear you down. It's a game. It's infinitely more fun than doing their homework."

"So I should have fired him?" I asked.

"Hell, no!" Susan said. "You hired him to build a house. You *make* him build the house – your way at your price and on your schedule. You make him do his homework, and clean his room, and take out the garbage."

"But that turns this into a full-time job," I said. I could see weeks of scrutinizing every detail of Joey's work. And, Susan was right: Noah had been out of the house for seven years and there had been a long stretch when I felt like I didn't have the energy to keep up with his teen- and pre-teen antics. Kate, by contrast, had been something approaching The Perfect Daughter; driven by her interest in marine biology. Except for the boys. Oh, lord, the boys…

Susan snapped me out of my reverie. "…do you want your house this year or let it sit, open all winter to anyone who wants to wander in and look around?"

"This year," I said. "Definitely, this year."

"Right answer," Susan said. "So the first thing we do is enforce the curfew."

I must have had a thoroughly baffled look on my face.

"It's noon," Susan said. "Where's Joey?"

She was, of course, correct. I looked around at the trucks assembled at the site. Framing Guy and his crew were hard at work starting to define rooms. The Window crew was taking their fifteen-minute lunch break. And the electrician was in the basement measuring for the power board. Joey had yet to put in an appearance.

"I have absolutely no idea," I said.

"Then what do you say we get his ass over here." Susan had a look on her face that said she meant business.

* * * * *

"I have other customers, you know," Joey said, his indignation setting on 'high'. "Some of those people have been my customers for twenty-five years." It was 12:45. There had been a phone call and a text to him every minute until he responded – eight minutes later.

It was clear to me Joey didn't quite know what to make of this woman – Susan – and her inexplicable attitude. The one other time he had seen her, she had been all smiles and good cheer. Wine and beer flowed freely and lobster rolls were there for the taking. Now, this incredibly attractive black woman was treating him like a truant.

"My other customers depend on me," Joey said, a bit of braggadocio in his voice. "I'm their go-to guy. And they don't call me all the time to ask where I am."

"What do they do, depend on you to tighten the hoses on their outdoor faucets?" Susan asked in a mocking voice. "You can't be here to supervise the construction of a house, but you can be at the McHelplesses to personally oversee the installation of a screen door?"

"These are major projects," Joey said. "My customers…"

Susan cut him off and gave him a Kerry-Washington-worthy scowl. "Your customers probably average eighty years old and they call you because they want company. They don't need a new bathroom. You flatter them and you tell them funny stories, so they think up projects for you. I bet they make you tuna sandwiches and cut the crusts. Meanwhile, there's a house here that needs your-full time attention, but you can't be bothered."

"That isn't true," Joey replied, though at least a few of the accusations hurled at him by Susan had struck a respondent chord.

"I got a major renovation going on at a house…"

"Or else you're scared to come here because you got caught cheating?" Susan said, her hands on her hips and a smile on her face.

Joey's face turned red. "I don't take that from anyone…"

"And, if I get my way, you won't have to," Susan said. I, in the meantime, was just standing there like a lamppost. I had no idea where Susan was going with this, but I was so fascinated that I made no attempt to stop her.

"I've been telling Anne about *my* contractor," Susan said, studying her fingernails. "He built my house two years ago. Did a *fantastic* job. Brought it in ahead of schedule and under budget. Green Brothers Construction. You know them?"

"Never heard of 'em," Joey said. But the swagger was gone and the look on his face said the conversation wasn't one of his choosing.

"Well, he'd *love* to take over this project," Susan said, beaming. "And stick you with the bills for everything you've done up to now. Because you're in breach of your contract and all that."

Joey shot me a dirty look. To Susan he said, "If your guy is so good, then he's booked out to the end of next year. So he must not be all that hot." His voice was sullen now.

"Oh, Mark will make room for *me*," Susan said, her smile still beatific. "He's been angling to build my new Cape house." Throwing her thumb over her shoulder at the construction behind us, she continued, "Believe me, the cost of this house will be a rounding error to the cost of my new Cape house. And he *really* wants that job."

What Susan was saying sounded incredibly persuasive. Except that Susan didn't build a new house two years ago. She and her family live in a Victorian in Needham that is surrounded by the most exquisite small garden in New England. No workman is allowed to get within a hundred feet of the place because, the last time one did, he trampled her peony bed. Further, Susan *hates* the Cape. You could deed her the entire Cape Cod National Seashore and she still wouldn't cross the Bourne Bridge to get there.

So, naturally, I just continued to listen.

"So, what do you say, champ?" Susan placed her hands back on her hips. "Is my friend going to get your undivided attention, or do I tap Mark Green's private cell phone number and let you explain to your subcontractors why you're going to have to work out a five-year payment schedule with them?"

"I was coming here anyway," Joey said, defeat in his voice. It was the same tone that my son, Noah, had used when he said, at age eleven, "I was about to clean my room anyway."

Joey went into the house and started yelling at subcontractors.

Susan turned to me and tapped the side of her head. "Psychology," she said.

* * * * *

For the next ten days, everything went swimmingly well. Closets and small spaces inside the house were framed, and the electrician and plumber snaked wires and tubes of various colors around the house. A siding crew appeared and long pieces of cedar began covering the Tyvek.

The foundation around the garage acquired a skeleton of two-by-fours and, in a matter of days, the outline of a garage appeared. Pilings were poured for the front and rear porches. I dispensed coffee and donuts and, in the process, began to acquire a smattering of Portuguese.

Joey mostly avoided me. He would already be at the site when I arrived. He would nod when he walked by me but would avoid eye contact except when necessary. He also spent at least two hours of each work day out in his truck, mostly on the phone.

Ostensibly, who he was talking to was none of my concern; the house was on track and that was what mattered. But I wondered who he could be speaking with so often and for so long. On the tenth day of that smooth-water stretch of construction, I saw Joey disappear around the back of the house for what I suspected would be a lengthy conference with the Siding Guy.

I casually walked down the soon-to-be driveway to where his truck was parked and just as casually opened the driver's side door. I'm not certain what I expected to see. Copies of *Playboy*, probably. What I saw instead was far more prosaic. The sports section of the *Boston Globe* opened to the coming Sunday pro football matchups. Several games were circled. There was no other papers or detritus in the truck cab.

Great. Joey was trying to decide which football games he was going to watch this weekend. Well, I couldn't demand he work seven days a week.

* * * * *

On the eleventh day, September 14, Fred the plumber took delivery on four large cartons of equipment, which went on dollies down into the basement. I waited an hour, then went down to see what was going on.

"Your heating system," Fred said, indicating the largest carton.

Fred was the senior citizen member of Joey's subcontractors. I would guess his age at about 65. He was nearly bald, stood around five-feet-six, and was well over 200 pounds. Plumbers, I imagine, don't need to fit into tight corners or lift heavy objects.

I went over to investigate the box. *'Nu-Heet Whole House Combi Tankless Boiler'*. The box was maybe 24 inches by 36 inches and 12 inches deep.

"This is going to heat our house?" I asked.

"This is what Joey says you ordered," Fred said.

"You've installed a lot of these, I imagine," I said.

Fred shrugged. "There's a first time for everything."

I looked at the back side of the box. *'Manufactured by Nu-Heet Technology at the Kaesong Industrial Complex'*.

"Are you going to install this today?" I asked.

Fred laughed. "It's going to take me a week to figure out *how* to install it."

"Don't be in a hurry," I said.

Fred laughed again. "Until you get gas in here, I can't be in a hurry. I can get the plumbing in place, but that's about all."

I didn't go to Joey to demand an answer. I needed to have my facts in place. I went home.

I pulled out our copy of the architect's plans and specification list. I ran my finger down to 'heating/ventilation/air conditioning':

Heating system shall have an efficiency rating of better than 96% and may be tankless or employ one or more auxiliary hot-water tanks.'

Frustrated, I called the architect's office.

Cummings & Longworth is a fairly large design firm based in the Fresh Pond area of Cambridge. A few years ago, they got themselves into what Matt called a 'slow death by strangulation' situation because of a contract no one had bothered to read. The firm purchased a piece of design software that never worked as advertised. So, they stopped using it and returned the software with a strongly worded letter that expressed outrage that a software firm could bring a not-ready-for-prime-time product to market.

The problem was that the user fee invoices kept coming, and escalated at an annoying rate. Cummings & Longworth's in-house counsel finally read the contract they had signed two years earlier. There was no 'return' clause, just an escalation clause that kicked in as the design firm added workstations; a measurement the software company watched with eagle-like attention.

Matt was called in when the monthly invoices hit $85,000 and the unpaid balance plus late-payment penalty was $2.2 million. He went through the contract not just line by line, but word by word, as well as every piece of correspondence between the two companies. He found what he needed not in the contract or correspondence, but in the original sales presentation given by the software company, one hard copy of which was still in the file.

Then, armed with what he needed, Matt flew out to Denver to pay a visit on the software vendor.

After a brief but forceful seminar put on by my husband on the subject of legal penalties for fraudulent representation, the software company not only apologized, but paid Cummings & Longworth the sum of $1.1 million for the corporate equivalent of pain and suffering. When Matt mentioned last year he was going to build a new home, the CEO of Cummings & Longworth insisted that their firm would do the plans without charge.

It was a great story and it almost had one those everyone-lived-happily-ever-after endings except for the fact that Cummings & Longworth doesn't design houses. They design factories and power plants. But they turned loose a third-year architectural associate with a computer and she sat down with Matt and me for about six hours getting down on paper every idea we had about our dream house.

Rachael, now a junior partner, of course wanted to know how the house was coming and I took ten minutes to wax enthusiastic about how the execution was every bit as good as the design. Then I said I needed to talk about the heating system.

"You didn't specify anything," I said.

"That's because the technology is changing really, really fast," Rachael said. "I mean, it's totally in flux. So I just picked, like, a really, really high efficiency level as a placeholder."

Millennials speak differently than their parents. I get that. It is a product of having grown up in a world where texting and instant messaging have become ascendant technologies that have driven the spoken word to the sideline. Rachael is a great architect who designed a wonderful house. I braced myself, gritted my teeth, and filtered out the 'likes' and 'really reallys'.

"My builder is trying to palm off a heating system the size of a large pizza, except they don't make pizzas in South Korea," I said. And then added, "At least I hope it's South Korea." I read her the information I had copied off of the box.

I heard tapping of keys. "Ohmigod," Rachael said, tapping more keys. "Ohmigod."

Great, I thought. *Armageddon.*

"Well," Rachael said, "theoretically, it's a South Korean company, but the Kaesong Industrial Complex is in North Korea. It's a joint venture. Except that there's some kind of pay dispute and the place keeps shutting down."

I did not like where this conversation was headed.

"The Nu-Heet Whole House Combi Tankless Boiler is an adaptation of Korean 'ondol' technology," Rachael said. "It has exceptional efficiency because Koreans don't have a lot of energy to waste."

"The plumber said he had never installed one of these," I offered. "Are they new?"

More tapping. "They just started selling them in America last year. They have a distributor in Riverside, California."

I realized I could get most of this information myself and I didn't need to tie up an architect's time, even if my husband's birthday was a company holiday.

As soon as I was off my house phone, I retrieved my iPhone from my purse.

"Siri," I said. "Find me reviews of the Nu-Heet Whole House Combi Tankless Boiler. Show me newest reviews first."

You will be amazed at the number of websites that review things as arcane as a tankless boiler.

A website called, 'ContractorStraightTalk.com' had a review less than a week old.

"The Nu-Heet system is a total piece of shit," wrote 'R.C. from Boise'. *"It arrived with roughly a quarter of the parts missing, took ten days to install, and continually shut itself down for diagnostics. When it did run, it emitted a smell not unlike a burning diaper, fully loaded, of course. They practically give these things away, and they're still not worth it."*

That was one of the gentler reviews.

Other sites added the useful information that no one answered the telephone in Riverside. All calls went straight to voice mail and were returned, on average, in three days. The spec sheet and installation diagrams were written, according to another reviewer, "in English, but as translated from Korean via intermediate stops in China, Bangladesh, and Cameroon."

No one – not a single reviewer – had a good thing to say about the product.

I drove back out to River Street where Joey was nowhere to be seen and Fred was in the basement surrounded by parts, a perplexed look on his face.

He saw me and said, "I don't think they sent all the parts."

"Put it all back in the boxes and ship it back to wherever it came from," I said, retrieving my iPhone. "Just read a couple of these."

Fred expertly scrolled through my saved list, alternately grinning and saying, "Oh, boy." At the end, there was just a perplexed look on his face.

"You're wondering 'why'?" I said.

He nodded.

"Almost everything in the house is specified down to model number," I said. "Except for the heating system. The architect specified an admirably high efficiency level but left the equipment choice open. Joey found a way to put some money back into his pocket that he lost on the foundation."

Fred nodded slowly. He understood. I took a plunge.

"Is he paying you by the job or by the hour?" I asked.

Fred physically took a step back from me and put up his hands as if to ward me off. "That isn't something I discuss with…"

I saw where he was going, and added, "I'm asking because, if you took a fixed amount for plumbing the house, then he intends to stick you with all those unbillable hours to put this together to make it work."

"I've worked with Joey on a lot of jobs," he said. "He's never done anything like this."

I pointed to the parts on the floor. "If this was your house, what would you install? Something highly energy efficient, but reliable and not out-of-this-world expensive?"

Fred thought for a moment. "There's a company down in Fall River…"

"Call them up and order a system to suit this house," I said, full of confidence that I wasn't certain had a foundation.

"And what do I tell Joey?" Fred asked.

"Tell him the truth. Tell him I told you to do it," I said. "In fact, tell him I *forced* you to do it, because that is what I'm doing. And, if you're uncomfortable, tell him to come see me."

"I can handle Joey," Fred said. There was a look on his face and a tone in his voice that told me that this was a fixed-price contract and that he, too, suspected that Joey intended to recoup his own profit by making Fred work harder with a lousy piece of equipment.

But then Fred added, "Of course, none of this means anything unless we get gas in here before it gets cold."

I realized I had just signed a declaration of war.

* * * * *

Heat. MassGas.

There wasn't a day I didn't call someone and ask if they could help me or who they knew.

Because of my work with the Hardington Garden Club, which pays for and maintains dozens of wayside gardens around town that would otherwise come out of the town's budget, I have gotten to know the folks in the Department of Public Works really well. Will Koslowski, the head of the DPW is an affable guy. You ask if he can spare a cubic yard of dark brown pine mulch for the planting site at the town library, and the mulch is there the same day, placed exactly where you want it.

During the horrific winter when Will's crews were working eighteen-hour shifts, the Hardington Garden Club kept kettles of soup going in the DPW break room and hosted a lasagna dinner when the snow was at its worst.

But when I asked Koslowski if he knew anyone at MassGas, he had only a pained expression on his face and an even more painful story to tell.

"We work with those guys every week," Will told me. "We do road cuts, we make certain they have access to town sites. For fifteen years, back when it was Pilgrim Gas, there was one guy whose job it was to make certain everything went smoothly in Hardington, Overton, and Oakley. I had his pager number, his home phone number, you name it. Then Pilgrim got acquired by Bay State and this guy had two more towns to deal with, including Cavendish. Then came MassGas, which is really some outfit out of Texas called Reliable, and there's a new guy with a 'district' that covers thirty towns in an arc that starts in New Bedford and goes up to the New Hampshire border. Every year, the shape of the 'district' changes and there's a new guy, whose job is to call me and demand that *we* do stuff. Please don't talk to me about MassGas."

It was still mid-September. I had my state senator and assemblywoman working on it. I had sent entreating letters – honest-to-gosh letters on cream-colored stationery – to the President of the New England Division (based in New York, of course). I had posted 'help me!' notices on Facebook asking if anyone knew anyone or had a back door into MassGas. No one could say I hadn't been a busy beaver.

What I still didn't have was an appointment to get my gas connected.

Chapter Thirteen

Two days after I told Fred to send back the Korean heating system, Joey reappeared, tearing into the makeshift driveway, his oversized tires throwing crushed rock in every direction.

He stepped out of his truck, cinched up his tool belt, and started walking toward me like a gunslinger, one hand on a power drill in its holster attached to the tool belt like a Colt 45. His other hand was clenched around several sheets of paper.

The look on his face said that I was getting my first good look at Really Angry Joey.

Now, you are probably wondering at this point, 'Where's Matt?'

What a great question. Matt was supposed to be my partner in all of this. The person ready to play Bad Cop or to read the riot act. Matt was supposed to step in front of me to take the bullet or the drill bit or whatever Joey had in mind.

Matt was in Singapore.

Remember that quick foray to Geneva to take the temperature of his best clients? Well, one of his clients seemed quite nervous and, when a client moves around in his or her chair, Matt probes. He keeps asking uncomfortable questions until he gets to the root of the problem and, in this case, there was an incipient crisis brewing.

Companies in Switzerland have no enemies. They have a charming habit of making problems go away by dispatching bales of Swiss Francs. But in this case, their pharmaceutical partner in Kuala Lumpur had been caught on video making a problem go away in just such a manner in the graft-free island city state of

Singapore. Technically, Matt's client was guilty of nothing. The guy in Kuala Lumpur was acting strictly on his own.

Matt patiently explained to his Swiss drug company client that quote-unquote 'technically' had a different meaning in Singapore than it did in the comfortable confines of the Swiss Confederation.

Of course, Matt did not tell me any of this. You don't say that kind of stuff over the phone and you certainly don't put it into an email. Instead, I got a call from him saying that he might be a few days late getting home because he needed to take care of a 'hiccup' in a negotiation.

'Hiccup' is our private code for 'hell breaking loose'. I wouldn't get the specifics about the 'hiccup' until his return. In the meantime, Matt was traveling the world with two changes of underwear, three clean shirts, and half a tube of toothpaste.

Why that image – Matt running out of toothpaste in Singapore – flashed through my mind is beyond me, but by the time Joey got within two feet of me, I could see him visibly shaking with anger.

"Where have you been?" I asked, assuming that taking the high moral ground was a good starting point. "This place needs…"

"None of your goddam business!" Joey exploded. He held the sheets of paper over his head in a fist. "You do not tell my crew to send back equipment!"

So that was what was in his fist.

"I would have told you except that you haven't been here," I replied. I was amazingly calm given that his other hand was still around that drill.

"I don't care," he screamed. "You don't talk to my people. You don't tell them to order different stuff."

"Even if the 'stuff' is garbage?" I managed to arch an eyebrow.

"The architect said better than 96%." Joey lowered his voice. But now his face had that, 'I got you dead to rights on this one' look. "I read that contract. The system I ordered is 97% efficient. Best of its kind." His lip turned up in a curl. He must have practiced that sneer in front of a mirror.

A little alarm bell went off in my head. That alarm bell doesn't function with complete accuracy but, when it sounds, I listen to it. The alarm bell was reminding me to think back to a conversation Matt and I had the night that we signed the contract with McCoy Contracting. Matt pointed out what he called his 'finest achievement' – the incorporation of Joey's full proposal into the final contract. Including all that happy language about using the finest materials and best workmanship.

Gotcha, Joey!

"Joey, do you remember giving us a proposal to build this house?" I asked.

The simplicity of the question caught him off guard. His anger and smugness were momentarily replaced by confusion. "Of course, I remember," he said.

"You promised to use the highest quality materials," I said.

"I'm using exactly what's in the architect's schedule," Joey said. "You can't do better that 97%. You get Nu-Heet." He shrugged. "Unless you want to *pay* for something better."

He was waiting for me to take the bait. No way.

"Joey, Nu-Heet is garbage," I said. "You know it and every contractor who has tried to install it says the same thing. Do you read the reviews? On the rare occasion the system works, it smells like someone put a match to a soiled diaper."

Joey shrugged again. "That's your opinion. Mine is that it exceeds the architectural specs. You can substitute something else, but it's on your nickel."

"No, Joey, it's on yours. And you never explained why you've been off site for – what? – four or five days." I crossed my arms across my chest, waiting for the answer.

"Then we don't install a heating system until we figure out who is going to pay for it," Joey said. "And I've been taking care of a family problem, not that it's any business of yours."

My maternal instincts kicked in, and I blurted out, "I hope it isn't something serious." Even as the words were coming out of my mouth I was kicking myself. He had even given me an out, saying it was none of my business. Except that Joey obviously *wanted* me to ask.

"It's my daughter," Joey said, his head hanging low with worry. "She suddenly has no energy. I've been taking her around to specialists, trying to get a diagnosis."

"That's terrible," I said, and I meant it. But was Joey lying? Two of his previous customers said he used family illnesses as excuses when he disappeared without telling anyone.

"She's a little frightened," Joey said, his head still hanging down. "My wife is even more frightened. I'm sorry I lost my temper back there…"

"You do what you have to do," I said. I mean, what else was I going to say. *'Prove it?' 'Show me the medical reports?'* You don't do that stuff. Even congenital liars are sometimes telling the truth.

* * * * *

And then Joey promptly disappeared again. He didn't respond to phone calls or to text messages. His phone mail inbox filled up.

Matt came home two days into the Great Disappearance and we walked the project together. It was September 19. The framing appeared to be completed though it did not have the Building Inspector's signoff. This was a little worrisome because the target date had been September 15. Still, other aspects of the job appeared to be on or even ahead of schedule.

The garage had gone up quickly, the big timbers for the back porch were in place, and the front porch looked terrific. But only half of the siding was on and the inside of the house was a jumble of studs and plywood with electrical boxes every few feet. A fireplace kit we had purchased on that tax-free weekend sat untouched in its box in the living room.

"Tell me I haven't made some tragic mistake," I said, holding

Matt's arm. We were in the raw space that was going to be my Dream Retirement Kitchen.

"I've been dealing with imperfect people for the past two weeks," Matt said, weariness in his voice. "I realize I'm getting tired of saving the world."

He notably did not respond to the 'tragic mistake' question.

Matt continued. "But I will not allow someone with the delusion that he is a competent contractor derail our house. It's my fault; I wasn't here when you needed me."

"What do we do?" I asked. Note that I didn't relieve him of partial responsibility for this mess.

"We assess what has been done on the house so far," Matt said quickly, having clearly thought about a plan. "We talk to each of his subs. We find out where they stand financially with Joey and whether they'll keep working for us. Assuming they will, we track down Joey and formally fire him, in writing."

My Matt was a Man with a Plan.

And so we did a construction status of our house. It had been almost exactly one month since the foundation was poured. What we effectively had was a shell of a house, except that it was missing half its siding. The 'big' interior projects hadn't even been started – the kitchen, the snazzy bathrooms with their fancy tile, our fireplace, the hardwood floors. As we did our walk I made a list, which was as long as it was depressing.

With the first part of Matt's plan done, it was time to talk to subcontractors.

Paul, the electrician, was working in what would become one of the bedrooms. I had been bringing Paul coffee for three weeks and we had a nodding acquaintance. He looked to be in his mid-fifties, with a bit of a paunch and a gray handlebar moustache. Though he drove the standard electrician's van filled with equipment, I had a hunch that he was a weekend motorcycle guy. He kept a big, yellow DeWalt radio tuned to a classic rock station from the time he started work in the morning until he finished for the day.

Joey also had a DeWalt radio, which was apparently programmed to play nothing but heavy metal. He had a playlist that was heavy on ear-splitting 1970s and 1980s bands like Grand Funk Railroad, Iron Maiden, and Metallica. Usually they worked on opposite sides of the house. Sometimes they worked in adjoining rooms. The results were headache inducing. But that's a different subject.

We had to start somewhere; we started with Paul. Paul saw us and turned off the radio.

Matt did the talking. He asked about Joey's frequent absences from the site. Matt also asked Paul if he was getting regular progress payments. Paul listened and nodded before responding to any questions.

"I agree that Joey keeps strange hours," Paul said. "But he gets the job done and he pays his subs in full."

"What about the heating system he wants to install?" Matt asked.

"I heard about that," Paul said, giving no facial indication about where he stood on the subject apart from scratching his beard. "That's Joey being Joey. Talk to him. Reason with him."

"We don't think Joey is going to be reasonable," Matt said. "And, if he won't be reasonable, we'll finish the job without him. Paul, we want to hire you to work directly for us to complete this job."

Paul was silent for more than a minute. Matt is a paragon of patience about getting responses. Far more than me.

After that prolonged silence, Paul said, "I've done at least fifty jobs with Joey over the past fifteen years. This is my fourth job this year and my largest. You're asking me to give up a fifteen-year relationship and a steady source of work because you and he are having a problem."

"When we fire Joey, you stop working on this job anyway," Matt said. "What if we give you a ten percent bump on your fee?"

"You don't understand," Paul said in a firm voice. "If I drop Joey and go to work directly for you, I'll never work for Joey again. He'll never have me on another job. I'm not going to jeopardize that for a few hundred bucks. This is a business built on trust. Agreeing to go to work for you for *any* amount of money would be the deal breaker of all time as far as any contractor was concerned."

Matt's plan to become our own general contractor had just hit an insurmountable obstacle.

* * * * *

To reason with someone (or to fire them), you first have to find them.

We had a phone number and an email address for Joey. For purposes of our contract, Joey provided a post office box number in Overton. The state's website for Construction Supervisor Licenses yielded a street address: 525 Industrial Drive North in Overton.

Overton is the town that allows other communities like Hardington to be 'charming'. Overton has all of the 'necessary-but-evil' things that make suburban life possible. It has a McDonalds and a Burger King so you can stop your kids from whining on a Saturday afternoon. It has a Costco and a Home Depot and three or four other big-box stores that allow you to get, in one or two stops, everything you need for a project or a party. All of these enterprises are spread out along an incoherent, three-mile-long stretch of highway interspersed with Chinese restaurants and strip malls housing lesser chain stores. The result is a thoroughly depressing town, but one that gave its soul so that four or five adjacent neighbors could proudly boast that they were WalMart-free.

The next morning, I drove to Overton and found Industrial Drive. It was a short street filled with more or less identical Butler buildings, all of them roughly the same 1980s vintage. Number 525 was the second on the right; there were two trucks parked in front of the building, one of which looked as though it had not been moved in weeks. Neither truck was Joey's.

The door – frosted glass with a crack running from side to side – was unlocked and I went in. The inside of the building yielded little evidence of commerce. The interior was dimly lit and musty. In the middle of the floor was a Bobcat and a pickup truck, both covered in thick dust. There was also thick dust on the floor but no visible footprints leading to the vehicles, and I wondered if they were abandoned by some previous tenant. One end of the building was filled with random stacks of lumber and a pallet filled with bags of something – perhaps cement. The overall effect was decidedly creepy.

One end of the building had been partitioned into offices. I walked over and tried the door which was also unlocked.

As I turned the knob, someone inside yelled out, "Who's that?"

I opened the door. Aided by the illumination provided by yellowed overhead fluorescent fixtures, I saw three flimsy desks and half a dozen filing cabinets inside. At one of the desks was a stocky, sweatshirt-clad, white-haired man wearing a 'Grainger' baseball cap. In front of him was a small printing calculator and an inch-high stack of papers.

I introduced myself and said I was looking for Joey McCoy.

The man laughed. "Yeah, I forgot," he said. "This is Joey's official place of business."

"Do you expect him soon?" I asked.

The man laughed again and shook his head. "I don't think Joey could find this place without GPS. He hasn't been here in months."

"But the state lists this as his headquarters."

The man nodded and leaned back in a chair that squeaked loudly from the change of position. He folded his hands over his ample belly. "You gotta understand that every guy in this business has the same 'headquarters'," he said. "It's the cab of his truck. But the state wants a street address. I probably got a dozen guys like Joey with businesses that use this as their mail drop for state paperwork."

"So, where do I find Joey?" I asked. I know there was more than a hint of exasperation in my voice.

The man shrugged. "You call him." He made it all sound so logical and easy.

"He's not answering his phone and his voice mail is full," I said, and added, "And he's not responding to emails."

The man rubbed his chin. "Then I don't know how to help you."

"Do you have his home address?" I asked. "This is really important."

Slowly, the man opened his top desk drawer and began riffing papers. He brought out a notebook and began looking at each page. After perhaps thirty seconds, he found a slip of paper. My pulse went up a notch.

"All I got is a post office box," he said, suspecting I already had that information.

"Does he live here in Overton?" I asked.

The man scratched his chin again, looking off in the distance.

"Maybe," he said after lengthy consideration.

I gave the man my thanks and went to the Overton branch of the United States Postal Service. Ten minutes of standing in line earned me six seconds of scorn for even asking such a personal, confidence-in-the-integrity-of-the-system destroying question.

"We are not allowed to give out personal information about box holders. May I help the next person in line?"

I left Overton ready to scream.

* * * * *

And so I went home and went to the information source where

there are neither limits nor rules: Google.

I typed in, *"Home address Joey McCoy contractor Massachusetts"*.

I got back 614,000 results in 0.37 seconds. Isn't technology wonderful?

And every result in the first three pages gave the same answer: 525 Industrial Drive North.

But there were all those enticing ads in the right-hand frame. *"We found Joey McCoy. Get arrest records, DUI reports, alimony, date of birth…"*

I clicked on the least sleazy looking ad.

"We found 139 J., Joe, Joey, Joseph McCoy in Massachusetts. Please enter credit card information to refine search…"

I had a queasy sense that the mere act of clicking onto the site was uploading viruses, Trojan horses, spyware, and keystroke loggers onto my computer. I did a hard shutdown and turned off my router. It was probably too late and my bank account was being systematically emptied by pirates in Moldova, but it was all I could think to do.

In my files, there was a folder marked 'River Street construction' that dated back to when we purchased the property. I went through the fifty or so sheets of paper in it hoping Joey might have slipped up and accidentally provided a home address or telephone number.

No such luck, but in the folder was Joey's original list of references. My finger came to rest on the line for Harold Berry, the guy who had been one of Joey's customers for more than two decades. Joey had provided a telephone number and an address in Dedham. I remembered my conversation with Berry. If anyone should have an inner pipeline to Joey, it would be Harold Berry.

* * * * *

Half an hour later I was in front of a sprawling Cape on Country Club Road in a quasi-rural corner of Dedham. Joey had certainly been a busy carpenter. The original house – which I assumed was the center section – likely dated from the 1970s. Now, an enormous solarium hung off the south end of the house and a new-ish looking three-car garage graced the north end. Who knows what had been appended to the rear of the house.

Having nothing to lose, I rang the doorbell. A minute later, the door was opened by a portly guy in Bermuda shorts and a Red Sox tee which, when he turned around, revealed himself to be one of the rapidly vanishing breed of Manny Ramirez fans.

Berry graciously welcomed me into his house with a broad smile. He appeared to be in his mid-seventies with a fringe of white hair and black-framed glasses with thick lenses. He walked with a noticeable limp.

As he led me through his house I explained that we had spoken on the phone a few months earlier and that I needed to get in touch with Joey McCoy. I suspected I would have received the same welcome had I said I was with the Jehovah's Witnesses and wanted to know if he had heard The Word. This was a lonely man and I was unexpected but welcome company.

We went into that solarium where a 50-inch television displayed two talking heads conversing wordlessly above a stock ticker. Copies of the *Wall Street Journal* and the *New York Times* were spread open on a coffee table. The Keurig system I had imagined during our long-ago conversation sat on a bar counter at one end of the room.

Berry would not take 'nothing, thank you' for an answer to the question of what I wanted to drink, and so I settled for a small bottle of Perrier, which he poured into a glass and added ice. He then placed the glass on a small tray and added three Milanos.

"I remember your call," Berry said after he sat down in an oversized leather recliner. "You're building a house in…." He snapped his fingers. "Hopkinton."

"Close," I said, smiling. "Hardington. That's OK, you're not the only one. Come Patriots Day we get busloads of people asking where the race starts."

The comment drew a grin from Berry. "Joey is a helluva guy. Known him for more than twenty years." Berry waved his hand at the ceiling. "You see that? Solid oak rafters and webs. The bead board is a custom-carved job. Joey did that three years ago. It's my favorite room in the house now. I live in this room until mid-September."

"Joey is doing a great job of my house, too," I lied. "My problem is that he seems to have – disappeared. I can't reach him by phone or email and I really need to speak with him. We have a deadline on some important decisions."

"Not answering his phone?" Berry's face showed deep concern.

I said, "The last time he and I spoke, he said he was trying to find a specialist for his daughter…"

"She's in college now, I think," Berry said, his brow furrowed. "B.C.? B.U.? Something like that. I hope it's not too serious."

"I hope so, too," I lied again. "But if I miss these deadlines, it will throw off our construction schedule. It's getting awfully late in the season to do outdoor work." I leaned in toward him. "Do you have a home address or a phone number for him? It would really help me." I put a note of urgency into my voice.

Berry eased himself out of the recliner and slowly walked over to a book case filled with binders. He pulled down a blue one and walked it over to the bar counter. For two minutes he shuffled through papers, much as I had done an hour earlier at my own home. He gave out a couple of 'hmmpfs'. I munched on a double-dark-chocolate Milano.

"No home address and just the one cell phone number," he said. Testing his own theory, he brought a piece of paper back over to the recliner, where a telephone sat on an adjoining table. He slowly and meticulously punched in the number and listened as he, too, got that 'voice mailbox is full' message.

But there was a silver lining to this trip. Perhaps Joey was avoiding me. Perhaps he scrolled through his missed calls and pulled out the names and numbers that were 'safe' to return.

"If, for any reason, Joey calls you," I said, "please tell him I hope his daughter is better but we need to discuss half a dozen important things."

Berry said he would do so. I declined an invitation for lunch and headed for home after leaving Berry my name and number. I hadn't found the secret number or address for Joey, but I felt strangely satisfied. As long as Joey's subcontractors kept showing up, progress would be made on the house. And, if Berry called me to say Joey had returned his call, then I knew it was 'just' me that he was avoiding. It wasn't a long term solution, but my sense of panic faded.

* * * * *

The next day, Berry phoned me to say that Joey had returned his call. Yep, Joey wasn't avoiding the whole world. Just little old me.

* * * * *

Joey returned after a week's absence. I didn't have the opportunity to ask him where he had been because, well, there was screaming going on in our garage. Bruno DiNapoli, the Hardington Building Inspector, his face impassive, listened as a red-faced Joey spewed invective and some inadvertent spittle in DiNapoli's direction.

"I've *never* had to do that on a job in any other town!" Joey screamed. "It's the *stupidest* thing I've ever heard of! I don't believe you'd make *anyone* do crap like this!"

At this point, allow me to say that, while the above quote from Joey accurately conveys the gist of his comments, it is not verbatim, nor are the ones that follow. What Joey actually said incorporated different words. I am no prude, but we live in a sufficiently coarse world that I have no desire to further add to its debasement. Just add whatever verbs, adjectives and gerunds you desire to my expurgated version to create your own version of Joey's full-throated soliloquy.

"I mean, this is pure garbage," Joey continued. "You're picking on me. You've got one set of rules for the out-of-town guy and a sweetheart version for your regulars. I guess I need to start giving you little 'gifts' like they do. Right?"

DiNapoli listened, his face showing that the obscenities and accusations being directed at him were not having the intended effect, assuming that intimidation and a sudden change of heart were Joey's desired outcome. Instead, Joey continued his rant, oblivious to the hole he was digging for himself.

I might also add that, as soon as I heard Joey's shouting, I positioned myself so that I could be that proverbial fly on the wall. I was inside the house, Joey's back was to me, and DiNapoli was in three-quarter view.

From what I could gather, Joey or his subcontractors had screwed up on multiple aspects of the garage framing, and those screw-ups had the potential to call into question other work that was now hidden by things like, say, siding and roof shingles. The problems involved plywood panels that had been placed in the wrong direction, and insulation with a lower rating than what was called for under the town's current building code. Further, the inspector had discovered that non-code bolts were being used to anchor the garage to the foundation.

All of these things were going to need to be corrected before DiNapoli would provide that next red signature on the Building Permit. And, until that signature was in place, Matt and I had no obligation to write another check.

When Joey had finished ranting, DiNapoli said, "Mr. McCoy, I'm sure you were aware that Hardington adopted the 'stretch' code last year, and that, for the past eighteen months, we've been in a 100 mile-per-hour wind zone. As a contractor, you're obligated to keep up with zoning changes. They're all on the town website. In fact, I remember telling you about it when I inspected the foundation."

I thought Joey was going to throw DiNapoli through one of the garage windows.

"No town around here has *ever* had a hundred mile an hour wind," Joey screamed. "It's insane. I've used these bolts on every project I've done over the past decade. No building inspector has ever said a word about them. If they don't meet code, why does my building supply house offer them?"

That last tirade employed an especially impressive number of colorful words.

"Mr. McCoy," DiNapoli said. "It's all in the code. I'll be around on Friday and expect that you'll have corrected these problems and have proof of compliance on the other items. Otherwise, I'll defer inspection for a few weeks until I'm certain you've done it properly."

"Yeah. I'll have it done," Joey said, using his sullen, whipped puppy voice.

DeNapoli departed. Joey sat on a large box, writing notes. I waited a decent interval and then knocked on the two-by-four stud that I hoped would soon become a doorway.

"Glad to see you back," I said brightly. "I hope your daughter is better. Am I interrupting anything?"

"Did you just get here?" Joey asked suspiciously.

"I just pulled into the driveway," I said, a look of innocence around me like a halo. "Am I late?"

Joey stood up and tapped his notebook with his pencil. I could see little, tiny gears in his head spinning wildly; coming up with a plan.

"I've been going over your architect's plans," he said, making it sound like I was about to be told I had six months to live. "She apparently wasn't familiar with Hardington's building codes and she specified some things that are going to cost a lot more money to build in order to comply with those codes. I'm thinking $50,000 to $60,000. Maybe more."

"That's a lot of money, Joey," I said. "You'd better give me some specifics."

Joey walked over to the area where the twin garage doors would be installed. He knelt down and pointed his pencil at one of the bolts coming out of the foundation that tied to the garage wall.

"These bolts are rated for 75 miles per hour of wind," he said. "The problem is, Hardington's building code calls for 100 mile per hour winds. I'm going to have to replace these."

"And these particular bolts are specified in the plans," I said. I tried to keep the skepticism out of my voice.

"Pretty much, yeah," Joey said. "I brought it to the attention of the Building Inspector, hoping he would let it pass, but he was adamant."

"Let's focus on what, 'pretty much, yeah' means," I said, dropping the Little Miss Sunshine act. "If I go to the architect's plan, I'll see a notation that instructs you to use these particular bolts, and not some other ones rated for a higher wind speed. Is that right?"

"What you'll see is that the architect *failed* to say that the higher rated bolt would be required," Joey explained. "Architects have an obligation to keep up with building codes for the town where the house will be constructed."

I think Joey had convinced himself he was the innocent party in all of this. It is amazing what feats of acrobatics the human mind is capable of performing.

"Joey," I said, "to get a building permit, you had to submit a copy of the architect's plans. Is that right?"

"Well, yeah…"

"And the Building Inspector goes over those plans with a fine-toothed comb to see if anything doesn't meet code. Is that also right?"

"Well, up to a point…"

"And our architect's plans came back with the building permit without any changes. No notations that some other size bolts would be required." I was on a roll.

"That doesn't mean…"

"So, in the eyes of the Building Inspector, the onus is on the *contractor* to pick up on things like proper bolt sizes and what direction plywood ought to be mounted and whether Hardington adopted the stretch code."

I had let the cat out of the bag. Now, Joey knew I had overheard the exchange with DiNapoli. I paused, smiling slightly. Waiting for the capitulation.

"We'll split the cost," he said. "I'll pick up a third, you pick up two-thirds, as a show of good faith."

"No, Joey," I said. "We don't split the cost. You screwed up and DiNapoli caught you. Worse, you started blaming him. If I heard right, you accused him of taking bribes. Joey, you don't go around making enemies of the people whose job it is to approve your work."

"It was his fault," Joey said in a whining voice. "I'm not going to lose money on this house." He had a look on his face that mixed equal parts sullenness with defiance.

"Joey, *you* screwed up," I repeated, changing only the emphasis on who was the culprit. "Man up, re-do the work, and read the damned building code so that DiNapoli doesn't catch you flatfooted again. And go apologize on bended knee to DiNapoli for that 'gifts' crack."

But Joey wasn't listening. Instead, he had a gleam in his eye. "Don't think I don't know what you and your husband were trying to do," he said. Then he grinned. "Paul gave me the straight stuff. My guys stand behind me a thousand percent."

He stopped and applied a hint of malice to his look as well as to his voice. "Oh, and getting back to that contract. It says that both sides will work toward a goal of a late November Certificate of Occupancy. But there's nothing cast in concrete about that date. And, you know, I've been thinking. What with all the problems you've caused me by constantly looking over my shoulder, that Thanksgiving Day thing has become just plain un-doable. Plus you don't have gas so I can't install the floors. So, unless you're willing to up the payments – and up them a lot – we're going to have to push back the completion date by a month or two."

Then he snapped his fingers. "Damn," he said. "I forgot. You sold your house. You promised to let the buyers move in on December 1. Well, you're just going to have to go back to them and ask for a postponement. To sometime in January. Or maybe February. I'm sure they won't mind. Or, maybe you can put your house back on the market. Be sure to tell everyone, though, that the reason the schedule slipped is that you kept interfering with the contractor's chain of command. They'll understand."

And, with that, Joey hurriedly collected his notebook and tools and walked right past me with neither another word nor a glance backward at me.

A skirmish had just been fought; maybe even a battle. And I had no idea who had won. What I knew with certainty was that Joey thought *he* had been the victor.

Which is when I saw the folded sheet of paper on the garage floor that had slipped out of Joey's notebook. I assumed it would be notes from his conversation with the Building Inspector; a list of things he needed to correct. I picked up the paper and opened it.

Instead, they were notes of an entirely different nature. They read *Patriots Dolphins over (+130)/ under (-115) 45.5 points 250.*

There were similar entries for three other pairs of professional football teams. Each was for the same dollar figure.

Now I understood. Those incessant demands from Joey for

more money, and his continuing search for ways to substitute inferior products were driven not just by his ineptitude as a contractor, but also by a deep and probably longstanding gambling habit.

My Thanksgiving occupancy date was quickly becoming a shattered dream.

Chapter Fourteen

"Hot compost," said Susan Williams, my Master Gardener best friend. "My CSA is going to heat a greenhouse with fifty cubic yards of manure to grow winter vegetables. They're going to move the pile in just a couple of weeks. The stuff will be four feet deep and the interior temperature will be at least 150 degrees. We bury Joey in that pile and, by the end of winter, there won't even be much of a skeleton remaining. By the time the CSA removes the pile next spring, there won't be a trace of him, not even teeth. Every speck of the jerk will have cooked away. And at least he will have done something useful for once in his sorry existence."

Susan and I were having lunch at my house. It was the day after The Great Confrontation. Susan had listened to my telling of the events and was of the opinion that Joey thought he had the upper hand.

"The man is *stupid*," Susan said. "He succeeded in making an enemy out of the Building Inspector. That's like a PhD in stupidity. There's only one solution to a guy like that."

Which is when Susan made the suggestion about turning Joey McCoy into compost. I tried to change the subject.

"I don't think you get it," Susan said, pressing on, pointing a fork with a piece of tortellini impaled on it in my direction. "Joey is so dumb he thinks he has the upper hand in all of this. He disappears for a week without a word of explanation. He got caught substituting cheap windows and didn't get fired on the spot. He gets reamed out by the Building Inspector and comes away thinking you'll pay for his rotten work."

Susan was just starting to hit her stride. "And it's all because of two things: you desperately want to get into your house by the end of November, and his subcontractors – or at least some of them – are loyal to him," she said. "And, on top of everything else, he is taking some part of every payment you give him and gambling it away. Blowing it, really because he's trying to recoup his losses by betting on idiotic things like the number of points scored. He's going to lose everything, and possibly cost you your house in the process."

I had to agree that Susan had summed it up beautifully.

"And Matt thinks that a contract is some kind of magic wand," Susan added, the tortellini still being waved around. "*He* doesn't understand the situation because *he* works with people who *respect* contracts. Joey has no idea that there is power in a contract. I'll bet you he still has never read it all the way through. And, if he did, he wouldn't understand it."

Again, Susan was right.

"So it comes down to finding a cure for stupidity," Susan said. "With hot compost, Joey just disappears one day…"

"Susan, I really don't like this conversation," I said, and meant it. My carefully prepared lunch was quickly losing its appeal.

"My apology for thinking out loud," Susan said. "Sometimes, my impulses get the better of my self-control mechanism, or at least that's what a psychiatrist once told me. But have you tried looking ahead? I want this house to go well for you. I know you've been excited about it for months. My fear is that Joey is going to hold you and Matt up for everything he can, and still do a lousy job."

My problem was that I *had* tried looking ahead. And, every horrible thing that Susan spoke of was in my vision as well.

* * * * *

After lunch I had an inspiration.

I drove to the Hardington Town House (if there's a difference between a 'Town House' and a 'Town Hall' it has escaped my attention, but every reference to Hardington's town government calls it the Town House). There, in the basement, was the Office of the Building Inspector.

'Office' is a bit of an overstatement. It's a large file room with a counter. On one side of the counter are the tradesmen – the plumbers, excavators, electricians and general contractors. They form a line. On the other side of the counter is the Assistant to the Building Inspector. He takes the tradesmen one at a time and answers their questions.

He was a nice looking guy. Early to mid-thirties, I would guess. He was in khakis and a plain blue cotton shirt. He wore an expression – aided by wire-rim glasses – that exuded confidence and intelligence.

I got in line and, for half an hour, listened to the pressing questions of moments: whether, at a certain address, the set-back limits for construction along the sides of the property were fifteen feet or twenty-five feet. A map was pulled. A street address was converted to a plot number. An acetate overlay was added to the map. The plot number in question was in Zone B or the 'orange zone', so the answer was twenty-five feet.

"Does that setback include paving work?" the tradesman asked. Instead of answering, the Assistant to the Building Inspector went to a shelf and pulled down a folder. The folder fell open to a page, and the tradesman and the Assistant to the Building Inspector together read that setbacks in Zone B specifically included outbuildings and miscellaneous paved areas, including sidewalks and driveways.

The tradesman, probably a paving contractor, turned around, a satisfied look on his face, and immediately pulled out a cell phone. I could hear a phone chiming on the other end as the tradesman opened the door to the outside of the building.

After seeing this happen four times on three different subjects, I concluded that the Assistant to the Building Inspector could have answered each of those questions – including translating the street address to a plot number – from memory. But the key was to completely close the circle. The tradesman left the building secure in the knowledge that there was no possibility of error in the information.

And then it was my turn. As it turned out, there was a lull in the action and no one was in line behind me.

I saw the Assistant to the Building Inspector – his badge said "Brian Marks" – looking me over. I had no roll of plans with me or anything else that gave a clue as to why I was there.

"Address, please," he said.

I told him, "131 River Street."

I thought Brian's eyes were going to bulge out of his head. He blinked. Twice. Apparently, my home had been the subject of some discussion within the Building Department.

"I was hoping I could catch Bruno DiNapoli," I said, smiling brightly. "He was out to my house yesterday to meet with my contractor, Joey McCoy."

Brian held up a finger, a sign asking me to wait. He disappeared around a corner. I looked around the area. The Office of the Building Inspector shared the basement with the Water Department and the Office of Public Works. Those offices shared a similar counter where, at present, an elderly man was waving his water bill and questioning the accuracy of the reading.

Thirty seconds later, DiNapoli emerged from around that corner. He, too, was eying me warily. Why was I here? Was I here to plead Joey's case?

I held out my hand. "Anne Evans Carlton," I said. "We met the day our foundation was poured."

"I remember," DiNapoli said. "Lobster rolls."

"I think we have a problem in common," I said. "Joey McCoy." The use of the word, 'problem' was intended to short-circuit the 'friend-or-foe' question.

DiNapoli laughed. "How did you get hooked up with him?"

"Believe it or not," I said, sighing, "he came highly recommended."

"I saw you out of the corner of my eye yesterday," DiNapoli said. "You were there for the fun part of the inspection."

I nodded. "Joey blames the architect for not writing in big, bold letters that Hardington is in a 100 mile-per-hour wind zone and adopted the stretch code."

DiNapoli shook his head. "He has no one to blame but himself, and I told him as much."

"Do you have any suggestions…" I started to say, but saw DiNapoli hold up his hands, palms outward, in front of his chest. Either I had just committed a 'pushing' foul or else this was Building Inspector sign language for 'stop talking'.

"Mrs. Carlton," he said, "I'm not allowed to offer homeowners advice on dealing with their contractors. I can provide you with a list of the deficiencies I found and I can explain those deficiencies to you. But ethics and the law prohibit me from taking sides or offering advice. That, you need to work out with your contractor."

"Then let me ask a general question that draws on your experience," I said. "A homeowner fires a contractor for breach of contract. Would it be unusual for that person's subcontractors to refuse to work directly for the homeowner? And, what does replacing a contractor usually do to a completion date?"

DiNapoli considered both questions and he lowered his hands. "Assuming we're talking non-union guys, they side with the contractor. He's their bread and butter. If the contractor gets terminated, his subs may never get paid for the work they've done, but the bond is still there. Unless the sub was new, I'd be very surprised if he would break ranks."

He paused before continuing. "As to a completion date, everything goes out the window. A new contractor may want to re-do a lot of what the old one did and you as a homeowner have almost no say. Also, there's almost always a lawsuit. The contractor wants his money and his reputation. He wants to be paid for everything he did up to the point when he was fired, and he'll want time-and-materials rates; not some percentage-of-completion computation. Even if you have him dead to rights, he has nothing to lose and everything to gain by suing you. It can get ugly."

"My husband is a contract lawyer," I said.

"That may help," DiNapoli said. "But it won't stop the demands. I repeat: a contractor who has been fired has absolutely nothing to lose and everything to gain."

I had one other question. "There have been times when I've had trouble getting in touch with Joey. His voice mailbox will fill up and he apparently won't be checking emails. Do you know of another way to get in touch with him? A home phone number or address?"

DiNapoli shook his head. "He mentioned to me that he drives here from Brookfield, but the only information I have for him is what's on his business card."

"Brookfield?" I said. Brookfield is a town about twenty miles northwest of Hardington. To the extent that anyone thinks about the town, it is for their annual fair. "His business card lists a post office box in Overton."

DiNapoli shrugged. "He said that the traffic getting down 495 was getting worse every year. That's all I can tell you." Then he paused and added, "When you said you had one more question, I thought you were going to ask me about what happens when a contractor displays either ignorance of or willful disregard for the building code."

"Are you allowed to answer that question?" I asked.

DiNapoli nodded and there was a hint of a smile in his answer. "The Commonwealth allows local Building Inspectors to use what it calls 'special scrutiny' when we find repeated failure to correct problems we've identified. It is how we make certain that the contractor doesn't try to hide something else."

"And is Joey McCoy subject to 'special scrutiny'?" I asked.

"You'll have to draw your own conclusions," DiNapoli replied.

* * * * *

A Google search showed six people in Brookfield with the name 'McCoy' and a listed telephone number. None of them were named Joey, Joseph, or started with the letter 'J'. I considered clicking on one of those ads running down the side of the research results, but came up with what I hoped was a better idea.

I had not spoken to Maria Olivera since the day of our foundation pour. She was one of my *Jeopardy* winner friends – sorority sisters, really – and her position in clinical trials management at Biogen gave her access to the kinds of databases that just might be able to pick a needle out of a haystack or, in my case, a reclusive contractor from a suburb.

It turned out Maria was thrilled with the idea. After I described the events of the past several weeks and Joey's disappearing act to care for his daughter, she offered a cute diagnosis of Joey: "Fifty going on fifteen with a bad case of adult-onset ADD."

An hour later, she called back with the information I was seeking, plus a multitude of surprises.

"Joseph Xavier McCoy lives at 760 High Street, Apartment 407, in Brookfield," Maria said. "That's the Brookfield Green complex just off 495. If Street View is any judge, Brookfield Green may be the most anonymous group of apartment buildings in New England. He and his ex-wife have been divorced…"

"Wait a second," I interjected. "Joey is *divorced?*"

"They've been divorced for about eight years and he has lived at that address for five years," Maria replied. "Do you want to know what he pays for rent?"

I ignored the offer of extraneous information. "Joey always talks about his wife in the present tense," I said. "He has never dropped a hint that he isn't married." It was a baffling revelation.

Usually, if a man is going to lie about such things, he says he isn't married when he really is. That was the first time in my life that someone implied they were married when they weren't.

"It gets better," Maria said.

"I can hardly wait," I replied.

"OK," Maria continued. "As to contacting him. He doesn't have a landline in the apartment. I'll keep a lookout for a second cell phone. Sometimes, guys like that have a 'secret phone' that they use so that some inner circle can always have access."

"Now, are you ready for the really good stuff," Maria asked, with a touch of the private detective in her voice.

"Don't hold back," I said, encouragingly.

"Mrs. McCoy, or should I say the former Mrs. McCoy, also lives in Brookfield," Maria began. "Shonda Rafferty – she remarried six years ago – is about three miles away in what I suspect was the former family home, at 34 Fern Hollow Drive. She's an O.R. nurse, an honorable profession if ever there was one. Here's the curious thing: there's no daughter. I went through the 2000 and 2010 census and there is one child shown, a son named Gregory. Joey invented the daughter."

All I could say was, "Wow."

"There's one more thing," Maria said. "Joey declared bankruptcy three years ago. Most of those records are sealed, but you're looking at a guy whose principal asset is that he knows how to be charming when he sets his mind to it."

"Is he a serial killer, too?" I asked.

"No arrests," Maria said, apparently taking me seriously. "At least not in Massachusetts. Any murder sprees were committed out of state."

Somehow, that didn't make me feel better.

Matt had been working down in his study while I was upstairs in the bedroom I used for my office. I tapped on the side of the door, not knowing what I might be disturbing.

"I just got off of the phone with Joey," he said. "He's coming over this evening for that Come-to-Jesus meeting."

I had so much to say that all I managed to do was say 'huh'.

"He says he has some ideas about how to make certain that our house gets completed on time," Matt continued. "I thought we ought to listen to him."

"Then you ought to hear about my talk with Bruno DiNapoli this afternoon and the talk I just had with Maria Olivera," I said.

* * * * *

I think that for one of the few times in my life, I actually managed to impress my husband with my research. Matt is the meticulous organizer in the family and the guy who makes 'to do' lists for everything from planning his work day to making a trip to the hardware store. As I told of my own travels and conversations, Matt filled two pages of a yellow legal pad with notes and he encouraged me to offer my view of how we ought to handle the meeting. I felt both proud and smart.

Three hours later, at precisely 7 p.m., Joey showed up at our front door. He was dressed in a sports jacket and khakis, with a plaid shirt and a burgundy-colored tie. In one hand was a bouquet of what I call supermarket flowers, in the other a green folder. Had he been 25 years younger, I would have thought he was calling to pick up our daughter for a date.

We met in our most formal room – the living room that we almost never used. I had no intention of putting Joey at ease.

"Mr. and Mrs. Carlton," Joey began. "I owe both of you an apology. My conduct over the past several weeks has been completely inexcusable." His tone was humble, his eyes were looking at the floor.

"I can be a real – and I apologize in advance for using the word, but it's the exactly right one – a real asshole. I tend to think I know what's best when I really ought to be listening to what my customers are telling me."

Joey looked up at us. "What I'm here tonight to tell you is that it's all going to change. I spent a lot of this afternoon thinking about things I've said and done, and I've kicked myself for being such a pri… for being so hard to work with."

Joey looked at Matt. "Mr. Carlton, you would be entirely within your rights to fire me. I wouldn't blame you if you told me to get out and never show my face again." He then shifted his gaze to me. "And, Mrs. Carlton, I've treated you with such disrespect, I'm ashamed."

"But I'd like to try to save this for all of us," he said, now looking directly at Matt and me. "If you fire me, you'll have to start over; find a new contractor. It will set back your timetable by six months, easy. I want this house to be finished on time, on budget, and to your standards. I think I know how to do that."

Joey opened the green folder. "I would start by saying that you should get the heating system you want. I had heard good things about Nu-Heet, but let's go with Fred's recommendation. He's the expert. I'll make certain that you're completely in the loop on any other decisions about big-ticket items that weren't spelled out by the architect."

"I promise I'll be on site every day." He looked at me again. "Mrs. Carlton, you've been great with the coffee and pastries. They crews really love you for it and I'm sorry if I implied otherwise. I hope you keep coming, and I hope you keep asking questions, because that's how this house will be built to your satisfaction."

Joey then went through a week-by-week calendar of what he expected to accomplish, leading to a Certificate of Occupancy the week before Thanksgiving. He unfolded a floor plan and spoke with conviction about getting every room completed to the architect's specifications.

When he got to the living room and dining room, though, he paused and tapped the plan with the eraser of his pencil.

"I'm worried about gas," he said. "You want top-quality red-oak flooring. I can bring in the flooring, but it has to acclimate to the house at a temperature of at least 60 degrees. If we don't have heat by the end of October, I can't install that flooring."

He looked at me. "I know you've been trying to pull strings, Mrs. Carlton. Please keep pulling until you find the right one. The alternative is a house full of electric heaters, and I know you don't want that. But there will come a point when we need to look at alternative heat sources for this winter."

At 7:45, Joey closed his folder. "I figure you guys want to talk about this privately," he said, his newfound humility on display in every word. "I'll be at the site tomorrow morning and you can give me your answer. What I wanted you to understand tonight is that the contractor you hired and placed your confidence in back in July is going to be on the job every day from now until November."

Matt said nothing. I was the one to jump into the breach.

"You forgot one thing, Joey," I said. I unfolded the sheet of paper with the betting information on it and handed it to him. Or, rather, I unfolded a copy. I had scanned the original and had it safely in an upstairs file. "I'm not sure I want to entrust the building of my house to a guy with a gambling problem."

"I was looking all over for this," Joey said, taking the paper from my hands. "What do you mean, 'gambling problem'?"

"Four football games for this Sunday's games with point spreads and a separate bet for total points scored," I said. "Two hundred and fifty dollars riding on each game. I would call that a gambling problem."

Joey looked at the paper and laughed. "I can see how you'd jump to that conclusion, Mrs. Carlton. But the only thing riding on this sheet of paper is a case of Sam Adams, payable next Sunday."

He saw the look of disbelief on my face.

"Every Sunday afternoon during the season, eight of us get together to watch one of the games," he said breezily. "One person has to bring the beer. Each week, we have to choose from one to four games being played that day and predict the outcome. We can assign as much weight as we want to each game. We bring our sheets to the game. By Sunday night we know who has to bring the beer the following week."

Joey paused. "But bet money on a game?" He shook his head. "I'd never do that."

He then looked up at me. "I hope that answers your question."

I was so dumfounded I couldn't say anything. He had a perfect answer. Of course, he had to have known that he had lost the betting slip and figured out I had found it. He had plenty of time to concoct an acceptable answer.

But did I believe him? Not for a second.

With that, he rose and we shook hands. As he came close to me, I could swear I smelled cologne.

Was it possible Joey had stopped by to see us on his way to a date? I pushed the thought out of my mind.

* * * * *

"What do you think?" I asked Matt when the taillights of Joey's truck had disappeared.

Matt didn't answer immediately. Instead, he picked up his yellow legal pad and turned pages, looking at things he had written during the meeting.

"Joey is a walking, talking Harvard Business School case study," Matt said. "On the face of it, we got complete capitulation this evening. He's going to give us everything we want. We've won."

Matt turned a page of his notes. "On the other hand, we're dealing with a guy who not only doesn't play by the rules; he doesn't even acknowledge there's a rulebook. Ignorance may be his greatest strength. Joey has no financial assets. He has nothing to lose and has been through a bankruptcy; he knows that drill and he knows that it isn't as painful as it sounds. 'Beating' him in court means having the dubious honor of taking over the lease on his truck and inheriting a stack of unpaid bills. On the other hand, anything he recovers from us is money in his pocket."

"And his answer about the betting sheet was worthy of a good defense lawyer," Matt said. "I don't believe it, of course, but he had a perfectly good alternate explanation. No jury could have convicted him."

Matt closed the legal pad. "What he's saying is, 'trust me', knowing full well that we won't trust him. But as long as he keeps hitting completion points, we're obliged to pay him. He has obviously crunched some numbers and decided that finishing the job is more advantageous than walking away from it. The problem is that his new attitude has no 'guaranteed good until' date. Tomorrow, or next week, or next month he could revert to the 'Old Joey'. We'd be right back where we started."

Matt took my hand and squeezed. "What it means is that you become a full-time construction manager; even more so than you've been up to this point. Are you prepared to do that?"

I saw my carefree autumn slipping away from me.

"Yes," I gulped. "If it means getting the new house on time."

Chapter Fifteen

'Joey: the Reboot' was on full display the next morning. He was busily ripping out non-conforming plywood and mixing concrete for new anchor bolts. He never asked me if he was still on the job; I guess he assumed that, if he was fired, I wouldn't have offered him a cup of coffee.

More likely though, Joey's feral instincts for self-preservation had been the entire motivation for the previous evening's performance. Apart from my question about gambling – for which he was fully prepared - Joey hadn't given us the opportunity to ask any penetrating questions, wait for answers, and then trip him up on his lies. Instead, he had pleaded guilty to whatever charges were in our indictment, meaning that we never got to *read* him that list of things he had done and ask the questions that Matt had prepared.

It was, in short, a brilliant performance on Joey's part.

But I couldn't resist a test. Later that day, I said to Joey, "Hey, you never told us if you found a specialist with the correct diagnosis for your daughter. How did that go?"

Without missing a beat, Joey said, "Through one of my clients, we finally got an appointment with the best internal medicine guy in Boston. Three days of tests and I know my insurance isn't going to cover most of it. But he gave her a clean bill of health. Just an iron deficiency anemia. She will have to take supplements for the next six months; the doctor will see her again in the spring. Great guy. I may be building him a home gym and sauna."

I marveled at the detail. Here is a man who doesn't have a daughter, and so the daughter, being imaginary, cannot possibly be ill. Yet Joey had fabricated an appointment with 'the best internal medicine guy in Boston' and his imaginary daughter had undergone extensive tests and had a diagnosis appropriate to the 'tired all of the time' symptoms he had described. Even though the imaginary bills for his imaginary daughter's treatment aren't going to be fully covered (hint, hint), Joey likes the doctor and may have an imaginary project on his calendar as a result of the encounter.

So, at least now I could be absolutely certain Joey hadn't given up lying. It made things much easier: if Joey was speaking, I should assume he was spouting falsehoods unless proven otherwise.

* * * * *

Through the next week, Joey kept his word on at least one major thing: the house construction moved ahead swiftly. A new crew – Joey's 'Interior Guys' – came on the scene and began putting up drywall and skim-coating for the interior walls of the house. (And don't think I didn't check every invoice and sheet of paper that came through the house to make certain that Joey wasn't trying to palm off some hydrogen-sulfide-infused Chinese product on us.)

By the end of the week I could walk through 'rooms' and begin to appreciate the flow of the house. I feared the master bath wasn't going to be large enough to fit the oversized Jacuzzi we had ordered and Joey thoughtfully put down tape lines to show that everything fit together perfectly. He even complimented me on choosing an oversize unit and said he hoped it would get a lot of use.

Doorways were framed and there was a rough cut in the sheetrock indicating where the living room fireplace would be installed. The Building Inspector made his appearance and, this time, found little to criticize.

Chloe Barnes, my friend from my jumping days, came by to see the progress. She, of course, looked gorgeous in cashmere slacks and an azure sweater set while I was in baggy jeans and a disreputable sweatshirt. I had briefed her via email on the high points of the construction progress but this was her first opportunity since the day the foundation was poured to see that a house was actually rising on schedule.

Chloe has an indoor jumping rink on her Dover property that is twice the size of my house, but it didn't stop her from saying all the right things about what a smart thing it was that Matt and I were doing. She listened intently to my travails with Joey and offered to provide an additional set of eyes on construction details.

Joey, of course, had to come over and re-introduce himself. He snapped his fingers and said, "I remember you from that day in August. Chloe, right?" He wore an ear-to-ear grin and his words oozed charm.

At least he didn't do the thing with his fingers in his belt loops. Chloe merely smiled.

"We're building a great little house here," Joey said, smiling broadly. "This house is going to be proof that small can be beautiful."

My God, I thought. *He's coming on to her.*

"Chloe is a doctor," I said to Joey. "Gastroenterology. You ought to run your daughter's diagnosis by her to see if she agrees with your specialist." To Chloe, I added, "Joey's daughter was just diagnosed with a hard-to-spot anemia. Joey got an appointment with the best internal medicine guy in Boston."

Chloe cocked her head. "Oh, yeah? Who did you see?"

"Joseph Levy at Brigham and Women's," Joey said without a moment's hesitation.

Chloe had a puzzled look on her face. "I know Don Levy at Brigham. He's great. Are you sure the name is Joseph?"

"I'll check the paperwork when I get home," Joey said nonchalantly, "but I'm pretty certain it was Joseph."

"Huh," Chloe said, apparently losing interest in the conversation.

The devil in me wanted to push the exchange further; make Joey talk about the diagnosis or inquire where 'Joseph Levy' kept his office. But the truth was that a) I was impressed that he had correctly paired the surname and hospital affiliation of a quality internist that Chloe recognized, and b) work was continuing nicely on the house and I didn't want to impede that progress.

I guess, though, when you peeled back the layers of my feelings, I was annoyed that Chloe had arrived at my house looking like she was just back from a full day beauty treatment at Bella Santé coupled with a side trip to Nordstrom, and I looked like something the cat had dragged in. Joey had descended on Chloe like a honeybee on a nectar-rich flower.

And no, I wasn't jealous. Joey was the enemy. And Matt was always citing a quote from Sun-tzu about keeping your friends close and your enemies closer. I didn't want my enemy getting even a little friendly with someone who was supposed to be squarely in my camp.

Chapter Sixteen

And then it was the second week in October. It was eight weeks since the foundation was poured and six weeks to a promised Certificate of Occupancy. The weather, though noticeably cooling, had stayed seasonable and dry. From the outside, the house looked like, well, a house. The garage was completed, the front of the house was painted, the front porch looked great and the screened porch, though rough, was readily recognizable as the space it would soon become. For people passing by on River Street, the house looked finished.

The focus now was on interior work and there, too, was a blizzard of activity. Ornamental moldings were attached to window frames, baseboards were cut and secured to the walls, and a crown molding appeared around the ceiling of the living and dining areas. Matt's study acquired a rich, oak paneling. It was a joy to walk into 'my house' every morning.

The kitchen and bathrooms cabinets were installed. PEX tubes of red, blue and orange snaked through the floorboards and rafters. The tens of thousands of dollars of products we had purchased during August came out of the basement of our Too Big house and, one by one, were fitted into the Just-the-Right-Size home. The HTP heating system arrived and Fred the Plumber whistled all the time he assembled it, a smile on his face because he was putting in the system that ought to have been delivered in the first place. There was a happy plumber in my basement.

Moreover, there was harmony. Subcontractors agreed on one radio station – not heavy metal – and stayed out of one another's way. No one blocked anyone else's truck and graciously moved their own when a large delivery was in the offing.

Matt and I visited enormous warehouses in Westwood filled with slabs of marble and granite and chose pieces to which our name was then appended. As soon as the stone was cut to our specifications, it would be affixed to those kitchen and bathroom cabinets. It was six weeks to Thanksgiving and I could sense that we were going to make it.

Everything was not perfect. There were nagging problems. The huge one hanging over our head was a gas connection. I continued to make calls and our state assemblywoman's 'constituent services' staffer said slow but steady progress was being made. That was a far cry from 'you'll get your connection', but I was down to grasping at straws.

* * * * *

Joey continued to be on good behavior. I say 'good' instead of 'stellar' because some bad old habits began to show themselves.

First, Joey began to take long lunches. In those early halcyon days after the 'Come to Jesus' meeting, Joey would make a fifteen-minute lunch run and eat in his truck while making phone calls. Half an hour later he would be back to inspecting and supervising. Then, after two weeks, the time in the truck began to stretch out toward an hour. In the past few days, he had left at 11:30 and not reappeared until one o'clock or later.

When I said something about ninety-minute lunches, Joey would look hurt and say that he was combining his lunch hour with errand runs. He would show me a box of nails or some pieces of arcane metal that he said were necessary to connect something in the attic. Because everything was still moving forward, I elected to let it pass.

There was also the little matter of painting the back of the house. A few paragraphs above these lines, I wrote that, for people passing by on River Street, the house looked finished. That's because only the front of the house had paint on it.

The back of the house had never been painted. Joey's 'Painting Guy' was Ernesto and he was a one-man crew. He hadn't been to the site in three weeks and my fear was that it would soon be too cold to paint the exterior – I checked the cans and it specified that it has to be at least 40 degrees for exterior paint to adhere and cure.

I raised the question with Joey and he initially dismissed my concerns. "Ernesto had to fly home for a week to take care of something going on with his parents," Joey said.

"We haven't seen him in three weeks. Is he back now?" I asked.

"Yeah, sure," Joey said. "I texted him. He said he'll be here tomorrow."

Unhappy with the response. I pressed for a better response. "What if he isn't here tomorrow?"

"He'll be here tomorrow," Joey said, starting to sound annoyed.

"Have you just texted him or have you spoken with him?"

"These guys are good about responding to texts," Joey said. There was a testiness in his voice.

"Why don't we call him," I offered. "Just to hear him say he'll be here tomorrow."

Joey let out an exasperated sigh. "To tell you the truth.."

Let me stop right there. There are five words in the English language that, when placed in a certain order, tell me that whatever follows those words are going to be a lie. Those words are, 'to tell you the truth'. Using that phrase acknowledges that all the words that came before were inaccurate, wrong, fibs, prevarications, inventions. And it tells me that the words that follow are going to be equally mendacious.

"To tell you the truth," Joey said, "I had to let Ernesto go."

"You let him go in the middle of a job?"

"Well, yeah," Joey said, as though firing your one-man painting crew when there are, maybe, five days of exterior painting weather remaining is something right out of the *Contracting for Dummies* handbook. "He wasn't doing the job. I've got another painter lined up. That painter will be here tomorrow."

"You said you were being honest," I was calm as I said this. "Did Ernesto quit or was he fired? And, if I called him, what would he say?"

Joey clenched his jaw and rubbed his chin, a firm, manly stance that tried to convey that he was trying to be patient with someone who does not understand The Way of the Contracting World.

"It doesn't matter what Ernesto says," Joey replied. "I fired him. I don't keep guys in my crew that won't put my jobs first on their priority list."

At last! A nugget of truth amid the lies. Ernesto was alive and well as was his family. He was also happily employed. He just happened to be painting someone else's house.

"So, Ernesto is working on another job and will get to this one when he has finished that one, if it hasn't gotten too cold to paint."

Joey realized he had said something he shouldn't have. It took him a moment to recover. "Look," he said. "I'll have my new crew here tomorrow. You have my word on it."

What could I possibly say in response? I had caught him in yet another lie although he would never acknowledge it. Joey's word meant nothing. Absent the miraculous appearance of a new Painting Guy, tomorrow would come and Joey would simply push out the painter's start date by yet another day. He could keep making the same promise until the snows around the house were a foot deep.

But tomorrow got postponed. Joey emailed me to say he needed to take three days off from our house to 'do some emergency work' for one of his 'oldest and most reliable customers'. I called him as soon as I got the email, and my call went straight to voice mail. The most annoying thing was that he didn't ask permission. He more or less informed me with absolutely no notice that he wouldn't be at the site. Joey's email was couched with promises that he had texted his subcontractors thorough instructions and that he would be just a phone call away if any problems arose.

And, of course, the new painter didn't show up.

The problem with those three days was that it gave me the time to examine jobs that were ostensibly completed, but that on closer inspection required a lot more work. Two items stood out above all the others.

The first one was nail depressions in the siding. If you've ever watched a house get built, you know that siding goes up one piece of wood at a time. Two guys put the piece in place, make certain it is snug and leveled, and then affix it to the frame of the house with air-pressure-powered nail guns.

In a perfect world, the air pressure driving the nail through the wood is set so that the nail head is flush to the surface of the siding. Too *little* pressure and the nail head is popped out above the siding. Too *much* pressure and the nail head is depressed into the siding. When I looked at the house, I saw hundreds of nail head depressions. Joey's 'Siding Guys' had been in a real hurry and they had not adjusted their air pressure.

It was something I had pointed out weeks earlier. But Joey had a ready explanation: when the house was painted, the paint would fill those depressions and render them invisible.

"Happens all the time," he assured me.

Well, now the front of the house was painted, and those nail depressions were just as prominent as the ones on the back of the house where there was bare cedar.

The second problem was the master bedroom closet.

There were three parts of our new house that we replicated from our starter castle. Matt got his study, we both wanted a screened porch just like the existing one, and I wanted a master bedroom closet that was a clone of the one we would soon be leaving behind.

My attachment to the closet was far from hedonistic. It's a huge room, fifteen feet long and seven feet wide. In our starter castle, those 105 square feet get lost in the round-off of a 4800-square-foot monstrosity. But in our 'just-the-right-size' house, those 105 square feet would represent five percent of the total footprint of our new home.

The genius of those 105 square feet is that it allows all of both Matt's and my clothes to be displayed in a systematic and intelligent way. The closet eliminates the need for seasonal storage. I have a rack for slacks and one for dresses. Matt has one level for winter suits and another for sports jackets and lightweight summer suits. I have shelves for shoes and others for sweaters. In short, all of our clothes are in one place. There is no need to go rummaging through drawers in the spare bedroom (and soon, there would be no spare bedroom to harbor such things).

Moreover, the closet in our old house *looks* good. The wood is high quality, everything fit together beautifully, and there are little architectural flourishes that speak to this being a custom installation. Joey promised that the new closet would be an exact replica of the old one.

Joey took photographs and careful measurements of our existing closet to ensure that the new one was an identical twin of the one we would leave behind. When the interior crew put sheetrock over the frame, we used tape to sketch out the closet in its new space, ensuring that everything fit and looked exactly as it should.

Except that it didn't. Joey brought in his 'Closet Guy' who assembled the new space in two days. As soon as I saw the completed space, I was unhappy. Our existing closet is built from solid oak and pine planks, stained to highlight the grain of the wood. The shelves are finished with caps, bullnoses and ornate trim work.

'Closet Guy' had used boards made of compressed sawdust with a plastic 'oak' laminate cover, all connected together with plastic clamps. All corners were squares and showed seams where pieces of laminate had been glued. Yes, it was the exact dimension of our existing closet but, to me, it looked as though it was straight out of a double-wide trailer.

It looked cheap and I used those exact words with Joey.

"Wait until your clothes are in it," he said soothingly. "The wood and the hardware will disappear. And I can get my guy to put decorative caps on the end face of the shelves."

On the second day of Joey's 'emergency work' for another client, I started dismantling 'Closet Guy's' handiwork. I stacked the compressed sawdust boards neatly into a corner and consigned all of the cheap plastic hardware to the oblivion of a Home Depot bucket.

* * * * *

When Joey returned on October 14, his 'three-day emergency' completed, things started to fall apart.

No. That's wrong. Things didn't start to fall apart. They fell apart. They crashed and broke into a thousand, irretrievable pieces.

I was waiting for Joey when his truck pulled into the driveway a few minutes after ten (gone were the days when he was on the site at 7:30 every morning). I didn't even give him time to pull on his tool belt. "Come with me," I said, and I quickly walked to the siding that covered the street side of our bedroom wall. I pointed to an area where the nail depressions were especially deep.

"This is not acceptable. You've got to fill these depressions and repaint the entire area," I said, then moved around to the side of the house. He followed me, glowering.

"You barely notice them," he said. "Come on, Anne, it's great."

Joey had also recently taken to calling me 'Anne'.

"Joey," I said, pointing to the next batch of nail depressions that made the house look like it had a case of smallpox, "your subcontractor did a lousy job. They were in too big a hurry to get it done and they didn't take the time to fix their mistakes. Worse, you didn't hold them to the quality they promised you."

Joey was silent for several moments. Then, he said, "I can't get those guys back here. They've been paid and they've moved on."

"They're not part of your 'A Team'?" I replied. "There weren't your 'Go-To Crew'? You just found them on some street corner? That's not the way you described them when they were here."

"My regular guys were tied up working on an apartment house job," Joey said, his voice defensive now. "The guys who did this work were highly recommended. But they won't come back. And the work is fine. The wood will fill around it and we can slap some more paint on it if you like."

I exploded. "We can WHAT? We can 'slap some paint' over the holes and make them disappear?" I was livid, my face beet red and my fists clenched.

"Calm down," Joey said. "I'll figure something out."

"No," I said. "I won't 'calm down' and you won't 'figure something out'. You'll bring in a crew tomorrow and they'll fill each and every nail hole. And then you'll re-paint any areas that need additional work. You'll re-paint the whole damned house if need be. And you'll finish it before it gets too cold to paint."

Which is when I led him indoors and into the master bedroom closet.

"And you're going to get this crap out of here and build the closet with the materials you're being paid to use," I said.

Joey's jaw dropped. "You dismantled the whole thing…"

"Tell your 'closet guy' to find the original boxes and take his sawdust back to whatever WalMart he bought it at." I can have a really cold voice when I set my mind to it. What came out of my mouth was pure ice.

"That's six thousand bucks worth of materials," was all Joey could say. He was still focused on the bare walls. "These are name-brand products…"

"Tell him to come back and use real wood this time," I growled.

"That would be, like, triple the cost," Joey whined.

"You said you would build a closet that was an exact copy of our current one," I said, my teeth gritted. "Not one with a picture of wood glued on top of sawdust."

"I won't pay for it," Joey said, an adamant tone of finality in his voice.

"You are contractually *bound* to pay for it," I said, my voice rising. "You may have forgotten, but you signed a contract. 'Highest quality workmanship and materials'. That's what you promised to deliver."

"Listen, Anne…"

"And you don't call me 'Anne'," I said. "You haven't earned that right. It's 'Mrs. Carlton'."

My last statement was undoubtedly pushing things too far. The world where 'tradesmen' could be called by their first names but customers were always addressed as 'Mrs. Smith' is a convention that went out with doctors endorsing Camel cigarettes. It's the sort of thing that, in a jury trial, would backfire on a grand scale. *(Mr. McCoy, did the plaintiff ever demand that you exclusively call her 'Mrs. Carlton' while she consistently called you 'Joey'?)*

But I was royally pissed. For eight weeks I had deluded myself that this house was going to be finished on time. I now realized that there was no possibility that we would serve Thanksgiving dinner here. We probably wouldn't serve Christmas dinner. Maybe Easter. More likely a Fourth of July cookout nine months from now, with a three-page punch list of still-undone items and Joey promising he would get to them 'real soon'.

Joey was screaming at me but I wasn't listening. With him following me, I walked through the plywood-floored unfinished living room, sidestepping the still-untouched fireplace kit box. I passed through the kitchen with its wires hanging out of walls and topless counters that had no hardware. All the while, Joey continued to scream and workmen looked up from their tasks at the stoic-faced woman and the wildly gesturing man. I reached the back door and walked down the steps into the garage and then out onto the gravel stmp that would one day in the dimly visible future be our driveway.

I took a deep breath of cool, October air. And as I did, I came to the unchangeable truth that the reason we would not be in our house was that Joey McCoy was a monumental screw-up. That diagnosis of fifty-going-on-fifteen was dead-on accurate. Joey was a little boy inside a man's body. He had a case of ADD that ought to be in a medical journal, and it would have been funny except that, instead of not turning in homework, Joey had lost interest in building my house.

There is a house in Hardington. It sits at the junction of two secondary roads and I drive by it three or four times a week. Ten years ago, someone decided to turn a modest ranch house into a colonial by adding a second story and a two-car garage. For a full year the second floor was a work in slow-motion progress. Then, the progress stopped. And for nine years the house has sat at that intersection with the silver Tyvek flaking apart and the stickers still in place on grime-covered windows. The exposed plywood is gray and swollen and open boxes of never-installed once-pink-but-now-black insulation still are stacked on the porch. I assume the house is abandoned; no one could possibly live there amid all that squalor and neglect.

My house was destined to suffer that same fate.

All of the frustration, all of the anger, and all of the hurt that my house was about to become one of those abandoned, never-finished houses you see in distressed communities. It all came boiling out. I turned to Joey, who was still ranting and waving his arms.

"So, what do you want, Joey?" I snapped, and he was suddenly quiet. "Is this a holdup for money? Had you planned on Matt and me being your personal ATM for the next two years? Did you figure we were good for another hundred thousand? Or was it more like a quarter million? Were we your next big score? The sucker customers you could bleed dry? The one that would keep your bookie off your back?"

"No one talks to me that way," Joey growled. He saw the anger in my eyes, though, and backed away.

"Well, *I'm* talking to you that way," I said, taking a step toward him. "I am talking to you the way every one of your customers *ought* to talk to you. You... are... a... screw-up. You... are... *incompetent.* You can't hire or keep good people. You have no idea what you're doing. And Matt and I are going to *put you out of business.* You are going to lose your license and we're going to make certain you *never* get it back. You are never going to louse up another house and another family. We are the last customer you will ever have."

I was standing less than six inches from Joey. My breaths were ragged, I trembled with rage. My eyes were full of tears.

Which is why I did not see it coming. Joey, with a primeval roar that emanated from somewhere down inside him; possibly the depths of his soul, reared his arms back and, with all his considerable strength, grabbed my slender shoulders and pushed me to the ground. I fell backwards onto the gravel like a slab of stone, my head and back hitting the ground simultaneously.

Dazed and in pain, I was dimly aware of his footsteps fading into the distance. I heard the engine of his truck come alive and I heard gravel being spit out as his tires sought and found traction. I wondered for a moment if he was going to finish me off; back his truck over me and leave behind just a corpse. But the engine sound receded rather than coming closer.

What I had not been aware of was that our argument had

attracted a crowd. Six workmen including Fred the Plumber rushed to my side even as Joey raced to his truck. Six voices asked how they could help me. Someone brought me a Thermos cap filled with water.

"Do you want the police?" Fred asked in a soft voice filled with genuine concern. "I saw the whole thing. Joey can't do that to people. He ought to be under arrest. Let me call the police. Let me call an ambulance."

I tried to sit up but found I was shaking too badly and my back and head hurt like hell, so I lay prone. I shook my head. "No," I said. "No police. I need to work this out." I pointed with my chin toward the house. "My purse is in the bottom right cabinet by the refrigerator hole. My phone is in there. Just tap the phone icon and you'll see 'Matt' at the top of the screen. Call him and ask him to come get me."

With that final trickle of energy expended, I closed my eyes and passed out.

Chapter Seventeen

When I next awakened, I was in a white hospital bed in a small room. An IV tube ran into my wrist and sensors were attached to my fingers and chest. Display panels beeped and gave multi-color readouts. I was in a pale green hospital gown. Matt was stroking my hair, a cool, wet cloth was on my forehead. My throat felt parched.

"What time is it?" I croaked.

Matt looked at the wall behind me. "About four o'clock," he said.

"What happened?"

"You're in the ER for observation," Matt said. "And you're safe. That's all that matters."

It turns out a great deal had happened in the preceding hours. Fred the Plumber had called Matt and Matt had called the Hardington EMTs. Matt took a cab from his office in the Financial District and met the EMTs as they pulled into Newton Wellesley Hospital.

When Fred described how and where I fell, Matt's protective instincts took over. Thirty-two years earlier I had been thrown by a horse and I landed on my back, a modest-size rock smashed into my spine. It nearly cost me my ability to walk and Matt was taking no chances. He spent part of the cab ride on the phone with the EMTs, relaying my medical history and making certain that the urgency of the situation was conveyed to the ER staff.

Matt spent the rest of his cab ride on the phone with the Hardington Police, who dispatched two officers to take statements from everyone at the work site. Each subcontractor told the same story: there was a heated argument outside the house, then another argument inside the house. Then I had wordlessly walked outside the house with Joey trailing me, screaming at me. When we were out on the gravel driveway, I said something to Joey, who screamed one last time and pushed me to the ground with a force and fury that took everyone by surprise. As soon as he saw me lying motionless on the ground, Joey ran and then hurriedly drove away. I regained consciousness only long enough to ask the crew to call Matt.

Joey, in short, was in a world of trouble. Based on the information provided by Matt, Hardington's town detective was en route to Brookfield to take a statement from Joey who, naturally, wasn't answering his phone.

While I was still unconscious, I had been sent upstairs for an MRI to see if there was any spinal swelling and we were waiting for that MRI to be read by a specialist. I had a pair of contusions on my shoulders where Joey had shoved me, and a litany of bruises on my back and minor cuts in my scalp where my head hit the gravel. I was sore from head to foot.

Matt told me all of this as I chewed on ice from a plastic cup. I marveled at his efficiency. I loved that he didn't hesitate about taking action. I loved this man for caring about me.

With the help of the ice, my voice was returning.

"Matt, what do we do about the house?"

Matt turned the washcloth on my head to provide more cooling. "We'll talk about that later," he said.

I shook my head, which didn't hurt as much as I thought it would. "No. We talk about it now."

Matt gave me an exasperated look. "Anne, you've just been assaulted by the guy we hired to build that house."

I managed a wan smile. "So I guess we don't give him another chance, huh?"

My response drew the first smile I had seen from Matt since I opened my eyes. "I think that boat has sailed," he said.

"So, what do we do?" I gave him my best pleading look.

"We…" Matt's phone buzzed. He extracted it from his jacket and looked at the ID. "This is the Hardington Police," he said, pointing at the phone.

"Take it," I said, and smiled as best I could.

Matt answered the phone. Mostly, he listened, throwing in a lot of 'uh huhs' and 'rights'. Four minutes later he tapped the screen and put the phone back in his jacket.

"That was Detective John Flynn," Matt said. "Joey is not at his apartment. He hasn't used his EZPass transponder. Flynn says he knows his counterpart in Brookfield and is going to stop and have a chat with him about places Joey might have gone."

"Don't forget his ex-wife lives in Brookfield," I said.

"I already told him that," Matt said.

"We were about to talk about the house." I sucked on a fresh piece of ice awaiting his reply.

"We go see the Building Inspector," Matt said. "We explain the circumstances. Joey's name and license number are on the building permit. Can we transfer that without his permission? Then we go looking for another contractor…"

Matt was interrupted by the tap of a knuckle on the wall. We both looked over to see a tall man in a white coat carrying a large tablet computer.

"Anne," Matt said, "this is Dr. Tillis."

I waved at him, trying to read his face. Was he coming in with good news or bad?

"Mrs. Carlton," Dr. Tillis said, nodding in my direction. Then, to both of us, he said. "I have the preliminary results of Anne's MRI and I won't keep you in suspense. There's no evidence of soft-tissue swelling and no spinal area lacerations. Anne took a clean fall."

"I can go home?" I asked.

"You're going to be stiff for a few days," Tillis said. "We'll give you something for the discomfort.   You were extraordinarily lucky." Then, to Matt, Tillis asked, "Any word from the police?"

Matt shook his head. "Our contractor didn't go straight home, which is no big surprise. Let's give them time. They'll catch up to him."

Tillis nodded. "We had a run in with the contractor doing work on our house last year…" Then he caught himself. "Take care of the back, which means get up and move around, but nothing strenuous."

An Uber driver took us from Newton out to Hardington. We decided Matt would pick up my car at River Street and the Uber would take me home. Thankfully, the EMTs had retrieved my purse before they took me to the Emergency Room; it was always good that an unconscious passenger had some form of ID.

When we got to the job site, my car was there, all alone. The workmen had decamped. They had likely taken their tools because they expected they would never return to this property. The sight brought tears to my eyes as I remembered the horrible feeling – just before Joey pushed me – that 131 River Street would become a derelict, never-to-be-finished house.

The Uber continued through the center of town and past the police station, where I suspected paperwork was being filled out to document what had happened this morning. At some point the police would want my statement.

I would tell them the truth. The guy I had entrusted to build my house had slipped back into being the 'Old Joey', full of excuses and outright lies. I would tell them that the fundamental problem was that my contractor had lost interest in building my house because there was no pot of gold for him. I would tell them of my sense of desperation; that this was the morning when I got it through my silly head that this house was not meant to be. It was jinxed. And so I had goaded Joey; invaded his personal space. Yes, he had pushed me, but I had threatened – no, I had *told* him – that I fully intended to make certain he never worked on another house as long as he lived. Joey's pushing me was as much an act of self-defense as it was an unwarranted assault.

I was still musing on what I would say when we pulled into the driveway of our starter castle, which was probably now destined to be our permanent house. Oddly, there was a gray panel van there. Even more oddly, it said 'Swearingen Plumbing'. This was Fred the Plumber's truck. What was he doing here? Probably demanding to be paid. In cash.

My car, with Matt behind the wheel, was right behind me. The driver explained that my husband had already paid the fare and held open the door for me. As I headed toward our front door, the driver side of the van opened and Fred emerged. He went to the sliding door where he kept his tools.

He took out a giant plant. From thirty feet away, I would guess it was a hydrangea.

OK, a plant. That was a nice going away present. And I owed him my thanks for being the person who called Matt. He ambled over to me, the plant waving from side to side.

"Your husband said you'd be home about now," Fred said, puffing. Plumbers are not used to carrying heavy weights. They have assistants to do such things. "I need to tell you something and I wanted you to hear it in person."

"I have a pretty good idea of what you want to tell me," I said. "And I want you to know that I understand. It's OK."

Fred had a confused look on his face. "May I put this down?" He indicated the plant with his chin.

"Of course," I said.

"Look, Mrs. Carlton, we all saw what happened this morning…"

"And I heard you all spoke with the police," I said. I think I was getting tired and I didn't need any more bad news in one day.

"Joey was so far out of bounds…" Fred started, then waved his hand as though erasing the idea. "What we – and I mean everyone working on the job – what we know is that Joey isn't coming back. But we want to finish what we started. We owe that to you. It's the least we can do after what he did."

My mouth was open but no words came out.

"What I'm saying is, if you'll hire us, we'll finish the house."

I think I was starting to cry again.

"You've been super to us," Fred said, still selling his idea. "We know what has to be done…"

"Yes," I whispered.

Fred actually had a look of surprise on his face.

Now I was crying.

* * * * *

The next morning I was more than a little stiff, but I also felt as though the weight of the world had been lifted off my shoulders. Joey was gone.

Matt the husband turned into Matt the lawyer. "Firing him will be the easy part," Matt cautioned. "Figuring out what we actually owe him will be much harder. He will, of course, claim we owe him tens of thousands of dollars for unreimbursed carpentry work. He will claim a management fee and demand reimbursement for every bill he can lay his hands on, whether or not it is related to our house."

Matt had created a spreadsheet that was the size of a 5,000-piece jigsaw puzzle. "It's partly my fault," he said as he printed out the last sheets of paper. "I wanted a contract that was three pages or less. I didn't spell out obligations under termination for cause. Of course, the Remodeling Contractor Arbitration Panel will side with us, but I'd rather this be a clean break with no loose ends or appeals."

Matt placed the last piece of tape on his gigantic spreadsheet which he planned to use to sway the Building Inspector that we were capable of managing the project. All of Joey's known subcontractors were there and all of the known tasks were listed. There were sub-cells for percentage of completion and materials. This was a dazzling piece of work. I hope Matt could make the Building Inspector understand it because I certainly didn't.

"The Building Department is open until 11 a.m.," he said. "I can do this on my own or you can come with me if you feel up to it."

"I definitely feel up to it," I said.

* * * * *

Brian Marks, the Assistant to the Building Inspector, saw me standing in line and did a screwball-comedy-quality double take, nearly knocking over a vase of fragrant roses on the counter that separated the Building Department's employees from those who sought its advice and approval.

There were two men standing in line in front of us. The first one had a question about zoning for a chicken coop. Instead of pulling down plot books and regulations, Marks said, "Yes, you can do it." The second man got out half his question about a variance for an in-law apartment. Marks interrupted him and said, "No way in hell. Don't even think about it."

And then we were up. Marks pulled a 'Closed' sign out from under the counter. Matt's eyes bulged and my face must have had a crushed look because Marks said, "No, no, no. That's not for the two of you. That's for anyone else who comes in. Come on back and let me find Bruno."

Which was when I learned that everyone associated with the building trades or law enforcement in eastern Massachusetts had heard about what happened the day before. The Fire Chief had heard all about it from his EMTs. The Police Chief told the head of the DPW and the Town Supervisor. They all wanted to hear the inside story.

Matt, who worries about things like tainting the jury pool,

protested that all we needed was to transfer our building permit from McCoy Contracting to 'self-managed'. He unfurled his spreadsheet along with the building permit.

"Jesus, just give me the sheet of paper," said Bruno DiNapoli. He crossed out Joey's name and license number on the Building Permit, added Matt's and my name, and initialed it in six places.

"Done," he said. "Now tell us the story."

By now, Will Koslowski, the head of the DPW, had also shown up along with the head of the Water Department and both of their office administrators.

And so I told the story. I didn't embellish and I didn't spare details. I went through the entire litany of Joey screw-ups leading up to his three day 'emergency repair' absence. I ended it with my waking up in the hospital, coming home, and finding my plumber waiting for me with the first plant for my new garden.

"He's toast," Koslowski told the group. "John Flynn says he has enough to go to the Norfolk County DA with both assault and battery and flight to avoid prosecution. He's getting a fugitive warrant."

"Is there anything else you need from the town?" DiNapoli asked. "You've been through six kinds of purgatory. There ought to be something we can do."

"Sure," I said. "Issue a warrant for the President of MassGas to appear and get us a gas connection before the end of the month."

That drew a laugh.

Will Koslowski, though, had a thoughtful look on his face. "I remember you asking me about that back in August. You mean you never got to anyone?"

I explained that my application had been 'accepted' and that a woman from the MassGas Engineering Department had come out and approved the site, but warned me that I was probably too late to get on the Construction Department schedule because crews were booked ten weeks out. And, of course, we had failed to meet the deadline because it was Joey who had failed to call two weeks earlier.

"And only the head guy for MassGas can pull the strings to make this happen?" Koslowski asked, a puzzled look on his face.

"The person who came out to the building site said in order to get us added, I needed to find someone as high in the organization as possible."

Koslowski turned to a woman sitting next to him. She was his office administrator; someone with whom I had what I call a nodding acquaintance.

"Donna, don't you deal with someone at MassGas?"

Donna, a woman in her forties with long brown hair, said, "Yes, but she's not an executive or anything. She's a secretary."

"Well, who does she work for?" Koslowski asked.

"The guy who sets up crew schedules."

There was a collective intake of breath around the room.

"Donna," Koslowski said, "why don't you call your friend – right now – and tell her that MassGas can earn some hard-to-come-by brownie points by adding an hour to a crew's schedule sometime between now and the end of the month?"

* * * * *

That afternoon I was paid a call by the Hardington police.

Hardington is a town of roughly 10,000 people. We have, for the most part, quite a law abiding citizenry. The 'Police Blotter' feature in the Hardington *Chronicle* seldom has anything more rousing than reports of bored teenagers smashing mailboxes with baseball bats, fender benders getting in and out of Starbucks, or the noise at parties getting out of hand. We pride ourselves on being bucolic and maybe even a bit boring, crime-wise.

But last year, Hardington twice made the news in spectacular fashion. The first time was when a revered retired English teacher (whom I knew as a member of the garden club) was found murdered in her home. Two more people would be dead before that case was closed. The second was when the body of a town selectman was found at the staging area where the *Ultimate House Makeover* show had come to town to build a home for the Cardozo family.

Except for Boston and a few other cities, homicides in Massachusetts are investigated by the state police. The murders in Hardington were solved by John Flynn, a retired Boston PD detective who thought he was joining a quiet police department in a peaceful town. In just a few months, Detective Flynn (aided and abetted by Liz Phillips, our garden club president) became something of a celebrity.

And now he was standing at my front door.

According to the newspapers, Detective Flynn was 55, but the man ringing the doorbell looked younger than Matt. He was trim and athletic under a brown sports jacket with close-cropped brown hair sprinkled with a few grey hairs. I invited him in.

He told me he had come to take my statement and to answer any questions I might have. The construction crew had given almost spookily consistent descriptions of what happened, so he was focusing on Joey's 'state of mind'. We talked over coffee in the Great Room.

I led him through Joey's multiple disappearances during the time he supervised the project. In turn, Detective Flynn was interested in my theories about where he was during those 'lost days'.

"I wish I knew," I told him. "He wouldn't respond to text messages or emails and he didn't answer his phone. That was the frustrating part."

"What would he tell you upon his return?" Flynn asked.

"He would lie," I said.

"How would you know he was lying?" Flynn tapped a pen against his cheek.

I answered by using the example of his needing to find a

specialist for his non-existent daughter.

"How did you know he didn't have a daughter, Mrs. Carlton?"

I started to answer but quickly closed my mouth. If I told the truth, I was about to implicate Maria Olivera, and I didn't want to get her in trouble.

"Do I have to answer that question?" I asked.

Detective Flynn grinned. "You don't have to tell me anything. But it might help me find Mr. McCoy."

I settled on generalities. "When he disappeared back in September, I started trying to find him and discovered that no one had his home address. Bruno DiNapoli, the Building Inspector, told me Joey had once commented to him that the traffic coming down Route 495 from Brookfield was getting worse every year. So, I did a Google search but there weren't any Joey McCoys or 'Joseph' or 'J' and I didn't want to use those 'we've found Joey McCoy' ads. I'm afraid of what they would do to my computer."

Detective Flynn smiled and nodded.

Here I paused. "I have a friend. She works for a company that has an ability to compile a lot of information about people lightning fast, and she is in a position to be able to make a request of that kind without raising eyebrows. She found Joey's home address in an hour, and she also had the information that Joey was divorced and had a son but not a daughter. She also said he had filed for bankruptcy a few years ago."

Detective Flynn nodded. "Your friend was exceptionally resourceful. Mr. McCoy seemed to go to great lengths to make information about him difficult to obtain. People with financial problems frequently do that."

Detective Flynn finished his cup of coffee. "Did he ever mention friends? Male or female?"

I thought for a few moments. Joey had never revealed anything about himself. At least anything that was true. "Joey claimed he and a group of friends get together to watch football on Sunday afternoon. That may or may not be true. He only said it after I found a betting slip for pro football games in the garage."

"Betting slip?"

"Joey apparently has a gambling problem," I said. "I found a sheet of paper with spreads and point totals for four games, with what looked like $250 riding on each game. He claimed it was all about *hoops*."

Detective Flynn made a lengthy note. "Anything else about his personal life?"

"Joey hardly ever talked about himself," I replied. "And, when he did, he wasn't the most reliable source of information. For example, he implied to me he was married. Maybe I'm the wrong person to ask. He has a number of long-term clients. He may have been more open with them. I have the list of references he gave me."

Detective Flynn nodded. "I think I have those as well. He used the same subcontractors from job to job, and they've provided me with a list." It was Flynn's turn to pause. "One of those references said he met you a few weeks ago. Harold Berry."

I nodded. "That was when I was trying to locate Joey."

"Mr. Berry said you told him that Mr. McCoy was doing a great job on your house."

"I was lying," I said. "I feared that, if I told him the real reason, he would protect Joey and never tell me anything."

Detective Flynn again nodded. "I appreciate your honesty." Then he added, "May I have another cup of coffee?"

I had a sense the conversation was going to go off in another direction. I poured and he asked.

"Mr. McCoy had never been physical with you," Detective Flynn said. It was a statement.

"No," I said. "In fact, I don't think he had ever touched me except to shake hands. Well, until he shoved me."

"There was never anything…" Detective Flynn left the

sentence hanging in the air. I knew exactly what he was asking.

"No," I said. "I think Joey fancied himself some kind of 'ladies' man', but he never turned his charms on me, and I wouldn't have been interested."

Detective Flynn was silent, thinking perhaps I might add something. I had nothing to add.

"What do you think made Mr. McCoy assault you?" he asked.

"Yesterday, I realized that he had lost interest in completing our house," I said. "He had disappeared for three – really, three and a half days – without explanation. During those three days I had an opportunity to look at the slipshod work he had allowed. When he showed up, I took him on a tour of his handiwork. He said there was nothing he could do about the nail depressions in the siding because he paid his subcontractors and they wouldn't come back. His 'Closet Guy' used the cheapest materials to build our master bedroom closet. Joey said a better closet would cost a lot more money."

"There were raised voices," Detective Flynn said.

"There was screaming," I corrected him. "I screamed at Joey, he screamed at me. It was the first and only time that ever happened. After the tour of the closet, I came to the realization that our new house would likely never get completed. Joey just didn't care. I walked outside, with Joey hard on my heels. I have no idea of what he was saying."

"He was screaming that nothing he did was good enough for you," Detective Flynn said, without referring to any notes. "You were never satisfied."

"When we got outside, I let him have it," I said, then thought about my choice of words. "I *verbally* let him have it. I told him he thought that Matt and I were a couple of sheep to be fleeced and I asked how much more money he thought he was going to get out of us. I told him he was a total screw-up. That's when he pushed me."

"That's exactly what the other witnesses said."   Detective Flynn drank some of his coffee. "Do you have any idea of where he went?"

"Not a clue," I said. "He left, and it was like this weight was lifted. The amazing thing is that his subcontractors want to finish the house." I smiled. "I even think I'm going to get a gas connection this month." I shifted in my chair. "What happens from here?"

"That's hard to say, Mrs. Carlton. We need…"

I interrupted him. "No, Detective Flynn. I've been completely candid and forthright with you. How about you being the same with me?"

Detective Flynn smiled. "That's almost exactly what someone told me you would say. OK, here's what happens. A warrant will be issued for Mr. McCoy's arrest. The charges are simple assault and fleeing the scene of an investigation. That will happen as soon as I leave here."

Detective Flynn continued. "But Mr. McCoy hasn't been back to his apartment. He hasn't contacted his ex-wife or any of those long-time customers. He must know he's in a lot of trouble because he immediately went to an ATM at his bank and tried to take out a large cash advance on his credit card. He wanted two thousand, he reached his limit at seven hundred and change. He hasn't used his EZPass transponder and he hasn't used his credit or debit cards."

Detective Flynn drank more of his coffee. "In short, he is hiding out. You were absolutely right about Mr. McCoy thinking of himself as a ladies' man. Several of his subcontractors told me that he was more than a little friendly with his female customers. He may be staying with one of them. My problem is one of resource allocation. On a scale of crimes, what Mr. McCoy has done is relatively minor and he has no priors."

"Bruno DiNapoli tells me that the state licensing board has a zero tolerance policy for assault or harassment," Detective Flynn continued. "Mr. McCoy will have his contractor license yanked and he won't be able to re-apply for a minimum of three years. He goes back to being an off-the-books carpenter for whomever will hire him."

Detective Flynn finished his coffee, set down the cup, and folded his hands. "I can put out an APB. I can put out a description of his truck. But no judge is going to let me find him by tracking his cell phone and Chief Harding isn't going to turn me loose to spend a week knocking on the door of every client he's had for the past five years. What will happen is this: he's going to run out of money and he's going to wear out his welcome with his friends. When he does, he'll turn up at his apartment or he'll use a credit card. I'll arrest him. If he has any sense, he'll accept a plea bargain – a fine that he can't pay, six months or a suspended sentence, something like that."

Detective Flynn rose from his chair. "He'll get what's coming to him. He may have some old friends that will hire him for carpentry, but he can't hire subcontractors. His life as a contractor is over and, apparently, that's for the good of everyone involved."

I thanked Detective Flynn for his honesty. Joey had pushed me and, in that simple act, he had self-destructed. Fortunately, Joey had done no lasting physical harm to me.

Joey was gone. He was out of my life, and my house was going to get built.

But not quite yet…

Chapter Eighteen

One by one, all my friends learned what had happened and then called or came by to commiserate with me. Those who came by brought flowers and soon both my 'old' home and my soon-to-be-new home were filled with the wonderful scent of hyacinths, freesia, roses, and lilies. Most were surprised that I was so willing to allow time and the justice system do its job. Some urged me to pursue alternate avenues of justice.

"Snow farms," said Susan Williams, my Master Gardener best friend. "The year that Boston got a hundred and something inches of snow, the city started dumping the stuff in a giant vacant lot by the Convention Center. By the end of winter it was seventy feet high and it took until sometime in July for the last of it to melt. Here's what we do: we find Joey, we keep him on ice until the first big snow fall, then we stash him at the bottom of that snow farm. Nobody sees him until the middle of next year and the weight of all that snow and ice will probably have crushed him to about an inch thick. They pulled all kinds of stuff out of that pile – parking meters, shopping carts, bicycles..."

Susan and I were having lunch at the construction site. It was the Monday after Joey disappeared. I had related Detective Flynn's prognosis for Joey, and Susan was dissatisfied with the prospective outcome.

"I don't care," I said to Susan. "Look at all this." I gestured with my hand at the work going on around me. Julio, Joey's 'Framing Guy', had a cousin who ran several painting crews. This morning, two men were going over every nail depression and smearing on a pink goop that would harden to the consistency of wood in an hour. Later today, it would be painted. By the weekend, I would have a house with perfect, painted cedar siding. *All* of the house; not just the front.

The ductwork and venting for the fireplace, something Joey had said for two months he would 'get around to' was being installed by Primo – Joey's 'Roofing Guy' – who as it turns out had done hundreds of such projects. And a marble installer was expected at 2 p.m. Life was good.

"But you can't let him get away with it," Susan said, a determined look on her face and a stubbornness in her voice. "He could have paralyzed you."

There was no dissuading her from her view. "I liked the hot compost ideas better," I said. She seemed satisfied by that response.

* * * * *

An unexpected call came the following day.

"My name is Shonda Rafferty," a voice on the other end of the phone line said. "I was once married to Joey McCoy. I'd like to meet you for coffee."

We met the next day – a Wednesday – at a Starbucks in Natick. Shonda Rafferty was an operating room nurse at the nearby MetroWest Medical Center and was attired in hospital scrubs. She was apparently taking her lunch break, as she carried an indefinable scent of hospital sterilizing agents. She was attractive, though with a 'hard' look on her face; the kind that comes from being dealt more than your share of hard knocks. I guess being married to Joey would give even Scarlett Johansson a hard look.

"I cried when I heard what Joey did," Shonda said. "I wish there was something that I could have done. I am so sorry for what he did to you."

I reached across the table and took her hand. "You aren't responsible for his actions. You've *never* been responsible for them. And, when he finally shows up, he's the one who will have to take that responsibility."

She looked across the table at me. "You're probably wondering why I ever married him, or why I stayed married for as long as I did."

The thought had crossed my mind, but it isn't the kind of subject you bring up with someone buying you a five-dollar cup of coffee.

"My mother warned me," Shonda said. "She told me, 'you're marrying a hound dog'. And she was right. But I was determined to be out on my own and, from my perspective, my mother had never been right about anything. So we got married. And three years later I was a mother. I thought being a father would make Joey settle down. It didn't."

Shonda toyed with her coffee stirrer, looking at the table instead of at me. "He liked – and apparently still likes – them young and, if he can't find them young, he likes them rich. He has a certain boyish charm that works wonders on women who are starved for attention. By my best guess – putting the clues together years after the fact – he had his first fling just a few months after we were married. After Greg was born, he apparently had two or three affairs every year. I put up with it for two years and then threw him out. Thank God I had my nursing career. And thank God I was still young enough to meet someone else."

"Joey paid alimony and child support," I said. "At least that's something."

Shonda shook her head. "Start with the fact that Joey has a gambling problem, especially at this time of the year. He thinks God gave him some special gift of being able to predict football scores. Back when we were married, I'd see some of his betting sheets. For every winning week he had two or three losing ones. I hear from people who still stay in touch with him. From what I can tell, it has gotten worse since he has been on his own. It's an addiction, of course, and we're supposed to look upon addicts with sympathy. I have a hard time sympathizing with those who make no effort to confront their problem."

She took a sip of her coffee. "Joey constantly argued to my lawyer that I made more money than he did, and that I ought to be paying *him* alimony. And, of course, I had a W-2 showing my full income while Joey was taking discounts for cash and declaring everything a business expense. Child support? He was supposed to pay five hundred dollars a month until Greg turns twenty-one, and I can count on the fingers of one hand the times the check was there on the first of the month. I saw the last check… five or six years ago."

"But he told me he was deeply involved with his son," I said. "The night he came to our house to drop off his estimate, he said he had to pick up his son from a night baseball league, and…"

The look on Shonda's face was one of pure disbelief. I stopped talking.

"He told you that?" Shonda said.

I nodded.

She shook her head. "In the last eight years, I think Joey has shown up for fewer than a dozen of Greg's 'big' events. And in the past five years, he has been totally off of the radar. When I remarried, Greg finally got the father he never had. My son is only vaguely aware of who his biological father is. In the past five years, Greg has not once mentioned Joey's name." Shonda gave a bitter laugh. "Baseball game."

"Joey also invented a college-age daughter," I said. "Why would he do that?"

Shonda shook her head, a saddened expression on her face. "I've heard about that. It is a sickness I can't fathom."

I am not a mind reader. I am, however, a reasonably good judge of human nature. There was something about that expression on her face and the quaver in her voice that told me Shonda Rafferty *did* have an inkling why her ex-husband would have conjured up a college-age daughter. But it was not my place to press or to pry. She had been kind enough to seek me out and offer an apology for Joey's actions. Nothing more was needed.

We parted after less than thirty minutes. As Shonda summed up her relationship with Joey, she said something chilling: "Religion teaches us that everyone has some goodness in them. Everyone is on this earth for a purpose, and everyone deserves to be remembered for the good they did." Shonda paused. "I respectfully disagree. Joey is one person who has left behind nothing but a trail of misery behind him. If he is never seen again, I think there will be a universal sigh of relief."

* * * * *

And then, on my way home from that coffee with Shonda, there was the Great Bagel Shop Revelation.

Please understand: I wasn't trying to hunt down Joey. I was glad to be rid of him; glad he was going to be punished at some point down the line. I had no desire to launch a one-woman investigation into his motivations, gambling habits, or sick psychology. Had I not been contacted by Shonda Rafferty, and had I not just forty-five minutes earlier been handed a valuable insight into my now-ex-nemesis, what happened next would not have taken place.

I was pushing a near-empty grocery cart through the Hardington Roche Brothers, trying to remember what I had written down (and failed to place in my purse) on my weekly shopping list. I bumped into another cart and mumbled an apology. I looked up to see the face of a woman I had seen somewhere before.

The woman saw who had bumped her. Her eyes grew wide and her face paled.

Tumblers turned and clinked into place. Chestnut Street in Hardington. Four weeks earlier. I had been looking for Joey. She had answered the door, knew instantly who I was, and slammed the door shut in my face. *What was her name?*

I smiled and spoke her name. "Ashley Harris?" Sometimes the synapses and neurons fire just right and a name pops into place. Of course, more often than not, I draw a blank and stand there looking stupid.

"I don't know you," Ashley said. Trailing behind her were two girls, probably seven and nine, adorable younger versions of Mommy.

Ashley tried to push her cart around me. I sensed this was my one chance to add to what Shonda had told me over coffee. I parried her cart thrust and would not let her pass. Our carts clanked noisily.

"Get out of my way," she said through gritted teeth.

"I want to talk to you," I said. "Five minutes. That's all."

"I'll yell out for store security," Ashley countered.

"I've got a better idea," I said. "Let's both yell out for store security. And then ask for Detective Flynn to come get our stories."

Ashley blanched. "You wouldn't do that." Behind Ashley, her two children looked up, trying to puzzle out the fascinating adult conversation taking place.

"Five minutes," I said. "At the bagel shop next door. Please. Do this and I'll never bother you again, so help me God."

Ashley looked dubious. She looked down at her cart with its half dozen jars of spaghetti sauce and several boxes of pasta, and then back at her daughters.

"Let's do it now," she said, leaving her cart in the aisle.

* * * * *

We were seated in a booth at the Silver Spoon bakery, a coffee and bagel shop that had not only survived the Starbucks onslaught, but thrived. On a Saturday afternoon, though, we had the place to ourselves. It was quiet except for the sound of a jackhammer cutting through pavement in the parking lot outside the shop. I felt cold and wrapped my hands around a cup of coffee. In an adjacent booth, the two girls munched on the blueberry bagels I had paid for.

"I heard he slugged you," Ashley said in a low voice. She was in her thirties, with a round face, blue eyes and, based on her skin tone, naturally blonde hair. She wasn't what most people would describe as knockout beautiful and she carried ten or fifteen pounds of what I call 'baby residue'. She was nonetheless attractive and she augmented her looks with a wonderful floral perfume.

I shook my head. "Pushed me down hard." Like her, I spoke in a voice barely above a whisper, ensuring that not even Ashley's daughters could eavesdrop.

"Lovers' quarrel?" Ashley asked, cynicism dripping in the question.

I shook my head again. "Not Joey's type, according to his ex-wife. I'm too old and I'm not rich. This was over calling him on sloppy workmanship."

"Ex-wife?" Ashley looked surprised and her eyes widened.

"Divorced for something like eight years," I said, my hands still holding the coffee cup against the shop's chill. The jackhammering outside had reached a fevered pitch.

Ashley nodded. Her eyes went off to look at some distant place on the far wall. A memory, likely.

"But you were…" I stopped. I didn't want to use any words or phrases that would end the conversation. So, I just said, "What happened? Please. It goes no further."

Ashley looked back at the adjacent booth and her daughters, who were contentedly tearing apart their bagels into ever smaller pieces.

"Joey remodeled our bathroom," she said. "About four days into the project, he came on to me, said we ought to try out the Jacuzzi together to see if it would hold two people." She paused and looked up at the ceiling, her eyes misting. "I was stupid. Don – my husband – is away a lot and when he's home, he's in front of the TV or playing with the girls. He stopped having time for me after Emma was born."

Ashley again looked back, making certain she wasn't being overheard. "It went on for about three weeks while Joey was working on the bathroom and the girls were at Don's parents on the Cape. Then, when the job was done, he presented me with the bill. The bastard was charging me from the time his car left his driveway in the morning to the time he pulled back into his driveway that evening. 'That's the way contractors do it when you're billing time and materials,' he told me." Then real tears started falling. "He was also charging me for the time we were in bed." She reached for a paper napkin and dabbed at her eyes.

"What did you do?" I asked. I reached across the table to take her free hand. She reflexively pulled it back. This was not someone who wanted to be comforted by a stranger.

"I told him he was a bastard for,.. putting that on the bill," Ashley said, still wiping her eyes. "He said he had no choice. That his wife made out all the bills and was always suspicious of him so he had no choice but to charge for every hour."

"And so you paid him," I said.

"Don wrote the check," Ashley said. "My own husband, who ignores me, paid for my affair. It's pretty funny when you think about it." Her voice told me she thought it was anything but funny.

"That day you came to the door," Ashley added, "I thought you were his new girlfriend. Joey had told me back in July he was going to build your house and so I drove by and checked out both your current house and where the new one was going to be. The night you gave him that first check to get started on the foundation, he texted me and wanted to know if I would go with him down to Foxwoods. He said, 'tell your husband your mother is sick and you're staying over'. I had mentioned to him at least four times that my parents live in Florida. Which kind of proves he wasn't really listening."

"I'm sorry for what happened to you," I said. To be honest, I couldn't think of any other response.

Ashley shrugged and began collecting her purse and keys. "It isn't your fault," she said. "I was stupid. I was flattered. I'll pay for it in the form of low self-esteem for the next ten years. If Don ever finds out, I'll probably pay for it with my marriage."

Ashley rose from the table. "I actually owe you a thank-you. I haven't talked to anyone about this; not even my closest friend. And, after having said it once, I don't feel the need to ever say it again. I hope he goes to jail." As she turned toward the door she said, with considerable viciousness. "And, when he does, I hope his cellmate is two hundred and twenty pounds of muscle and a strong need for sex with whatever is close by." She turned to the next booth and said in a normal voice. "Come on, girls. We've got grocery shopping to do."

I stayed at the Silver Spoon for fifteen minutes. I wanted to give Ashley ample time to shop without encountering me again.

I also stayed because I was shaking, as much as from the chill of the shop as from what I had learned. Two women. Both of them victims of my contractor. I had learned more about Joey in half a day from two strangers than I had learned working alongside him in three months. Joey was, if not a sexual predator, a sociopath who preyed on women in need of attention, choosing those who were most vulnerable.

It seemed fairly obvious that, while he was working for me, he had one or more 'involvements' going on that kept pulling him away from the job. Were they previous clients or just women who caught his attention? I really didn't want to know.

Was Joey placing bets with the money we were paying him? Did his painting contractor quit because Joey wouldn't or couldn't pay him? Was Joey hiding from people to whom he owed money?

Maybe the real reason I was shaking was because I had completely missed the signs. My 'sixth sense' for aberrant behavior was usually pretty good. In this case, it had failed me completely. I had looked at Joey strictly as someone to build my home. I never added in the personality component. I began paying attention only when his absences and sloppy work threatened something I wanted.

Was Joey that good at hiding who he really was, or was I that blind?

And that started turning the wheels of my mind. Maybe Joey really hadn't 'fled'. Maybe he was regrouping. It was entirely possible that he had revenge on his mind.

The jackhammering stopped. I abandoned my idea of grocery shopping and, instead, drove to the Hardington Police Department.

* * * * *

As we sat in a cramped cubicle, Detective Flynn listened carefully and made notes as I recounted what I had learned from my two encounters. I did not use Ashley Harris' name; I had no desire to add any more stress to her life. To his credit, Flynn did not press me for a name. Perhaps he already knew her identity.

"My fear is that Joey is just biding his time," I said, summarizing my growing anxiety. "Everything I've learned about him tells me he's some kind of pathological liar and sociopathic monster. He thinks the rules don't apply to him."

Flynn finished writing on a notepad. He glanced up at a calendar on the side wall of his cubicle. "No one has seen Mr. McCoy for five days. Since that one bank transaction an hour after the assault, he hasn't used a credit or debit card and he hasn't been to an ATM. He hasn't used his EZPass. He hasn't been home. We know all that with certainty."

Flynn leaned in his chair until it touched the back of the cubicle. "That's a long time to be off the grid and an even longer time to be living on cash. You can't check into a motel; you can't charge a meal. He didn't plan to run. There was no unusual activity on his credit cards in the days before the assault. What it tells me is that he's staying with someone. It could be one of his girlfriends, it could be a good buddy although he appears to be a man with few close friends. It could also be one of those long-term customers. My money is on the customers."

Flynn continued. "I've spoken with each of those long-term clients at least three times since last Friday. I don't ask if Mr. McCoy is staying in their guest house or is camped out in their driveway. What I say is, if they hear from him, they should let him know that the Hardington Police urgently need to speak with him on a matter of some seriousness. They should tell him that it is infinitely better that he comes to see us on his own rather than being apprehended by us or by another police department."

"Do you think that will work?" I asked.

Flynn nodded. "I'm certain Mr. McCoy has heard the message loud and clear. It sends a separate message to whomever is giving him shelter: they're harboring someone with an outstanding arrest warrant. That tends to shorten the time the welcome mat is out. In a period of time that will take him by surprise, Mr. McCoy will run out of hospitality. He'll weigh the fact that he isn't making any money."

Flynn scratched his temple, a sign of a new idea. "Based on what you told me, it wouldn't surprise me if he chose to take all his remaining money for one last night at Foxwoods or Mohegan Sun, thinking he's going to run the tables and have seed money to start a new life. You can't formally bet on football there, but I suspect there are people around who would be glad to take the action. When he walks out with nothing in his pocket but gas money, he'll understand that he is truly out of options. I think I'll send his photo down to Connecticut and ask them to give me a call if he shows up. It would be interesting to be there when he goes bust. It would likely make for a much easier arrest."

He rose from his desk and placed his hands in his pants

pockets. "But revenge? No. I agree with you about Mr. McCoy being a congenital liar. He is the kind of guy who seduces a woman and then sends her a bill for his time. That's his style. And, if he saw you again, he would do his damnest to charm you into dropping charges – not understanding that felony assault is not something that you can un-charge. If that didn't work, he might well try threatening you with whatever he thought he had as leverage. But physically hurt you? That isn't who or what he is – unless he is truly pushed into a corner. The armchair psychiatrist in me says the exchange you had with him touched a raw nerve. You spoke a truth that he keeps hidden even from himself. He exploded, and he's not the kind of guy who explodes, which is why he panicked."

"So you don't think I have anything to worry about," I said.

Flynn cocked his head. "I try not to think in absolutes. Should you be on your guard? I would say 'yes'. But here's what I can do: I'll make certain a patrol car goes by your house every hour, looking for any cars that don't belong and especially for Mr. McCoy's truck. If he were to decide to keep an eye on your house – looking for that opportunity to approach you – he's going to see that patrol car and I'm reasonably certain that it will dissuade him from staying around. It just might be enough to get him to turn himself in. You have my word that someone is going to come around and check on you every hour."

I departed the police station with a sense of relief. I had walked in with a vague plan to drive into Boston and check into a hotel for a few days. But doing so would be both giving into fear and ceding that Joey had somehow 'won'.

I drove home to await Matt's arrival on the 6:36. I prowled around the wine cellar and found an impressive Grand Cru Burgundy Matt had bought on impulse a decade earlier. I freshened one of the arrangements of lilies someone had brought me and placed it in the center of the table. When he walked in the door he smelled a delectable veal dish and other odds and ends I found in the refrigerator.

"You must have had an extraordinary day," Matt said, observing the dining room table set formally with linens and candles.

"Sit down and I'll tell you all about it," I said.

Chapter Nineteen

What a difference a day makes.

My meetings with Shonda, Ashley and Detective Flynn had consumed just one work day, but I came back to the work site to find a palpable sense of excitement.

Fred the Plumber greeted me as soon as my car pulled into the driveway. "You missed it!"

Because the grin on his face didn't adequately convey exactly what it was I had missed, he slowly pointed a finger across the front of the property. I saw a freshly dug and re-filled trench. And, at the end of the trench, against the house, an orderly tangle of pipes.

A gas meter.

"Oh, my God," I said, and started walking toward the contraption. I patted it to make certain it was real.

"Yesterday afternoon around three," Fred said, his pleasure obvious. "Two MassGas trucks and a backhoe. Two hours and they were out of here. It's obvious that somebody up there likes you."

There is no way to hug a gas meter, but I stroked it. It was like Christmas in October. Since August, this meter had been my unattainable quest, my Great White Whale. Had Joey called the gas company just a few days earlier, the meter's installation would have been a non-event; just something ticked off on a checklist. Now, it was a symbol of hope, a talisman. Yes, my house would be completed on schedule.

"…I'm finishing the connection to the heating system," Fred was saying. "By sometime today we'll have the house warming up nicely. Julio knows the floor people Joey uses. We'll see if the wood order was already in…"

I listened to this efficient recitation of work details and felt tears coming into my eyes. A group of guys who, two months ago were strangers to me, had banded together to ensure that the *senhora do chefe com café* got her house built. Out of the incompetence of one contractor had come something like a miracle.

And, the next day, Jorge Silva's truck bashed into the driveway with an enormous load of red oak destined to become the flooring for our home. The temperature inside the house was a pleasant 68 degrees.

Jorge introduced himself, said he had heard what happened with Joey, and apologized that a *corrompido* like him would lay a hand a *bela senhora* like me. He also asked if it was true that I served Colombian Extra Dark Roast from Starbucks and said that his crew liked theirs with a lot of sugar. When I asked what he would need by way of an advance payment, he looked at me as though I had just insulted him.

"You pay me when my men are finished, and when you are happy with what they have done. Not a *real* before that." I didn't think Jorge expected to be paid in Brazilian currency, but I got the drift.

It took three days for the bundles of oak flooring to rise to the temperature of the house. Once Jorge was satisfied that the wood would neither contract nor expand, he brought in his crew. For the next two days I watched as workmen – more like artisans – pieced together the beautiful red oak floors. Joey, of course, had tried to talk us into using the prefinished composite panels. ('They look just as good, they don't need to be sealed, and they wear forever.') No thanks, Joey. None of your second-rate Lumber Liquidators trash.

Finishing the floors would require sealing them with three coats of polyurethane, each coat applied two days apart. During the week the polyurethane was being applied and was drying, no work could go on in the interior of the house. And, once the floor was coated, it would limit what could be dragged in and out through the house. Accordingly, sealing the floors was deemed to be an 'end of the punch list' item, something that would be done in the second week of November.

In the meantime, workmen buttoned up the outside of the house. A few cosmetic patches were applied to the foundation wall, the inside of the garage was plastered, gutters went up on the back of the house, and the garage door openers were installed. Every day, the house looked more finished.

The screened porch acquired screens. I had fought with Joey for weeks over something as simple as whether the architect's specifications required him to put an insect screen under the porch decking. He, of course, said it was an extra charge. I pointed out that, without such a screen, bugs would have free run of the space. Because of the impasse, the porch sat week after week in its incomplete state. With Joey on the lam, two workmen put a fine-mesh insect screen under the decking in less than an hour.

I wrote checks to work crews as they presented invoices. Matt kept track of everything on his massive spreadsheet. We carefully reserved funds we believed would be owed to Joey and earmarked them in a separate account. While he was, according to the Building Permit, no longer the contractor of record, we wanted no room for disagreement when he finally re-appeared and was arrested.

Bruno DiNapoli came around the house every few days. I'm sure he was stretching whatever boundaries govern what Building Inspectors are and are not allowed to do. For one thing, he suggested the name of a competent carpenter who completed dozens of projects Joey had left half-done. The same carpenter also came to our home, photographed and measured our existing master bedroom closet, and re-created it perfectly in two days.

Bruno also ensured that work was progressing in an orderly

way. He answered questions from the crews. He pointed out problems before they became a matter of expensive re-work, including areas where Joey had taken – and hidden – shortcuts. He found that the vent from the dryer simply disappeared into some Fiberglas ceiling batting in the basement. A toilet vent exited into the attic but never quite found its way to the outside. The basement stairs lacked a code-required handrail. I came to admire Bruno and his sense of responsibility for my project.

Detective Flynn also came around several times. On the eighth day after what he called 'the incident', he recounted a report of a 'Joey sighting'. Flynn had made his regular round of calls to Joey's long-time customers. A call to one of those customers, Phil Vonn, produced something other than the 'I'll tell him if I see him' response. Vonn had said, "That's exactly what I told him when I saw him."

"You saw him?" Detective Flynn had said.

"Yeah, he came by last night, looking for a place to stay," Vonn had said. "I almost felt sorry for him. He's got a three- or four-day growth of beard and I don't think he's had a bath. He wanted to borrow money. Money I don't think he'll ever be able to repay. He said he couldn't do any work because he can't go out for materials. So I told him maybe he ought to turn himself in and take his medicine. He got mad, called me names, gave me the finger, and took off in that truck of his."

"So, he's out there," Detective Flynn told me. "It's unlikely he has been able to accumulate any additional funds, so leaving the area isn't an option. When he travels, he almost certainly does so by night to draw less attention. I'd say he's getting desperate. Most perps don't last this long on the run but, in the end, they all come crawling in."

Then Detective Flynn added, "Just to be on the safe side, I'm continuing to have the patrol car stop by your house. "

* * * * *

It was Tuesday, October 25. Joey had been gone for ten days. If he never came back into my life, that would be just fine with me.

After I swore for the fiftieth time that I was fine and had no lingering pain from my fall, Matt finally decided that it was safe enough for him to travel, and he headed for four days of client meetings in the San Francisco Bay area. Because everything was going so smoothly at the work site, I drove my husband to the airport. He promised to be home on the red eye Saturday morning. We kissed at the terminal entrance.

I was feeling light-headedly good about everything as I left the airport. The end was in sight on my new home. Everything was on track for the sale of what I now thought of as my 'old' home. The Pollard's had a mortgage commitment and a closing date had been set for November 22. Brooke Pollard had been out twice to photograph and make extensive notes on the garden. A story that had seemed doomed just two weeks earlier now appeared bright.

I was just coming out of the Ted Williams Tunnel from the airport when my cell phone chimed.

And everything changed.

Chapter Nineteen

My caller ID said 'Chloe Barnes,' so I answered, "Hey, what's up Chloe?"

"Can you come to my house?" Chloe said. Her voice was disturbingly subdued; she sounded nervous.

"Today?" I asked.

"Right now," she replied. "I mean, as fast as you can get here."

Dover, Massachusetts is not the easiest place to get to in the Boston area, and I'm reasonably certain it's by design. If you look at a map of Greater Boston, Route 128 makes an inexplicable inward bend just before it gets to Dover – Dover wants nothing to do with anything as vulgar as superhighways. There are nearly five million people in a 70-mile-long swath of densely urbanized land that stretches from Providence, Rhode Island to Nashua, New Hampshire. Yet Dover, which is only twelve miles from the Financial District, has just 5500 people leisurely scattered across its fifteen square miles, and probably twice that many horses grazing in paddocks. I made it there in an amazing twenty minutes.

Chloe Barnes fits right into Dover. I've known her since I was twelve when we competed on the junior riding circuit. My career ended with that spill when I was seventeen; Chloe went on to glory in Seoul, winning a place on the jumping team. While she didn't medal (European nation teams more or less owned jumping for a couple of Olympics), Chloe has accumulated enough trophies and ribbons to furnish a barn, though she displays just a few of those mementos of her accomplishments.

Chloe went on to Med School after college though. She married a few years after I did, to a newly minted surgeon with an exceptionally bright future. Chloe was in practice until about two weeks before she gave birth to her first child, after which she took down her shingle. She raised two preternaturally smart and well-behaved children, the last of whom went off to college last year. For the past fifteen years she has been seriously into show jumping both as a breeder/trainer and as a participant. Her horses have shown well at the Prix des States and the Grand National Championships.

I offer this capsule biography because it is the made-for-the-silver-screen picture of a woman who is uncommonly smart, athletic, and possessed of nerves of steel.

The woman who stood in the driveway of her twelve-acre farm was a quivering, nervous wreck. I got out of my car and hugged her. She looked like a woman who desperately needed to be comforted.

Chloe was in jeans – working jeans, not the designer kind – boots, a heavy Pendleton shirt, barn jacket, and a scarf to keep her hair out of her eyes. There was a fairly heavy 'horsey' smell to her clothes, indicating she had been working. "I don't know where to begin," she said.

We were standing in a meticulously raked gravel circle. Overhead was a brilliant, late-afternoon cloudless sky. Around her were sugar maples in their late October glory. Behind her was a white clapboard farmhouse large enough that it probably had its own zip code. It was a picture-perfect day in paradise. What on earth could be the problem?

"Come with me," she said, and took my hand.

"Where's Jeff?" I asked. Jeff is her husband.

"Fishing," she said without emotion. "Baja California. Courtesy of some drug company or equipment manufacturer. I didn't ask and he didn't say." Then she added, "He left Sunday afternoon. He'll be home Saturday. I think."

Though Chloe had never said anything to me directly and was

always the perfect spouse in his presence, I had long suspected that she and Jeff's marriage had not been an especially happy one, those children notwithstanding.

Still holding my hand and guiding me, we skirted around the house and came to the first of several paddocks where five horses stood at the gate, waiting to get back to their stalls and dinner. Having horses still in pasturage seemed a little unusual; It was just after 5 p.m. and sunset would be in 45 minutes. Horses are usually back in their barns by late afternoon.

Ahead of us was Chloe's indoor jumping rink, a roughly five thousand square foot Butler building but with a handsome stone veneer. I thought we were going there but Chloe instead turned left on another of those professionally maintained paths and headed for the barn, a beautifully restored edifice painted in country cream.

Chloe had not spoken in over a minute. As we turned, her grip on my hand became tighter; almost painfully so. Her breathing became more pronounced. I began to feel a sense of dread at where we were going.

We stopped at the barn door.

Still holding my hand, she turned to me. "I didn't know who else to call. All I ask is that you don't judge me. And I hope you have a strong stomach."

Chloe's barn consisted of eight stalls, four on either side of the central passage. At the far end was a tack room and a large work area suitable for grooming and farrier work. All this I know because I've been in that barn a hundred times.

We entered through the tall horse doors and passed by the empty stalls. A bank of overhead lights burned at the other end of the building. As we reached the end of the stalls, Chloe took a deep breath and released my hand.

Just beyond the last stall amid a jumble of barn tools and sacks of feed was the crumpled body of Joey McCoy.

* * * * *

In 49 years on this Earth, apart from funerals and wakes where the deceased was formally attired, makeup applied and laid out in a casket, I have never seen a dead body.

Joey appeared to still be in the same clothes he wore ten days earlier. The look on his face was one of surprise and his eyes were open, though most assuredly unseeing. His face and hands still had a certain degree of pinkness to them; whatever had happened was fairly recent.

His head was turned at an angle no contortionist could achieve; more than a hundred degrees of rotation. His body lay sprawled atop sacks of Purina Horse Chow but was slightly propped up. A quick look showed why: a pitchfork was impaled in his back.

"It was an accident," Chloe said. Her voice was even, as though giving a report.

"Then we should call the police," I replied.

Chloe shook her head. "No. We can't do that." Suddenly, her voice was shaking and she visibly trembled.

"Can you tell me what happened?" I asked. "We don't need to talk here."

Chloe again shook her head. "No. It may have been an accident, but I am responsible for this. Let's talk here."

There was silence in the barn for several moments.

"You remember the day your foundation was poured," she began. "That was a gorgeous day. I tried to get Jeff to come along but he had a 'big' surgery that morning and said he needed time to 'decompress'. If he had come along…" There was a wistfulness in her voice.

She shook her head. "No, it wouldn't have made a damn bit of difference. Men like Joey have a built-in radar for women like me. Affluent, neglected women, ripe for the plucking. We ought to have a club or something. Joey took one look at me and he knew exactly what to do. 'Oh, you live in Dover? I've done some great work there. I could give you some ideas…' All it took was a couple of words. A standard line."

"Two weeks later, he was up here, giving me some ideas. Yeah, he gave me some ideas. He walked into the Master Bath and said, 'the problem with this Jacuzzi built for two is that it has never had two people in it. I can fix that.' Less than an hour inside my house and we're naked in that Jacuzzi."

Listening to Chloe, I was startled to hear a second reference in a week to 'two people in a Jacuzzi'. Then I remembered the first one: Ashley Harris, also quoting Joey McCoy. Joey had apparently been a man who knew a handful of, 'can't fail' lines and employed them shamelessly.

"I'm a stereotype, Anne," Chloe said, bitterness edging into her voice. "That middle-aged housewife with a husband who's bored with her, looking for someone – anyone – to notice her. To pay attention to her. To tell her she still looks great. To make a real, honest-to-God pass at her."

There was a tear in her eye, but she continued. "No, I'm not some slut. I don't sleep around with every handyman who winks at her. But that morning, Jeff had been in one of his moods – a mood he gets in a lot these days. We got up at 6:30 and by 6:45 he was enumerating everything that was wrong with me and this house. He was going on that I wasn't supportive of his interests and career and that all I cared about was my horses. It all came out of nowhere and it was relentless. He stormed out of the house at 8:30, peeling out of the driveway in his shiny new Mercedes. And I felt as drained as old dish rag."

Chloe caught her breath. "I had completely forgotten Joey was coming. He showed up at 10 a.m. I should have told him it was a bad day. I should have said I was sick or that I had another appointment. But, instead, I let him in. And, what happened, happened. Afterward, I beat my head against the wall for being stupid."

"And, of course, Joey kept sniffing around, looking for a repeat performance. I let him know in no uncertain terms that he wasn't welcome. He eventually gave up, shrugged and said something like, 'you can't blame a guy for trying'."

"I thought that was the last of it," Chloe said. "You saw how we were at your house a few weeks ago. That day he told the cockamamie story about his daughter. I had done something stupid. I knew I had done it out of spite and I immediately regretted it. The saddest part is that I got no joy out of it."

Chloe looked at me for a reaction. My face was carefully neutral. "No," she said to the un-asked question that had nonetheless formed in my mind, "Joey wasn't the only one. In the past five years, as Jeff has grown angrier and more distant, it has happened a few other times. Never more than once and never with any of our friends."

Chloe walked over to Joey's body. "For Joey, though, I strongly suspect it was a regular part of his diet. Oh, was he smooth. After I turned him down, I'm sure he moved on to the next Chloe, or maybe a few more Chloes. Because there's an inexhaustible supply of pathetic women like me out there."

I thought about Joey's late arrivals and long lunch hours. I realized one of those must have been a morning with Chloe. How had Joey looked upon his return? Smug? Happy? I had never bothered to notice. And how many other days were spent the same way with other women?

Chloe turned back to me. "He showed up here this afternoon. I was here in the barn trimming hooves, doing a mustang roll on Sinbad. I heard a truck go by but didn't think anything about it. Everyone knows where to find me. About a minute later, there was Joey standing in the doorway. He looked awful."

She shifted her stance. "I was not especially pleased to see him and I let him know with a few choice words. He said he needed a place to stay, to sort things out. I told him he needed to find a lawyer and turn himself in."

Chloe sighed. "That's when it got dicey. Joey started screaming that lawyers were the problem with the world and cited your husband as 'Exhibit A' of a bloodsucker – his word – who was out to screw over guys like him, who were 'trying to make a decent living'."

"Sinbad doesn't react well to sudden loud noises in close spaces. I told Joey – several times and emphatically – to keep it down. His response was to get louder, which started making Sinbad nervous. He said if I wouldn't give him a place to stay, he needed money and we should leave and drive to an ATM. I don't know why, but I asked him how much he had in mind. He told me that two thousand dollars would get him staked."

Chloe shook her head. There was a sadness on her face, though not in her voice. "'Staked to what?' I asked him and that's when he got really angry. He said he could clean up on football this weekend; 'turn two thousand into twenty grand, easy,' he said. And that's when I laughed. I probably said something like, 'Good luck with that'."

"Which is when Joey got a gleam in his eye and said, 'Then I'll just hang around until your husband gets home. I bet he'll love to hear what you and I have been up to.'"

"Remember, I was carrying a rasp. That one." Chloe pointed to a heavy, foot-long file with a pick end. Joey was waiting for a response. He was probably waiting for me to get down on my hands and knees and beg. Instead, I laughed and said something like, 'be my guest'. I wasn't about to tell him Jeff was gone for four days."

"Joey looked surprised for a moment, then began shouting at me, 'I'm sick of waiting around here. We're going to that ATM right now or I'll shove that thing… you get the idea."

Her eyes went back to Joey. "He lunged. He grabbed me. I brought the rasp up into his crotch. He screamed and jumped back

– right into Sinbad's flank. Joey turned around – I don't know why – and started to scream something at the horse. Joey then made the mistake of slugging Sinbad's right flank with his fist. Sinbad did what any horse would do. He gave Joey the full treatment: two hooves right into his chest. He went sailing by me and hit the wall with a half turn."

Chloe's voice was calm. "I didn't just stand there. I'm a doctor, or at least I used to be. I checked for a pulse. But given the angle of his neck, I wasn't expecting anything. The pitchfork in the back didn't do him any favors. Given that there's almost no blood from the wound, I'd say he died pretty much on impact from a broken neck."

"I put Sinbad out into the paddock," Chloe said, turning back to the barn door. "You know horses and the smell of blood or death. I don't want to keep them out there after dark."

"It was an accident," I said. "There's no good reason not to call the police."

Chloe looked at me, choking back tears, her mouth open. "I thought you'd get it," she said quietly. "Let's start with the easy part. The police show up, they examine the scene. They look at Joey's body. They look at the twin indentations on his chest and what are likely half a dozen broken ribs and a fractured sternum. They look up Sinbad's record and read that, five years ago, he reared up when some stupid kid waved a shovel in front of him in a stall and ended up with a fractured collar bone. Sinbad gets put down because this time he 'killed' someone. How many times have you read about that?" She shook her head. "I couldn't let that happen."

Chloe continued. "But let's say I could persuade the police that Joey did everything but stick Sinbad with a cattle prod, and all Sinbad did was protect himself. It still leaves a bunch of questions hanging in the air. The biggest of which is, 'Tell us, Mrs. Barnes, how did Mr. McCoy come to be here in this building with you?'

That's the question I can't answer."

"I can answer," I said. "He came here to ask you to talk to me. He has met you twice. He knows we're good friends. He wanted to persuade you to get me to drop the charges. That works!"

"I thought about that," Chloe said, sadness in her voice. "That's when – just to be on the safe side – the police start investigating how many of your other friends were approached, and it turns out that I was the only one. So, how did he know where I lived? Since I wasn't in the house, how did he know to look for me in the barn? How did he know I *had* a barn?"

Chloe looked at me with a pained expression. "That's when they're going to start looking at what's on his phone. They're going to find phone calls and text messages. Uncomfortably explicit text messages. Because, after that morning, I started getting texts from Joey. Some with photos of the kind you'd expect from a sixteen-year-old. The texts detailed what we had done and suggested that there was lots more fun to be had. The messages I sent back were just the opposite: terse and negative. Joey's texts stopped after a week or so."

Chloe's gaze returned to Joey. "But the police will find those texts and they're going to see his being here in a different light. And that's when Jeff – who, by the way is probably being accompanied on that fishing trip by one of his pharma babes – is going to get a huge smile on his face because he has just been handed, on a gold platter, all the grounds he needs to get rid of both Chloe and that $200,000 a year he's dropping on Chloe's 'hobby' to keep her happy."

Suddenly, it was all crystal clear to me. I 'got it'.

Chloe looked around the barn. "The only part I'm having trouble with is Joey's wife and kids. He's no bargain, but I assume he was a good provider. His wife…"

"Joey isn't married," I said. "He has been divorced for something like eight years and she is remarried. And he doesn't have two children. There's just a son who hasn't seen his father in years."

Chloe's mouth made an 'O'. "But there's child support, alimony, life insurance…".

I shook my head. "I met his ex-wife last week. She called me. Joey apparently never paid alimony and gambled away what would have been child support. He was a real piece of work."

Chloe was quiet for several moments; she was obviously weighing options. Finally, she said, "What kind of trouble do you think I'd be in if I moved the body?"

"Moved it where?" I asked.

She shook her head. "Someplace that isn't here. Someplace that, when he's found, it can't come back to me."

"That question is way outside of my pay grade," I said.

Chloe spoke quickly, excitement in her voice. "No one is going to miss him. He wanted to get together a stake to start over somewhere else. He probably told that story to several people." She waited for my response.

I said, "Let's say – for the sake of argument – that you put him someplace where he isn't found for three or four days and it is fifty miles from here." I was doing some first-class thinking here. "Then somebody finds him and the police take the body to the Medical Examiner because they figure it's a homicide. The person doing the autopsy takes off his clothes. The first thing that person sees is a pair of hoof prints in his chest. I think the police are going to start talking to people with horses."

"Then I take him to some place where there are horses," Chloe said.

"Where's his truck?" I asked.

"He parked it in back of the jumping rink," Chloe said. "I guess he was nervous about being seen."

We walked outside. The horses now were whinnying at the paddock gate, reminding Chloe that it was time to let them back inside. We went behind the jumping rink. Right next to the manure pile was Joey's truck. Except that now, instead of that fresh-washed-every-morning look, it was caked in mud. Joey probably had been sleeping in his truck.

"We'd have to get rid of the truck, too," I said. And, as I said those words, I realized I had used the word, *'we'*. I wasn't going to let Chloe's life get ruined because of someone she only knew because of me.

"I hadn't thought of that," she said. "Maybe I ought to just call the police. Get it over with. It was an accident. I don't want to live with this for the rest of my life and I don't want to drag you into this."

It was right at that moment that a giant illuminated light bulb appeared over my head.

The manure pile.

Chloe was talking herself into placing the phone call I had wanted her to make as soon as I heard her story. She was saying that training jumpers was a young woman's dream and she could take up Scrabble or something. I wasn't paying attention. I was trying to reconstruct a conversation from a few weeks earlier. It was about manure… compost….

"Chloe," I said.

Chloe stopped talking and looked at me expectantly.

"I have an idea," I said. "If it works, it solves your problem. If it doesn't work, we're both in a world of trouble."

Chloe didn't say a word. She just looked at me with something like adoration in her face.

"There's one problem," I said.

"Tell me," Chloe said.

"We're going to have to tell someone else about this. We're going to need an expert in hot composting."

Chapter Twenty

Dover and Needham are adjoining towns and it took Susan Williams less than fifteen minutes to arrive. In those few minutes we managed to take at least fifty photos of Joey *in situ*, several of which showed the horrific bruising that came from being kicked by 1200 pounds of muscle concentrated into a few square inches of hooves moving at ten feet per second.

Then, while I dragged Joey's body back to his truck, Chloe hosed and scrubbed down the grooming area. The horses were back in their stalls and we were putting out feed when we heard the sound of Susan's Volvo crunching on the driveway in front of the house.

Having Susan come to Chloe's house hadn't been my original plan. I was going to have Susan talk me through the mechanics over the phone with Chloe listening in on an extension and taking notes. But Susan immediately jumped at the opportunity to have the meeting in person, and I had no plausible explanation of why she couldn't join us.

I had been rehearsing what to say and how much to reveal. I didn't want Susan to get in any trouble, and so I decided that we should hold our discussion strictly in Chloe's house; away from prying eyes.

"We were just feeding the horses," I said, smiling, as we rounded the corner of the house.

Susan had come in her gardening finest: coveralls, a Cornell sweatshirt that even her alma mater's Extension Service would have disowned as beyond wearing, and steel-toed shoes. She saw me looking over her wardrobe and said, simply, "Mowing leaves back into the lawn. Practicing what I preach."

I nodded. "Why don't we go inside?" It might have sounded odd that I was inviting Susan into the house that was not my own, but I wasn't certain how much strain Chloe could handle.

We seated ourselves in an ultra-comfortable room designed to be perfect for three. There were three beautifully upholstered chairs, a vase of fresh flowers, an antique pie-plate table, and a revolving bookcase with a decided equine theme. The artwork included at least one George Stubbs piece.

A year earlier, I had hosted a dinner for six with Chloe and Jeff and Susan and her husband, Dwayne. The three women had a wonderful evening with the conversation careening between child rearing, gardening, great vacation spots, and even horses. For the three of us, it was a matter of picking up the threads of conversations we had at luncheons and ladies' night out. Chloe is not much of a gardener and what Susan knows about the world of competitive jumping would fit comfortably on a 3x5 card with room left over for a complex recipe. But that evening Chloe asked insightful questions about organic gardening, and Susan kept asking Chloe to tell her more about the horse world's people and personalities.

The three men…. got drunk. Jeff quickly ascertained that Dwayne was a registered Democrat and was a senior vice president at Raytheon. Those two attributes made Dwayne someone who did not want to hear a diatribe about the waste being laid to the medical profession by the virtual socialization of medicine under the Affordable Care Act. Neither Matt nor Dwayne shared either of Jeff's twin sports passions of golf and deep-sea fishing. The common ground they found was that Matt's dinner wine selection was superb, and so they consumed four bottles of a 1982 Ridge Zinfandel. They were not only the final four bottles from the case Matt had put away three decades ago; there was a strong likelihood, Matt said afterward, that they were the last four bottles on the face of the earth.

I thought of that dinner as Chloe uncorked a simple red and poured each of us a glass.

"Chloe is thinking about creating a hot compost pile to help heat her barn this winter," I said. "You're my go-to person on composting. What should she do?"

Susan looked at me quizzically. "You said it was important…"

"Chloe wants to start this compost pile right away." Yes, I know that sounded incredibly lame. It was also the best thing I could come up with.

Susan turned to Chloe. "Are you using your own horse manure?"

Chloe looked at me and I gave her an imperceptible nod.

"Yes," Chloe said. "I have five horses. There are a couple of truckloads." She gave a wan smile and added, "Fresh supplies arriving daily."

"Are you using wood shavings or straw?" Susan asked.

"Wood shavings," Chloe replied. She didn't have to look at me for that one.

"You're more than half-way home," Susan said. "The bacteria that break down the manure into compost are thermophilic. The trick is to keep that high-heat phase going as long as possible by getting the right mix of carbon and nitrogen to make the bacteria happy. I'd lay down wood chips for a base, use straw bales to contain the edges of the pile, and then add a layer of manure, say twelve inches deep. Then get some four-inch plastic drain pipe and drill one-inch holes in it at one-foot intervals. That's to drain off liquids and excess ammonia. Lay those a foot apart. You're going to need to feed that into a second pile that serves as a bio-filter, but we'll get to that in a few minutes. Then put down another foot of manure and…"

Chloe shook her head and looked at me. Tears began forming. "This is hopeless. I can't do this…"

Susan said, "In fact, it's easy. The guys who muck out your stable can do this for you in a day once you've got the pipe drilled."

Chloe had a horrified look on her face. "I can't have someone else do this…"

"What?" Susan said, and looked back forth between Chloe and me.

I ignored Susan's implied suspicions. "We want this pile good and hot," I said. "I heard adding coffee grounds will do that. And I can help Chloe with the labor. That's not a problem…"

Susan shook her head. "No. No one cries over building a compost pile and no one I've ever met would turn down having someone else do it for them." She looked at Chloe, whose head was down, sobbing into her hands. Susan said, "Do you want to tell me what's going here?"

"No," I said. "Susan, I'm sorry I called you. I don't want you involved with this."

"Involved with what?" Susan narrowed her eyes. She looked at Chloe, who was still crying, and back at me. "She's my friend, too, you know."

I shook my head. "This was a mistake. Really. A bad idea…"

Susan held up a finger. "You call me at six o'clock and say you really need to see me, and then you start asking me how to build a really *hot* compost pile. The last time we talked about hot compost was when I told you about my CSA and how we could use it to…"

Susan looked at me in amazement. "Lordy have mercy. You killed Joey."

In the eight years I have known Susan, this was the first time I ever heard her use that expression.

"Actually, one of Chloe's horses killed Joey," I said. Chloe started wailing.

"Oh. My. God," Susan said. "We're going to compost the bastard." Chloe wailed more loudly.

"Would it work?" I asked.

"I don't see why not," Susan replied. "I was up at a conference in New Hampshire last week and a guy was telling us about using their compost pile to dispose of dead cows. Joey's a lot smaller." Then she added, "Do I want to know why we're not calling 911 on this?"

I shook my head. "No, you don't want to know."

"Can I at least see the body so I know what we're dealing with?"

"You don't have to be involved with this at all," I said. "This isn't your…"

Susan cut me off. "You're my friend. Chloe is my friend. Friends help one another in times of need. Joey put you through six kinds of hell – walking off the job whenever it suited him and trying to hold you up for more money. Sister, this will be a pleasure and a public service. Now show me the body."

Chloe was a little wobbly, but we walked out to the rear of the jumping rink. It was dark now, and Chloe threw on a pair of perimeter flood lamps.

"There's this woman down in Duxbury," Chloe said. "She is the worst excuse for a trainer I've ever known. We could leave Joey's body out in her paddock. She probably wouldn't notice him for a week…"

"And have the police trying to figure out what Joey was doing in a paddock sixty miles from his home," I said. "Or in *any* paddock. It wouldn't make sense. No, Joey has to disappear."

Susan was examining the body, doing so with a disinterested manner that I found mildly unnerving. People are supposed to shrink back from the sight of a dead body. Susan was turning him over with the steel-tipped toe of her shoe.

"What are these holes in his back?" Susan asked.

"Sinbad kicked him into a wall," Chloe said. "There was a pitchfork on the wall."

"How deep did the pitchfork penetrate?" Susan asked Chloe.

Chloe gave Susan a look of incomprehension.

"It could be really important," Susan said. "Not to get gross, but the guy in New Hampshire said that they… well, ventilated the cow to help drain fluids and prevent bloating…"

"I think I'm going to be sick," Chloe said.

"From what I saw, I'd say the tines were in three or four inches," I said.

"Three or four inches is better than nothing," Susan replied. "We can work with four perforations that deep. While part of me would love to put a few more holes in him… well, we don't have to."

"Chloe also said her horse probably broke some of Joey's ribs," I added.

"Broken ribs are also good," Susan said. "The bacteria only work on exposed surfaces; they digest around the edges. The more exposed surfaces, the better."

"This can really take care of the entire body?" I asked.

"If we construct it properly, there will be nothing left of Joey but the rivets and zipper from his jeans," Susan replied. "What we're going to do is build two compost piles, one inside the other. One heats the greenhouse, the other composts Joey."

"Greenhouse?" Chloe said. "I don't have a greenhouse."

"I do," Susan said. "Do you know what a CSA is?"

Chloe shook he head.

"Community Supported Agriculture," Susan said. "It's like a farm. Most people know them because they can buy a 'share' in what the CSA grows. The farm knows it has customers for what it grows, and it knows how much money they'll have to grow that food and make a profit. To keep costs down, volunteers do a lot of the grunt work. My CSA is adding winter vegetables for the first time and I happen to be the greenhouse advisor." She grinned. "Joey is finally going to do a lot of people a lot of good. He's going to help heat a greenhouse."

"Is it local?" Chloe asked. "There's one here in Dover, I know."

"You're talking about Powisset Farm," Susan said. "No, the one I'm working with is Saybrook Farm over in Sherborn. They're going into winter vegetables with two big hoop houses. I'm in charge of what they're calling the 'auxiliary' heating system which, if all goes as planned, will be the only heating system they need."

"And Joey will produce part of that heat," I said softly.

"We need a shopping list," Susan said. "Anyone got something to take notes on?"

* * * * *

And thus was born the Hot Compost Conspiracy.

I have admired Susan ever since I met her. She is incredibly outgoing, engaging, intelligent, full of humor, and horticulturally savvy. However, I never suspected that her talents included the composting of a human body, nor that she would manage such an undertaking with such relish.

We knew we had an exceptionally tight time frame. We had from Tuesday evening until Saturday morning to accomplish our mission. Saturday was critical for multiple reasons. First, Susan told us a work party was scheduled at Saybrook Farm: a dozen volunteers were coming to build a heat-generating compost pile under her direction. Five truckloads of manure would be on hand together with the other necessary elements. By Saturday morning, we had to have Joey in place but in such a way that, when the volunteers arrived, they wouldn't wonder why there was already a compost pile in the greenhouse.

Second, Chloe's husband and mine were due to arrive home on Saturday; mine on the red eye from San Francisco, Chloe's at a less determinate time, though she would try to pry that information from him over the next few days. Susan's husband, Dwight, was less of a problem. He was used to Susan going off at odd hours and coming back smelling of strange garden-y things.

We would have to do much of our work at night. Susan also said Saybrook Farm had a final field harvest in progress with lots of earnest volunteers underfoot, coupled with a full-time staff that would question why three women were building the compost system out of sequence. Questions from anyone were the last thing we needed. At night, there was only a lone resident manager. Susan said she had a way of dealing with that person.

There were two pressing needs. The first was to find a temporary home for Joey. At Susan's suggestion, we laid him out in the manure pile a few feet away from his truck, burying him under three or four inches of the manure and shavings.

"This kind of eases him into the idea of where he's going to be spending eternity," Susan said. We all took turns shoveling. It cemented the fact that we were in this together.

Our second pressing need was to make Joey's truck disappear as thoroughly as its owner. We had agreed to come back with ideas on that the following evening.

In the meantime, I had a gnawing question that I could not get out of my mind. To wit: exactly what laws were we breaking, and what were the consequences?

To answer that question, I phoned Michaela McDermott Wednesday morning and invited her out to lunch.

Michaela, you may recall, is one of my *Jeopardy* 'sorority sisters'. She is young – just 28 – and possessed of what I guess is commonly known as a 'trick' memory. She reads, sees, or hears something and retains the gist of it. It isn't that 'total recall' mind that Marilu Henner and a few dozen other people around the world have. In some ways, it's better: akin to having a music or film library in your head coupled with the *Encyclopedia Britannica*. You give her a sentence fragment from a book and, if she had read it, she can tell you its context, and then relate *that* fragment to half a dozen other relevant sources.

Michaela got out of college and planned to go to law school, but didn't have the money and was unwilling to saddle herself with more than a hundred thousand dollars of student debt. Instead, she landed a job as a paralegal at WilmerHale, one of Boston's largest law firms. Thanks to her *Jeopardy* winnings, she has applications out to three excellent law schools and the ability to pay their tuition. The law school that gets her as a student should count itself supremely fortunate.

If I were forced at gunpoint to name my favorite *Jeopardy* sorority sister, it would be Michaela. She is plucky, fiercely independent, and not the least bit shy about her intelligence. Michaela is always up for something different and thrives on a challenge. I love my daughter with all my heart, but I sometimes wish Kate was more like Michaela. Kate is single-minded to a fault. She decided at twelve to be a marine biologist and never wavered from that career. She applied only to schools with stellar marine science programs and married someone whose passion for oceanography matched her own.

But I digress.

After spending three hours at the construction site the following morning, I took the train into South Station and enjoyed the brisk walk to Government Center. We had agreed to meet at a Bertucci's around the corner from WilmerHale's State Street offices.

Despite her windfall from *Jeopardy* and what I suspected was a decent salary from her paralegal position, Michaela refused to upgrade her wardrobe from a small, revolving assortment of white and blue blouses, black slacks, and navy blue skirts. As it got cooler, she would augment that basic wardrobe with a handful of sweaters, but she said she essentially wasn't interested in clothes; that *Jeopardy* check was earmarked for law school tuition and nothing else.

Michaela arrived a few minutes later. We hugged and ordered. All the time, of course, I was carefully cataloging and rehearsing the phrasing of my questions, but my mothering instincts were also aching to get this woman to a hair salon and a day spa. Michaela is far from unattractive, but neither is she a natural beauty. Her nose is a little too prominent and her chin a bit recessive. Cosmetics and a good hairstyle can minimize those flaws, but Michaela's shoulder-length straight brown hair and near absence of makeup leaves those shortcomings out there for everyone to see. At least she was wearing a good-quality floral perfume. Maybe she was starting to take more of an interest in how other people perceived her.

"You said you had some theoretical legal questions for me," Michaela said as our soup arrived.

I nodded. "I'm trying my hand at writing romance fiction. I've got a great story idea, but I want to make certain I'm not getting my protagonist into a box she can't get out of."

Michaela gave me an appreciative nod in return. "A legal box," she said.

"Exactly," I replied. "My protagonist, Rebecca, has a dead body on her hands. A mysterious stranger trespasses on her remote, windswept farm and breaks into her barn with a plan of hiding out for the night among her cattle. He's on the run. Rebecca encounters him the next morning and they fall in love. But two passionate days later, she discovers that this stranger is almost certainly a thief after she finds a piece of jewelry missing. Roberta orders him to leave…"

"I thought you said her name was Rebecca?" Michaela asked.

"I'm sorry," I continued. "Rebecca orders the stranger – his real name is Antonio, but that doesn't matter – to leave. He isn't really a thief; it was someone else who took the jewelry, but even as he agrees to leave, he gives her one last passionate kiss. As he turns to say goodbye, he falls through a rotten floorboard in the barn and breaks his neck on some machinery below."

"What year is this set in?" Michaela asked, a disturbingly quizzical look on her face.

"Um, the present," I replied.

"And where is it taking place?"

"Um, here?" I was hoping to get Massachusetts law, but I hadn't expected and hadn't prepared for any questions.

Michaela nodded slowly. "This is a remote farm in Massachusetts in 2016," she said. "It has a barn with rotten floorboards that won't give way under the weight of a cow, but when a man steps on one of those floorboards, it disintegrates and he falls down into a cellar filled with machinery."

"Put that way, it sounds like I need to tighten up my setting," I said.

"A little," Michaela replied. "But tell me the rest."

"Rebecca fears that, although it was definitely an accident and he was trespassing, she will be blamed for his death. Now, some people are looking for Antonio. He jumped off a sailing ship and may have a price on his head…"

Michaela looked at me, that quizzical look turning to one of incomprehension. "You said the story is set in the present, but he jumped off a three-masted schooner, and there's a price on his head?"

Flustered, I said, "It's one of those replicas that sails around the world, and it had Salem as a port of call." Needless to say, I was ad-libbing as I went along. I went into this genuinely thinking that Michaela would just listen and then quote me applicable law.

"So, this remote, windswept farm is within walking distance of Salem Harbor. Go on," Michaela said.

I did not like the look on her face.

"Rebecca decides, rather than calling in the police, that she is going to bury Antonio on her farm and tell no one. She fears that, even though Antonio had no family, she could be sued by the ship owner, and burying him privately is the best solution."

"How about, she is worried that her family will find out about those two passionate days and her husband will leave her,"

Michaela offered. "That sounds more plausible."

"Roberta is single," I said, much too quickly.

"*Rebecca* is single," Michaela corrected.

"Are either of them breaking any laws?" I asked, exasperated.

"Wow," Michaela said, drumming her fingers. "Where do I begin? First of all, as soon as she discovers Antonio is dead, she has an obligation to leave the body in place and call the police so that a duly appointed representative of the state can determine the cause and manner of death. That could be the police or a medical professional."

"What if she took lots of photos? Like, fifty or sixty?"

Michaela shook her head. "Not even close as a mitigating factor. Moving the body is a misdemeanor, moving the body to make it more difficult to ascertain cause of death is obstruction of justice; that's a felony. Do we assume, then, there's not going to be a death certificate?"

"Definitely no death certificate," I said.

"Then Antonio becomes a 'missing person' and his case remains open for the balance of what could be assumed to be his natural life," Michaela said. "I take it Antonio is in his twenties or thirties?"

"I haven't decided," I said. "Let's assume he's twenty-something."

"Then the police will be investigating this until the year 2080 and there's no statute of limitations on any criminal charges," Michaela said. "How old is Rebecca?"

"Same age," I replied.

"She is going to have this hanging over her head her entire life," Michaela said. "Plus, because the death is unexplained on its face, Rebecca has an obligation to turn the body over to the coroner to determine cause of death. That's a separate felony."

"But Rebecca has the photos," I countered. "That shows the cause of death."

"What that proves is that she is deliberately concealing evidence," Michaela said. "She should lose the photos. And the camera or phone they were taken with. She shouldn't store them or email them under any circumstances. Otherwise, they're certain to be discovered."

"How about the actual burial?" I asked. "How many laws is she breaking there?"

"Not as many as you might think," Michaela said. "She needs a burial permit from the town of Salem. Failure to have a burial permit is punishable by law, but I don't know if that's a misdemeanor or a felony. Whichever it is, it pales next to moving the body. Embalming isn't a requirement in Massachusetts and there's an evolving set of case law for 'green' burials, which gets around the usual requirement for concrete grave liners or gravel bases so long as the burial isn't in a cemetery."

Michaela paused and looked straight into my eyes. "Anne, are you in trouble?"

The look on my face must have given something away, because Michaela continued, "WilmerHale isn't the best place to find a criminal defense attorney. But that guy who was at the foundation pouring at your house – Lew Faircloth – is a legend…"

"I'm not in trouble," I said. "I'm… asking for a friend."

"Anne," Michaela said, "Paralegals in Massachusetts aren't officers of the court. I have no duty to report what I hear. But if you have first-hand knowledge of what someone else has done, you could be charged with what is called 'failure to come forward'." She paused to give me time for her words to sink in. "Do you want to tell me how much of that story about Rebecca and Antonio is true?"

"I don't think this is the place," I said.

Michaela looked around at the busy restaurant. We were in a corner; the tables around us were all occupied by people having conversations, some of them quite loud.

"Actually, this is a perfect place," she said. "I don't see anyone I know."

"Do you remember my contractor?"

Michaela nodded. "Joey the Pig. Leering at your friends, with his fingers pointing down at what I bet he thinks are the most exquisite family jewels ever to be bestowed on an adoring female. Yes, I remember him."

"He's dead," I said. "He was kicked by a horse…"

"One of Chloe's horses?" Michaela said excitedly.

I nodded. "It's a complicated story. Joey showed up at her farm, demanding money and threatening her. It all happened in her barn."

"And she didn't call the police because…" Michaela left the question open.

I shook my head. "I've had that conversation with her. It would start a chain of events that would be…" I failed to find the right words. "I understand why she would rather risk jail."

Michaela looked me squarely in the eyes again. "Anne, is there any question on your mind about what happened being an accident?"

"None at all," I said. "She called me as soon as it happened. Joey was still warm when I got there. And I saw the hoof marks. I know exactly what kind of impression they leave. The fall broke his neck." I left out the part about the pitchfork. My description was gruesome enough already.

Michaela slowly repeated back my words in a way that made the hair stand up on the back of my neck. "Joey was still warm when I got there… I saw the hoof marks… So you helped Chloe move the body?"

I understood exactly what she was saying, and my heart was pounding as I answered.

"Yes."

Michaela closed her eyes and silently nodded; processing the information.

"Then you aren't just an accessory," she said. "In the eyes of the judicial system, you have exactly the same culpability as Chloe." There was no quibbling in what she said. She was stating facts.

"I hadn't thought of it that way," I said.

"And you've help her bury the body," Michaela said.

"It isn't buried yet, and we're not exactly planning to bury it. Susan has a…"

"Susan Williams?" Michaela looked startled. "She's part of this?"

I nodded.

"Anyone else?"

"No, just the three of us, and we didn't intend to involve Susan except that she… she really disliked Joey. She volunteered."

"And what are you going to do with him?" Michaela asked, dropping her voice to a whisper and leaning in.

"You don't want to know," I said, vigorously shaking my head. "Except that, if everything goes as planned, Joey will disappear off the face of the earth. Forever."

"But people will come looking for him," Michaela countered. Everybody has someone who cares about them."

I gave her the truncated version of my conversation with Joey's ex-wife. As I explained, Michaela nodded an understanding.

"Then the *police* must be looking for him." Michaela's commanding sense of logic was on full display.

"To them, this is an assault case," I explained. "They assume he'll turn himself in when he runs out of friends or money. They aren't expending any resources on Joey."

"Have there been any sightings of him that you know of?" Michaela asked.

"Two days ago," I said. "I was told by the detective working the case that Joey tried to borrow money from one of his customers. The customer told Joey to get himself a lawyer and turn himself in."

Michaela nodded. "That's good for another few days. But when he doesn't surface on someone else's doorstep in the next day or two the police will start assuming something happened to him."

"The detective in Hardington says Joey will try to gamble his way out of it," I offered. "Trumbull."

"So, Joey was hitting up everyone he knew for money," Michaela said. "Which included Chloe. But when he disappears, the police are going to get suspicious…"

"No they're not," I said. "The detective I spoke with said Hardington's Chief of Police won't authorize any special effort because Joey will turn himself in."

Michaela tilted her head at me. The look on her face was serious. "Let me ask you a question. When you were given that update on Joey, did you go to a police station and ask to speak to the detective, or did the detective come to your home?"

"He came to the construction site," I said.

"So, in the eyes of this detective, this isn't just a case of simple assault," Michaela said. "If it were, the report would have been filed and that would have been the end of it." She leaned in again. "Anne, I know more than just the law. I'm getting to know how the police and prosecutors think. And here's what I know: yours is an 'interesting' case. It's interesting because you're a woman and a known quantity in your town. The police pay special attention to people like you. And, Joey ran."

Her voice dropped to a near whisper. "If he had pushed you, saw what he had done, called the paramedics, waited for the police, given a full and honest statement, and then apologized profusely for his actions, none of this would have happened. A guy like him could probably have talked his way out of everything but a fine and a slap on the wrist. But he ran. And, when he did that, there's a pre-programmed switch that clicked on inside that detective's brain. He isn't going to stop until Joey is behind bars."

Michaela sat bolt upright. "You had a town selectman found murdered at that TV show construction site last year. This isn't the same detective that…"

I nodded.

Michaela's eyes rolled. "Big-deal Boston homicide detective retires, gets itchy, gets hired by a sleepy suburb. Of course. Out-thinking guys like Joey is what your detective… what's his name?"

"Detective John Flynn," I said.

"Out-thinking guys like Joey is what your Detective Flynn does instead of solving a Sudoku or a Ken-Ken in the morning," Michaela said. "So far, Joey had done everything Detective Flynn expects him to do. And, the Good Detective has a little stopwatch and a personal bet with himself that, if Joey can't get down money on his favorite teams – or if he does and blows it all, which he will certainly do – then Joey will come crawling in on all fours to accept his punishment Sunday night."

"But Joey could leave town – start over somewhere else," I said.

Michaela shook her head. "Guys like Joey have never lived more than twenty miles from where they were born. Joey is a home boy. He couldn't make it in Worcester, let alone some alien city like Atlanta or Denver."

Then she frowned. "How did Joey get to Chloe's farm?"

"His truck," I said. "We're working on what to do with it."

Michaela exhaled loudly, a worried look on her face.

"This isn't your problem," I said. "I wanted to know where we stand legally. You've made it perfectly clear that, if this doesn't go like clockwork, Chloe and I are in big trouble."

"You're more than just my friend," Michaela said. "You're either the older sister I never had or the mother I *wish* I had but didn't. You understand me because there's a part of you that I bet was just like me. I can…"

"Stop," I said softly and held up my hand. "Chloe, Susan and I can figure this out. Susan has a plan. We'll figure out what to do with the truck."

Michaela shook her head furiously. "I've been around lawyers and law enforcement for six years now. I'm the extra set of hands you don't know you need yet. Before this is over, you'll need them and you'll thank me."

I sighed. My problem with Joey had just claimed its third conspirator.

Chapter Twenty-One

We met that evening in Chloe's house. Having outgrown the comfortable equine-themed room for three, we now sat at the country kitchen table. A lovely scent from multiple bouquets of flowers was an incongruous touch to the task we had before us. For fortification purposes, Chloe had set out two opened bottles of wine, all of which was poured within twenty minutes of our arrival.

I explained Michaela's presence as someone who 'understood both the law and the mindset of law enforcement', which caused Chloe and Susan to look at Michaela with new appreciation.

"If we do this right, we will be the only four people in the world who will ever know what happened," I said. "If we *don't* do this right, millions of people will know what we did, and that is not what we want."

Vision of lurid headlines on creepy websites flashed before everyone's eyes. I had made my point.

Susan opened a manila file folder and passed around a legal-size sheet of paper to each person at the table.

"I've slightly re-worked the passive heating system I designed for Saybrook Farm to account for Joey," she said. "There are two greenhouses – hoop-houses, actually – each one twenty feet wide and a hundred feet long. The 'special sauce' that supplies passive heating is a 'hot compost pile'. It's basically a giant pile of manure and organic material enclosed by straw bales. Bacteria and other microorganisms in the manure 'eat' the manure and organic material. They give off heat in the process. In the end, what's left is compost, suitable for spreading around a garden as nutrients for plants."

Susan continued. "What scientists have learned how to do is to tweak the heat level by a combination of venting and varying the mix of organics. The venting is done with perforated plastic pipe; the organics are modified by adding or subtracting things rich in nitrogen and carbon. The reason the tweaking is so crucial is that, done wrong, a compost pile can become so carbon-heavy that the bacteria stop doing their job. The opposite can also happen: the mixture can grow so rich in nitrogen that the heat kills off the bacteria, and so composting also stops."

Pointing to one area of the diagram, Susan said, "We're going to use a forced aeration system – a simple fan, in this case – and a biofilter to get rid of ammonia and other volatile components that might damage the crops growing in the greenhouse."

"The compost pile is the length of each hoop-house, roughly four feet high, four feet wide at the base and about three feet wide at the top," Susan said. "One of the greenhouses will have a perfectly normal system, just like the one here. The other will be exactly the same except for about ten feet at one end. The main compost pile will run at a temperature of about 140 degrees. The part we'll be building will run at 160 degrees. At that higher temperature, anything in that section will be reduced to something that looks and acts just like soil in about three months. Anything and everything." She thumped those last three words for effect.

Susan removed a second set of papers from her folder and passed them around. "It will look the same from the outside. No one except us will know it is any different or what's inside it."

The second sheet of paper showed a cross-section of what we were to build. In the middle of it was the outline of a human body.

Whatever wine remained in our glasses was quickly consumed.

"Friday night," Susan said, "we are going to build this section of the compost pile in the north greenhouse. For cover, we're also going to build one end of the pile in the south building tomorrow evening. To the volunteers building the heating system on Saturday, all we're doing is creating a demonstration template they're supposed to follow."

"How do we do this without getting noticed?" Michaela asked.

Susan gave a wink and a smile. "We get noticed tomorrow night. That's when we build the dummy section in the south greenhouse. Anyone who is poking around asking questions – probably the farm's resident manager – will get used to the idea we're there. Her name is Linda Corapi and she's one of the friendliest people you'll ever meet, but she's also whip-smart. We get to explain why we're there in the evening and why we brought our own manure. We let her poke around the pipes and piles to her hearts' content. We'll bore her and anyone else who pops in with a mountain of details. On Friday evening we'll be old news. People will stay away in droves."

"So, why are we there in the evening?" Michaela pressed. "Pretend I'm that resident manager and I'm curious about why you're in my greenhouse when normal people are at home with their families."

"These people are my guinea pigs," Susan responded, sweeping her arm to indicate everyone at the table. "They have day jobs. They are gung-ho to learn and they're willing to give up two evenings to be better gardeners."

Michaela nodded satisfaction with the answer.

"Which leaves the truck," I said. "We can't compost a truck."

"I've been thinking about that," Chloe said. "There are ponds up in New Hampshire that are filled to the brim with old cars and trucks…"

"We're not going to pollute a pond," Susan said with finality. "Don't even think about it."

"And those cars and trucks get pulled out of those ponds," Michaela said. "License plates and VIN numbers get matched. It would fairly scream 'foul play'."

"What about a chop shop?" I offered. "We drive the truck to some dicey part of Boston and leave the keys in it, wipe it down for prints, and wait for some enterprising crook to break it up for parts."

"That might have worked fifteen years ago," Michaela said. "Vehicle ID numbers used to be on two or three places on a car. Now, they're stamped on every removable part. It hasn't put chop shops out of business, but it has made the business less attractive."

"Do you have any ideas?" I asked, looking at Michaela.

She nodded. "Steal to order."

Around the table, everyone looked at the person next to them, seeing if anyone knew what Michaela was talking about.

"Joey's truck has to disappear, never to be seen again," Michaela explained. "Because of all those markings in the truck, you can't burn it, submerge it, or leave it in the woods. In a year or two years, someone is going to stumble on it and, when they do, the truck's history is a scan away, and it will set off alarms in the minds of every law enforcement agency interested in Joey."

Michela looked around the table at the gloom on our faces.

"However, there's one perfect way out," she continued. "There's a sizeable market for high-end vehicles, especially overseas. You put in an order that you want, say, a black BMW i8, a car that goes for around $150,000. The word goes out and thieves find one, disable the locator device on it, and deliver it to a container at a shipping port. In three weeks it gets offloaded in Colombia or Brazil. The buyer pays $75,000, of which the thieves get $40,000 and the middleman gets $35,000."

Michaela saw the dawning looks of hope on our faces and continued. "It turns out Joey's truck is a high-demand item. It costs about $65,000, so there isn't the kinds of margins thieves would want, but for every BMW, there's a demand for two or three Joey-type trucks. We hide Joey's truck in South America."

Chloe asked, "What happens when the police in Bogota pull

over that stolen-to-order car or truck and see that it's registered to someone in the United States?"

Michaela grinned. "That's the beauty of it. No one cares. No one checks. There's no database in Colombia of stolen American cars. In fact, if you see an expensive car on the streets of Bogota, you should expect that it was stolen."

"Now, all we need is for someone to order a Dodge Ram 3500 Longhorn," I said. "Oh, and put the truck exactly where thieves will be looking for it."

Michalea smiled at me. "Let's just say I have friends in low places and leave it at that. If we are all agreed, Joey's truck can be gone as early as Saturday morning and almost certainly by Sunday night."

I looked at Michaela with new-found respect.

"Unless someone has a better idea," I said, "Let's send Joey's truck to Bogota."

Everyone murmured their assent.

Susan wrapped up the meeting. "We meet here at 8 p.m. tomorrow. Wear old clothes. Bring gloves, a pitchfork or shovel, and boots if you have them. We need to load up Chloe's truck. I'll have the pipe pre-drilled."

* * * * *

On Thursday evening we assembled as requested. In less than an hour we filled Chloe's long-bed truck with several yards of manure and topped it with a dozen bales of straw. With a dozen sections of pipe hanging out of the back of Susan's Volvo, we made our way in two vehicles across the back roads of Dover and Sherborn to Saybrook Farm. We rumbled past the farmhouse that served as the CSA's offices and farm manager's residence and came to a stop next to a pair of hundred-foot-long greenhouses.

Susan turned on the light switches in the first greenhouse and we began offloading pipe and bales.

It took less than ten minutes for the headlights of a third

vehicle to appear.

"Show time," Susan said, indicating the approaching vehicle with her chin.

An olive-green truck with the Saybrook Farm logo on its side came to a stop. We all dutifully stopped what we were doing.

The truck door opened and a woman dressed in jeans and a sweatshirt alighted

"Hi, Linda," Susan said warmly.

"The woman looked at the four of us warily. "You're not supposed to be here until Saturday morning," she said. There was concern in her voice.

"Everyone," Susan said, "this is Linda Corapi. She's the resident manager here at Saybrook Farm." Then, to Corapi, she said, "I realized the other day that it was unlikely that any one of those volunteers for Saturday have ever built anything like this. They're either going to be getting in one another's way or else standing back afraid of doing it wrong. So, I drafted some friends to help build one, ten-foot section of the heating system in each greenhouse. That way, everyone can see exactly where everything goes. We're going to build one section tonight and the other section tomorrow night so that, on Saturday morning, it will be just like coloring inside the lines."

"Couldn't you do this tomorrow?" Corapi asked.

"I could," Susan replied. "But my friends have jobs and commitments. They can only play in the manure at night." Susan smiled broadly. "Want to stay and help? It's quite educational."

Corapi, a woman in her early fifties, tilted her head. "I do have some questions. I've been worried about what a real cold snap would do to the vegetables…"

Susan beamed. "Then grab a bale. You're in for an education."

For the next two hours we constructed the compost pile and piping that would connect to a fan and the bio-filter. We used tape and string to mark out the exact limits of each component for the full length of the greenhouse.

All through this, Susan kept up a running commentary on what each element of the system would provide, how temperatures would be monitored, and what safeguards would be in place. Corapi, to her credit, stayed to the end though it was clear that she had long since exhausted her questions.

We departed a few minutes before 11 p.m. The resident manager thanked Susan enthusiastically and complimented us on our energy and dedication. We just smiled.

When we were back in Chloe's driveway, Susan said we had all done our parts perfectly. "Tomorrow night, same time, same place," she said. "Tonight was the dress rehearsal. Tomorrow night is the real thing, but this time without the audience."

I fell asleep Thursday evening, exhausted.

* * * * *

Friday morning I checked in with each of my subcontractors and, in each conversation, there was the same, uniform optimism. The granite and marble countertops were due to be installed in the afternoon; another giant step forward.

I had planned to go home and take a two-hour nap in preparation for an evening of work. As I was leaving, though, a car pulled into the driveway. I recognized it as the one driven by Detective Flynn.

He had a look on his face that I had not seen before. It wasn't quite suspicion nor was it quite a look of worry. Maybe it was just his furrowed brow that caught my attention. There was no place to sit and so we stood on the newly screened back porch.

"I stopped by your home last evening to give you an update but neither you nor your husband were there," he said. He said it in such a way that I sensed he was waiting for an explanation.

"Matt is on the west coast until tomorrow," I said, adding, "Business." Detective Flynn waited for a further comment. "I had a girl's night out with some friends." I said the words with a friendly smile. It was technically true though I had no intention of sharing where I had been. I did not need for the Hardington Police to have Saybrook Farm's name on some evidence board.

Detective Flynn's furrowed brow did not become any less furrowed. "I am concerned about your safety," he said. "That's the reason I'm here."

He shifted his stance and I again felt the unease.

"Joey McCoy has fallen off the radar screen," he said. "He went to see Phil Vonn, one of his regular clients, on Monday evening, asking for money. Judging from the way Mr. Vonn described him, I had a sense we were about to come to closure. Joey has to be nearly out of money and he has no place to turn."

Detective Flynn again shifted his stance. He reached into his coat pocket and retrieved a notebook. He scanned several pages. "I've spent the last two days canvassing every known friend and customer. Because I've pressed people for information, I got several acknowledgements that Joey had been around earlier. I even found someone who had put him up for a night."

Detective Flynn closed the notebook. "But all of those contacts were before Monday evening. No one has seen or heard from him since that time. It's going on four days."

"Could he have made a run for it?" I asked. "Decided to make a new start somewhere that people don't have many questions of newcomers?"

Detective Flynn shook his head. "Joey knows this area. It's *all* he knows. He has no idea of how to fit in or how to start over."

Which is exactly what Michaela had told me.

I asked, "Could he be laying low until after the football games over the weekend?"

Detective Flynn again shook his head. "As best as I can tell, he has not been able to tap any of his friends or customers for money, so he has nothing with which to bet." He paused for a moment before continuing. "I found out he also is already into at least one bookie for a couple of thousand dollars. When someone taps out a line of credit and then disappeared, the word gets around. No one is going to take his bet unless he clears up what he owes."

Detective Flynn took an unnecessary half step toward me. It wasn't quite an invasion of my personal space but it also wasn't *not* an invasion.

"Mrs. Carlton, is there anything you haven't told me? Anything that might help me find Joey McCoy?"

He left the question hanging in the air. I, of course, had the information he needed. *Of course Detective, Joey is dead. He was currently buried under an inch or two of compost on a horse farm in Dover. If you come out to Saybrook Farm tonight, you can verify this for yourself.*

"I'm trying to think of anything Joey said in the last week," I said. "Did you ever find out for whom he was doing those 'emergency repairs' that kept him away from the job for three days?"

Detective Flynn nodded. "A woman in Weston. You can probably guess the rest." He reached back for his note pad. "This is probably grasping at straws, but you've had friends over while he was here. Did he ever – excuse the expression – come on to them?"

I forced a laugh. "Yes, and Joey wasn't their type. He has this thing he does…"

Detective Flynn smiled. "I've heard about it. It's really juvenile, but some women respond to that kind of an overture."

"The women I was with laughed themselves silly," I said. "I know them all well enough to be certain none of them slipped Joey their phone number."

"Could I get their names anyway? I really need to cover every base."

Reluctantly, I gave him the names of my friends that had been at Matt's and my party in August.

All, of course, except for Chloe. She was now the weak link in my chain.

* * * * *

At 8 p.m. the four of us began our task in silence. We filled Chloe's truck with manure and topped it with hay bales. Susan's Volvo already contained the pipe needed for the project. Also in her car were multiple poly bags filled with fresh chicken manure, a nitrogen-rich product that would heat the area around Joey to a higher temperature than the rest of the compost pile. All that remained was to move and load Joey, for which Susan had thoughtfully supplied several yards of biodegradable burlap.

There wasn't room.

"We need another truck," Susan said. "We also need more manure. We were light last night."

The only available truck was Joey's.

"Isn't it dangerous taking it out on the road?" I asked.

"It's seven miles over country roads," Susan said. "I think we can risk it."

And so Joey's truck was pressed into service. Joey lay at the bottom of another cubic yard of a mixture of wood shavings and fresh manure.

The ride to Saybrook Farm was uneventful. We arrived at 8:45 and, as we did on Thursday evening, Susan turned on the greenhouse lights.

We had just finished placing the first dozen hay bales when the headlights appeared in the distance.

"Linda Corapi," Susan muttered. "I'll get rid of her."

I looked more closely into the distance.

"There's more than one set of lights," I said.

There were, in fact, four sets.

Two SUVs, a truck and a station wagon came to a halt at the greenhouse. The truck's door opened and the farm manager fairly bounced out of the cab.

"I brought you some help," Corapi said. She was in high spirits.

"That isn't necessary…" Susan started to say.

"I was so excited about what you said last night," Corapi said. "I called a couple of members of the CSA Board. Once they heard about what you're doing, they said they had to see it for themselves and they're all ready to pitch in to help."

"Can't they come tomorrow?" Susan pleaded. "We're really not set up for…"

"They want to hear your talk," Corapi said excitedly. "I told them everything I could remember of what you said, and they want to hear more for themselves. They have so many questions. I think two of them have brought video equipment. This could spread like wildfire on the internet. It's exactly the kind of publicity I've been looking for."

Now there were nine strangers standing around in a circle. Their faces were full of wonder, expectantly awaiting Susan's words of wisdom.

Meanwhile, not twenty feet away was a truck belonging to a dead man, and that dead man was in the back of the truck covered with a veneer of manure. This was a nightmare come to life.

I saw another car was making its way down the dirt road. Thirty seconds later, it stopped just beyond the other vehicles. Out of the car stepped Detective Flynn. My nightmare was complete. Detective Flynn had his notebook open, ready to take notes… or my confession. The look on his face showed neither mercy nor sympathy.

And now, overhead was a brilliant white light. A searchlight, likely from a police helicopter called to the scene by Detective Flynn. He had put it all together and waited for this moment to pounce. I felt the sense of dread but could not move.

The light played over the greenhouse, then over the small crowd. It came to rest on me. The light was intensely white. I tried to close my eyes but someone was gently pulling them open…

Chapter Twenty-Two

"Anne?"

The masculine voice seemed familiar.

"Too much light," I whispered.

The light immediately snapped off.

"Anne," a different voice, this one feminine, said, "this is Doctor Remsen. We're bringing you out of sedation."

"Sweetheart, this is Matt. You're going to be OK."

My eyes opened. Everything was out of focus.

"Her vitals are fine," the voice of Dr. Remsen said. "I'll give you a few minutes. Remember that she is probably disoriented."

I tried to look around. My head was in some kind of a brace. "Where am I?" I whispered.

"Mass General," Matt said.

"I smell flowers," I said. They were outside of my field of vision.

Matt glanced around and smiled. "Yeah, there must be fifty arrangements in here. They've been coming in since about an hour after you got here. You've got quite a fan club."

"How long…" I couldn't phrase the question properly.

Matt nodded an unspoken understanding. "I better start from the beginning. Right after the incident our plumber, Fred Swearingen, called me from your phone. He said you were out cold. I called the EMTs and explained your history. After some consultation, they decided to have you MedFlighted here. The ER and trauma teams took it from there."

Matt took my hand. "Anne, you took a scary, hard fall. Joey really shoved you and, from what everyone said, you went down like a pile of bricks onto coarse and jagged rocks out in the driveway. The doctors didn't know whether to be more worried about your spine or your concussion. Everyone agreed that you needed to be kept immobilized and that required heavy sedation."

He squeezed my hand. "You've had cranial and spinal MRIs from every angle. The good news is that there's no soft tissue swelling around your spine. There are no spinal tears, and the area that required surgery when you were seventeen was unaffected."

A worried look crossed his face. "There was, however, a great deal of cranial swelling and a probable hairline fracture. You've had drugs to bring down the swelling and the doctors warned me that the combination of the two sets of drugs – those for the sedation and those to reduce the swelling – can produce some fairly vivid hallucinations."

"But you're going to be OK. The immobilizing neck brace is going to come off as soon as the Neurology head signs off…"

"What day is it? How long have I been here?" I asked.

Matt seemed startled. "Of course, you would have lost track of time. You came in Friday before noon. It's Sunday late afternoon."

"What's the date?" I asked.

"October…." Matt took out his phone. "October 16."

Two days, I thought. *It has just been two days…*

"Where's Joey?"

I asked that question with great trepidation.

Matt grinned. "Joey is in the Dedham lockup. He's not going anywhere."

"Dedham?"

Matt started to answer, then paused. "Anne, a lot has happened since you went under. Are you sure you want to hear it all?"

Matt gave me the kind of smile he gives me when the answer he is looking for is 'no, don't tell me'.

"My love," I said, "I have just had the most vivid – and frightening – dream of my life. Until a few minutes ago, I thought I was going to prison as an accessory to Joey's murder."

That one caught him off guard.

"Joey's murder?"

"Just tell me what happened," I said.

"Sure," Matt said, clearly taken aback. "You may or may not remember that after Joey assaulted you – and the charges he is facing from the incident is assault and battery plus leaving the scene of a crime – he took off in his truck. His first stop was an ATM where he tried to max out his credit card…"

"Please don't tell me all he could get was seven hundred dollars."

Matt gave me a puzzled look. "Seven hundred and twenty dollars. How could you have known that?"

"I'm not sure I want to know," I said. And meant it.

Matt continued. "He panicked. He apparently spotted a police car in his apartment complex and never went home. He started driving around to friends and customers, alternately demanding and begging money or a place to stay. Our police department…"

"Detective John Flynn," I said, closing my eyes and praying Matt would say someone – anyone – else's name.

"Right again," Matt said. "Are you sure you were under all of that time?"

"Later," I said. "Just tell me: has Detective Flynn been here?"

"Several times," Matt said. "He has been exceptionally conscientious about providing updates and wanted to personally see how you were doing. I think he has worked this case for 48 hours straight."

I nodded to the extent the neck brace allowed me to do so. "Go on," I said.

"Detective Flynn got a list of Joey's clients and started calling to warn them there was a warrant for his arrest," Matt said. "By last night, Joey was running into customers who met him at the door with the advice that he ought to turn himself in."

"By any chance did the calls placed by Detective Flynn include any clients or prospective customers Joey might have hit on?"

Matt just looked at me incredulously.

"Just please don't tell me Detective Flynn also asked for a list of our friends," I said.

"Only the ones who might have spoken with Joey."

"Oh, my God…" *Maybe it wasn't a dream…*

"But he didn't ask for them until this morning, and he never needed to call any of them," Matt said quickly.

"What happened?"

"This morning, Joey circled back to one of his long-time clients; an old guy who lives out by the country club in Dedham…"

"Harold Berry," I said.

Again, Matt's face showed consternation. "How did you know that?"

"I went to see him after Joey disappeared," I said. Or did I *dream* I went to see him? I could no longer be certain what was dream and what was reality.

"Right," Matt said, taking about five seconds to get out one word. He regained his train of thought. "Berry was in a different part of the house when Joey broke in. Unbeknown to Joey, though, Berry had installed an alarm system, which automatically alerted the Dedham Police when Joey triggered it. Berry heard something going on upstairs. There was some kind of an altercation that left Berry roughed up with a black eye, fractured elbow, and a dislocated shoulder. The police arrived just as Joey was getting into his truck with a pillowcase filled with a couple of super-expensive watches and a coin collection. He is being held on burglary and a second count of assault."

"Joey is alive," I said. It wasn't a question, *per se*. I just needed to hear those words.

"Of course he's alive," Matt said. "The police didn't shoot him."

"I've never been happier to hear those words," I said.

"That must have been one hell of a hallucination you had," Matt said, staring at my face closely.

"Tell me," I said. "Who has been to see me? Who has been in this room?"

"Well, doctors and nurses," Matt said. "I've been here. Several of your friends. Chloe Barnes has been super. She's been here most of the time. She and Susan Williams. Maria Olivera was here last night. Michaela McDermott was here just a few hours ago. Of course, you also went out for MRIs…"

"Did they talk to me?"

"Yeah," Matt said. "They talked to you. Read to you. Susan Williams went on about a composting project she's doing at a farm. I've never seen anyone get so passionate about the virtues of chicken guano."

"Oh, and the crew from the house has all been by," Matt said. "They're the ones who brought most of the flowers. Now that you're fully alert, maybe you can absorb one surprise. I promise it's a pleasant one." He leaned over me so I could see his face.

"I think I can take it," I said.

"They want to keep working on the house," Matt said, a broad smile on his face. "The whole crew. They all saw what happened. They know Joey is going to lose his contractor's license over this." Matt paused for dramatic effect. "Anne, they've promised we'll be in our house for Thanksgiving."

"It's like déjà vu all over again," I replied.

"What?"

"Yogi Berra. Nothing. I'm thrilled beyond words. Really."

And I *was* thrilled. But how could I tell Matt that I had dreamed – or hallucinated – all of this? If I told Matt the whole story he might ask the hospital to keep me for further evaluation. And I wanted to go home. I couldn't wait to see my house get finished. A thought came to me.

"What about gas for the house?" I asked.

Matt shook his head. "I guess that's still a problem. Maybe we'll have to install tanks for the winter. We can live with that."

At this point, my brain was beginning to comprehend what had happened to me. Everything from the time shortly after Joey shoved me onto the driveway until a neurologist shined a penlight into my eyes had been a drug-induced dream. I had one set of drugs in me to keep me sedated while doctors tried to determine if my spine was damaged. Meanwhile, another set of drugs kept down the inflammation in my head while a different set of doctors dealt with a concussion and skull fracture. The drugs had interacted and, as Matt had been warned, they produced hallucinations.

But my brain had produced a hallucination that was influenced – or maybe even directed – by what was going on in the little world around me. I smelled the flowers in my room and so my dream added perfume and blooms to match the reality around me. That jackhammer sound I heard in the bakery coupled with feeling cold could have been an MRI. Chloe, Susan and Michaela visited me, and my subconscious incorporated them as characters.

And my intuition was working overtime. All the bits and pieces of information that had passed through my hands over the past few months – Joey's obsession with football scores and his otherwise inexplicable absences – were neatly parsed and assigned plot lines.

I had once glimpsed Ashley Harris as she opened her front door. My imagination filled in the reason she was unwilling to speak to me. And Shonda Rafferty? I had been told by Maria Olivera that she was a nurse. Nurses had been in and out of my room for two days.

What to make of Chloe's failing marriage? I'm not even certain how I had ever heard the sobriquet 'pharma babe', but I must have heard it somewhere and it stuck in my brain, waiting for just such an opportunity. Perhaps I sensed something between Chloe and Joey in one of their meetings. Or it could have been pure invention. At least it had not resulted in a horse named Sinbad sending Joey into a barn wall with a pitchfork chaser.

I wondered just how far I could trust my hallucination? Nothing ventured, nothing gained.

"If we're able, I want to go to see Bruno DiNapoli on Monday morning," I said. "We need to transfer the building permit from Joey to us anyway, and there's some chance that someone who works in the Town House – maybe a secretary or clerk – knows a back door into the gas company."

"Let's see what the doctors say," Matt said, a certain amount of caution in his voice.

There was a knock at the door. With my neck in a stationary brace I could not see whom Matt was speaking with, but I heard him say, "I think she's up for a short visit."

Matt then said, "Anne, I want to introduce you to Detective John Flynn of the Hardington Police Department."

Detective Flynn leaned over me so I could see him. He was exactly as I pictured him, of course. Rugged good looks, flecks of silver in close-dropped brown hair, and with a firm jaw. Even the brown sports jacket was as I had dreamed him.

"Mrs. Carlton, I'm pleased you're finally conscious," Detective Flynn said.

"I'm glad I'm alive," I said.

"So is everyone I've spoken to," Detective Flynn said. "May I pull up a chair for a moment?"

He did so and explained to me that Joey McCoy was a man looking at a lengthy stretch behind bars.

"I've spent the past 48 hours getting to know Mr. McCoy," Detective Flynn said. "I've spoken with his ex-wife, many of his customers, his subcontractors, and what few friends he appears to have. I've also spoken with him."

Detective Flynn paused, seeming to consider his words. I couldn't see his face and so I listened carefully to his words for nuance. "I'm not usually one for philosophy," he said, "but would you allow me a moment to digress?"

I encouraged him to do so.

Taking a breath, Detective Flynn continued. "Our criminal justice system is predicated on punishment and rehabilitation. Someone commits a crime, they're found guilty, and they are incarcerated for an appropriate period of time. Once in jail, we do our best to rehabilitate the offender. Get them counseling, teach them a skill to get a job once they're on the outside. For some small percentage of offenders, rehabilitation is beside the point. They will never re-enter society and so we simply try to keep them occupied."

Detective Flynn continued. "There's another group of offenders for whom incarceration is a place of suffering. It isn't inflicted by the institution; thank God prisons got out of that business a long time ago. No, the suffering is self-inflicted, and it happens to the people like Joey McCoy."

I could hear Detective Flynn shifting his body in his chair. "I've spoken with Mr. McCoy twice since he was arrested. He is utterly indignant that he is being held, appalled that his customers and subcontractors haven't rushed to put up his bail; and angry that the Public Defender assigned to his case isn't some Johnny Cochran wannabee. He claims that *you* goaded *him* into pushing you; that he was only going for help when he fled the scene; that he was in Harold Berry's home only to check on the status of some repairs; and that Mr. Berry's numerous injuries were self-inflicted."

"When someone engages in that degree of self-delusion at the outset of their involvement with the justice system, it bodes very poorly for what is going to follow," Detective Flynn continued. "I have a sense that Joey is a man who has lived his life without ever thinking about the consequences of what he did to other people.

He fits the modern definition of a predator and he is going to be taken off the streets. He is going to have years to contemplate what he did – not just to you, but to dozens of customers and especially to those women on whom he preyed."

"Every morning, he will wake up in a cell, and every evening, he will go to sleep in that cell. And, because he will likely never come to terms with his responsibility for his actions, he will suffer. Instead of being the contrite, model prisoner who gets out in a year, he will be the angry one who continually finds himself in more trouble. There will be no early release, no half-way house. Just more suffering. He may even be unruly enough to find himself in a more serious prison. That happens."

"You had the misfortune to be his customer when it all fell apart," Detective Flynn concluded.

"So, I'm his last customer?" I asked.

"You are his last customer as far as his career as a contractor is concerned," Detective Flynn said. "And he has no one to blame but himself."

Epilogue

We served Thanksgiving Dinner in our new, 'just the right size' home. Noah flew in from Seattle and stayed through the weekend. Although there was a terabyte of data awaiting analysis back in Falmouth, Kate and her husband pulled themselves away from their lab long enough to be sociable.

I now know why I was fixated on being in our new house by Thanksgiving. That holiday, more than any other, is a celebration of 'home' and family. It is the time when we gather together to take stock of ourselves and those we love. We share our dreams and desires without fear of being judged.

Without children to fill it, our old house had become a too-large, half-occupied shell. Our new house is a perfect size for this, the next stage of our lives. It felt like home even before the first piece of furniture was put in place.

We closed on our old home on schedule. Brooke Pollard and I worked alongside one another to put my 'old' garden to bed in the first two weeks of November. When it awakens next spring, it will be Brooke's garden and I know it will be in capable hands. She will make the garden her own and I will cherish its transformation and lend a hand if asked.

Two weeks before Thanksgiving, 131 River Street received its Certificate of Occupancy and we had a different kind of celebration for the construction crew. It was our way of thanking twenty-two men for coming to our rescue when the easy thing to do would have been to pick up their tools and move onto the next job.

Joey's name was never mentioned. He has disappeared from their lives just as thoroughly as he had vanished from mine.

Indeed, Matt and I have not discussed Joey in quite a while. We have no time to look backwards. We are busy planning a month in Tuscany next summer. Matt has promised to clear his calendar. Perhaps my close call at the hands of Joey gave Matt cause to re-consider the balance between work and family in his own life.

And I still get together with my friends, especially Chloe, Susan and Michaela. I have a fresh appreciation for them, for their intelligence, and for their steadfast friendship, though I keep my reason for that appreciation to myself.

You can see the twin greenhouses from Saybrook Farm's access road. I have made a point of driving there a few times and I have stopped to contemplate those two building's role in what I can best describe as my 'inner life'.

But more than anything else, I cannot go past a compost pile without smiling. And wondering what secrets it might contain.

Acknowledgments

Some books are much easier to write than others. Some novels require monumental research to achieve verisimilitude; others flow naturally from first-hand observation or memory. Some characters are laboriously constructed from whole cloth; others are plucked, intact, from the people we meet in everyday life. This was an easy book to write.

My wife, Betty, and I built a new home in 2014 and 2015. Like Anne's situation, ours was a case of selling a much larger house and downsizing to a 'retirement dream home' of our own design. Too many of the absurd elements in *How to Murder Your Contractor* were drawn from our experience building that home, including the notion that our 'local' gas utility believes that Eastern Massachusetts freezes solid around Halloween.

I never had any idea that contractors were such a lightning rod until I began mentioning the proposed title of this book. Without fail, the immediate reaction from those with whom I spoke was, *"Let me tell you what happened to me…"* I am pleased to say that I was able to incorporate a number of those horror stories into my plot. There are too many people to thank in this brief space, but for those of you who see their favorite contractor vignette in these pages – you know I was listening.

At the head of my thank-you list for making this book possible is Betty, who manages to switch with ease between being my biggest fan and my sternest critic. It wouldn't be possible without you.

Several people contributed specialized knowledge. Chief among them are Lifetime Master Gardener Susan Hammond and

University of New Hampshire compost researcher Matt Smith. Both of these individuals threw themselves into the decidedly macabre question of how best to use hot compost in the service of heating a greenhouse while simultaneously disposing of a corpse. For those who wish to pursue the subject further, YouTube offers several instructive videos.

It takes a community to produce a book, and I am indebted to a group of readers who both castigate me for my inability to properly use commas and who subject my story line to tests of plausibility. That group includes Jan Martin, Faith Clunie, Connie Stolow, and Linda Jean Smith. Your assistance shows on every page.

Finally, what started three years ago as a handful of requests from libraries and garden clubs to speak about gardening and my books has mushroomed into something I could never have imagined. My three talks, 'Gardening Is Murder', 'Gardening Is a Mystery', and 'Strong Independent Women', now takes me all over New England (and with a growing number of availability queries from other regions). Those talks allow me to meet and interact with readers, and all I can say is, 'please keep the requests coming'. I continue to look forward to every presentation.

Made in the USA
Middletown, DE
22 June 2023

33178571R00161